SHERLOCK HOLMES

The LADY on the BRIDGE
and other stories

DAVID MARCUM, EDITOR

JAICO PUBLISHING HOUSE

Ahmedabad Bangalore Bhopal Bhubaneswar Chennai
Delhi Hyderabad Kolkata Lucknow Mumbai

Published by Jaico Publishing House
A-2 Jash Chambers, 7-A Sir Phirozshah Mehta Road
Fort, Mumbai - 400 001
jaicopub@jaicobooks.com
www.jaicobooks.com

Published in arrangement with
MX Publishing Ltd
335 Princess Park Manor
London, N11 3GX

SHERLOCK HOLMES
THE LADY ON THE BRIDGE AND OTHER STORIES
ISBN 978-81-8495-913-0

First Jaico Impression: 2016

Page design and layout: Special Effects, Mumbai

Printed by
Replika Press Pvt. Ltd.

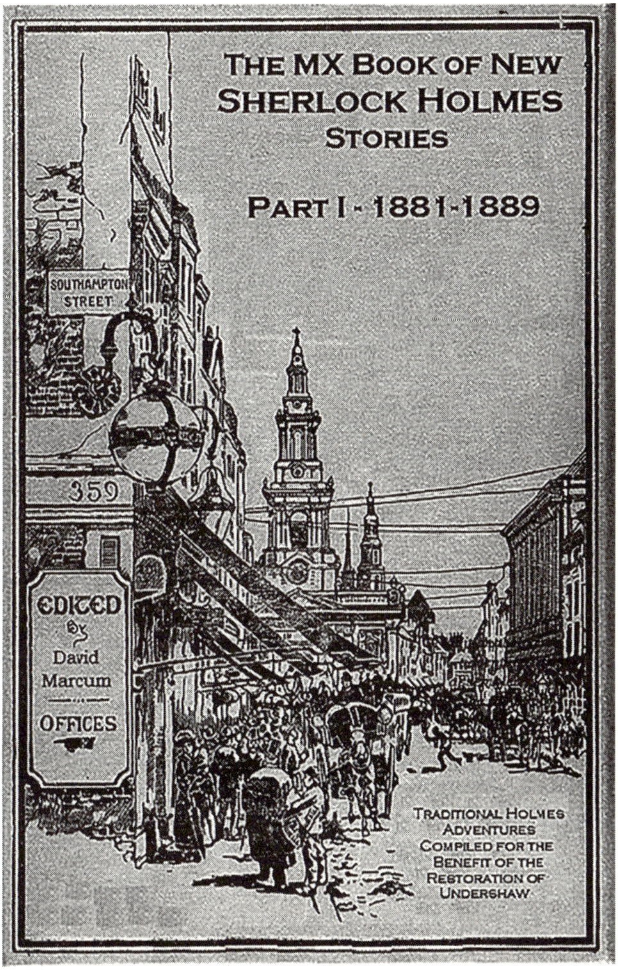
THE MX BOOK OF NEW
SHERLOCK HOLMES
STORIES
PART I - 1881-1889
SOUTHAMPTON
STREET
359
EDITED
By
David
Marcum
OFFICES
TRADITIONAL HOLMES
ADVENTURES
COMPILED FOR THE
BENEFIT OF THE
RESTORATION OF
UNDERSHAW

COPYRIGHT INFORMATION

Contents

SP

The Case of the Murderous Numismatist

by Jack Grochot

After I sold my medical practice in Kensington to Dr. Verner and returned to Baker Street to share rooms again with my friend Sherlock Holmes, life in the summer of 1894 became hectic. I had re-joined Holmes at a time when he was juggling three or four cases at once. Consequently, my own erratic schedule, to say the least, took me hither and yon unprepared, for I usually accompanied Holmes on his adventures, but now I was writing down notes of his movements or encounters haphazardly, with the hope that my memory of events would not fail me when I sat at our dining table to compose a magazine article about the ingenious methods and mind-numbing accomplishments of this peripatetic consulting detective. What follows is an example of my remembrance combined with those sketchy notes:

One day at lunch in our flat – a meal of turkey pot pies served graciously by our landlady, Mrs. Hudson – Holmes flipped a coin onto the tabletop and watched it twirl noisily until it came to a stop.

"What can you tell me about this piece, Watson?" he wanted to know.

I picked it up, examined it, and told Holmes the date the crown was minted, 1707, the very year it was introduced as currency to commemorate the Union of the kingdoms of

England and Scotland.

"Is that all there is to it?" Holmes persisted, as if to entertain himself.

"Only that this is a rare coin, a collector's item," I added.

"Wrong on all counts, as I anticipated," he blurted with an exaggerated wink.

"Wrong? How can you allege it?" I insisted.

"This is not a genuine crown. It is counterfeit," Holmes revealed, surprising me. "It is not solid silver, it is silver-plated and made of lead, weighing approximately a half ounce more than it should."

"Where did you get it?" I quizzed.

"From a new client, or I should say a group of clients," he answered. "Here is a letter from them that arrived in yesterday's post, along with the spurious coin." He unfolded a sheet of correspondence that was in his jacket pocket, then tossed it over to me, and I read it aloud:

"We, the undersigned, represent the Society of American Coin Traders, an organization of more than 200 members," the message began. "One of us, one whose identity will remain anonymous, purchased this coin by mail from a London dealer, a Joseph Smisky, for the sum of 90 dollars. This specimen is worthless, for it is a fake.

"We have sent a telegraph to Mr. Smisky to demand that the money be returned, and he has ignored our plea. Instead, he has continued to advertise in the newspapers that he possesses a 1707 crown for sale in mint condition. We suspect he actually possesses several reproductions of this valuable coin.

"We urge you to bring an end to his fraudulent scheme and to intercede for us with your Scotland Yard contacts to see that justice is served. We shall reward you with a fee in whatever amount you deem sufficient under the circumstances, providing, of course, that it is reasonable."

The letter gave the impression Holmes's task was a simple one, but he informed me otherwise. "If Mr. Smisky is to be prosecuted, it must be proven that he not only peddled a counterfeit, but that he knew it was counterfeit when he did so," Holmes advised. "Thus, the sticky wicket."

"How do you intend to establish he knowingly sold a bogus collectable?" I wondered with skepticism. "What was in his mind is hardly possible to decipher."

"My plan – " Holmes started to say, but a knock at the door interrupted him.

"It is only I, here to collect the dirty dishes," said Mrs. Hudson cheerily, letting herself in and directing a comment toward Holmes. "That pot pie should help put meat on your bones. The way you have been running about at all hours takes a toll on the frame, and you can't stand to lose any more than you have already."

"It was delicious and abundant, my lady, and no doubt it will amount to as much as a pound on my sorry frame," he responded, then charmed her with a compliment about her hair.

"Oh, Mr. Holmes, I didn't think anyone would notice how I did it up differently this morning," she giggled, blushing. "I'll be out of your way in a jiffy. You gentlemen have more important things to discuss besides my appearance. You approve though, eh?"

"It becomes you, Mrs. Hudson," I piped up. "No need for you to hurry off."

"All the same, I best get going, because I am expecting a gentleman caller," she disclosed, stepping away with the dishes in a rush.

"The word romance never would have occurred to me in a conversation about Mrs. Hudson," Holmes jested in a low voice after we heard her lively footsteps on the stairs.

"You were about to tell me your plan when she came in abruptly," I prodded, expecting Holmes to resume our discussion.

"Better yet, Watson, you can enthrall your readers even more so if you witness my stratagem unfolding, rather than listening to me explain it," he contended. "Come with me to Gravesend, where I shall acquaint you with a female constable who is also an amateur stage actress in her off-hours. Gertie Evans is the key to my grand design and its shocking aftermath for the likes of Mr. Smisky."

"Grand design? Shocking aftermath? What on earth?" I marveled.

"I suppose I should confide in you my ulterior motives for accepting this case, my good man. The investigation of a counterfeit coin is a means to an end. Dealing dishonestly in rare coins is but a minor crime for the nefarious Mr. Smisky, a commonplace infraction ordinarily not worthy of my attention. The fact of the matter is that I have another client, The British Fire and Casualty Company, which has its sights set on Smisky for a heinous insurance swindle. The company has engaged me to probe his responsibility in the destruction of a tenement he owned in the East End. A tremendous explosion and conflagration leveled the structure last April, killing six occupants and injuring a multitude of others."

"I recall reading about it, Holmes, but if I remember correctly, the police blamed a faulty gas valve for the tragedy," I interjected.

"The police suspect sabotage, but they didn't say as much to the newspapers to avoid arousing interest on the part of Smisky or the professional arsonist he employed," Holmes stated categorically. "Unfortunately, the authorities have been unable to assemble any evidence of a deliberate act. The insurance firm has come to me, therefore, to solve the puzzle so it can deny Smisky a settlement of 50,000 pounds."

"Good heavens, he committed six murders, for money. How disgraceful and malicious," I remarked scornfully. "His malevolence is unparalleled."

"As is my ambition to see him hang," Sherlock Holmes threatened. "Shall we go now?"

"I am as eager as you," I assured him, donning my bowler.

The afternoon sun was intense, so we rode in a hansom

to Charing Cross, where we boarded a train to Gravesend, down by the great river. On the train, Holmes spoke not a word, but tapped his toes to the rhythm of a song in his head and drummed his bony fingertips on his knees, his close-fitting cloth cap pushed forward onto the bridge of his hawk-like nose. When we reached our destination, he cautioned me on the platform not to let on in public that I knew Gertie Evans was a police official. "She works surreptitiously and wears no uniform," he observed, "and she is very careful to protect her true identity."

We met Gertie at the Boar's Head Pub, a raucous establishment on the waterfront with sawdust on the floor and medieval armour hanging on the walls. She waved warmly to Holmes from a corner table occupied by three surly men competing for her attention, one a sailor, another a businessman, and the third a football player wearing his colours. Gertie, aged about thirty, looked lovely in a dark blue dress and yellow blouse with ruffles around the neck and on the ends of her sleeves. Her auburn hair was done in large curls that draped over her shoulders and back, accenting a youthful, angelic face. As Holmes and I approached, she ordered the three suitors to "take a powder, boys, I have private business to discuss with these two gents." Grumbling, the men strolled to the bar.

"So this is your deputy and biographer, Dr. Watson," she said coquettishly to Holmes, who stood at the table until she motioned for us to sit. "It is my pleasure to see you in the flesh, Doctor, because I have admired your writings from afar," Gertie crowed. "And Mr. Holmes, I consider it an honour to collabourate with you once more." A waitress took down our preferences for refreshments and Gertie wasted no additional time getting to the matter at hand.

Speaking barely above a whisper in the din of the pub, Gertie outlined the step she had taken on her own. "My sergeant is a numismatist, and he loaned me five rare coins from his collection to offer them to Smisky for the right price.

Give me the imitation crown and I'll put it with them."

Holmes produced the counterfeit, which she inserted into a small paraffin paper jacket and dropped into her reticule. "Your plan will fall apart if Smisky buys back this hunk of junk," she frowned. "I'll memorise his words when he lays eyes on it. Now let's see what happens." We departed the pub together, Gertie hailing one cab while Holmes and I summoned another to take us to the railway station. "Best we're not seen together until this is over," Holmes theorised when we boarded separate cars for the trip to Saxe-Coburg Square, the location of Smisky's coin shop. Once in the vicinity, Gertie walked alone the two city blocks to the shop, with Holmes and me trailing about 20 paces behind. As she went in, we plopped down on a bench near the entrance so we could hear the banter between Gertie and Smisky, close enough to intervene in the event there was trouble.

"I wish to speak to the owner," she notified the muscular man with a handlebar moustache behind the counter.

"You're lookin' at him, lady," he snickered.

"Do you buy rare coins at a fair price?" she asked.

"What price I pay will beat any competitor's, so help me God," he swore.

"Well, then, I have six to sell. My dear father passed away and left me his collection. Before he went on to his reward, he told me which ones to part with if I fell onto hard times."

"I won't take advantage of you, miss," he pledged. "Let's see what you have."

Gertie reached into her handbag and displayed the coins on the glass countertop.

"Hmmm," Smisky hummed, examining each one and replacing them into a row. "This one is worth five pounds to me, this one a little more, and the rest about ten pounds apiece – except this one," he scowled, manipulating the counterfeit 1707 crown between his fingers, flipping it into the air with his thumb and forefinger, then catching it in the palm of his stubby right hand. "This one is worth nothing, not even face value," he claimed.

"What in heaven's name do you mean by that?" Gertie ejaculated, pretending to be stunned.

"It's too heavy. It's a replica, not the genuine article," Smisky laughed.

"We'll see about that," Gertie snapped. "I'm taking it back, in fact all of them – I shan't do business with a scoundrel."

"Suit yourself for today, miss, but I'll gamble that when you find I've been truthful I'll see you again," Smisky concluded arrogantly.

"You can bet your life on that," Gertie mumbled to herself quietly as she stomped out of the shop.

"A marvelous, convincing performance; I believed you myself," Holmes beamed, complimenting her at the train station. "Mr. Smisky is one notch closer to the gallows."

"I was tempted to clamp the irons on his wrists right then and there," Gertie admitted, "but I realised that would interfere with your plan, Mr. Holmes."

Gertie returned to the constabulary in Gravesend, while Holmes and I rode on to the Strand for a dinner at Simpson's, our usual Wednesday evening habit.

That night, dressed as an Episcopalian cleric with a grey beard and frizzy white hair, Holmes went on the prowl in the West End, searching the streets for Gunther Williams, a clever and stealthy informant who once served time in Dartmoor Penitentiary for a series of burglaries, and who was known in the underworld as Hobo Willie. Holmes, who had been instrumental in the convict's early release from prison, based upon testimony that he financially supported the orphanage where he was raised, came across Williams at midnight outside a cafe famous for its coffee and fresh-fried donuts.

"I have a job for you, Gunther," Holmes began.

"And who might you be with a job for me?" Williams retorted. "It is I, Sherlock Holmes, your benefactor," Holmes replied.

"By Jove! If it isn't you, Mr. Holmes. Preaching the gospel, are you?" a startled Williams quaked, to which Holmes responded with this quote from *Oliver Twist*:

"Yes, I'm preaching the gospel according to Charles Dickens: 'To do a great right, you may do a little wrong; and you may take any means which the end to be attained will justify.'"

"You want me to do something underhanded, then," the corpulent Williams predicted, stroking the fleshy portion of his double-chin.

"Skullduggery is more like it, Gunther," Holmes corrected. "There is a coin dealer in Saxe-Coburn Square who paid what the Americans call a torch to set an apartment building ablaze in the East End, where six people were burned alive and many others scorched. I want you to make a friend of him and learn the identity of the culprit who destroyed the building."

"That's an easy assignment, Mr. Holmes," Williams boasted. "I know the man, Joe Smisky, and he is a hard case, but I am more brainy. I'll betray him to you, yet never to the coppers, though. They would make me go to court and expose myself as a snitch."

"I shall protect your role in this, Gunther, rest assured," Holmes promised.

"Your word is your bond, I know that for a fact," Williams conceded, then was ready to disappear into the darkness until Holmes delayed him with the story of Gertie Evans and the counterfeit 1707 crown. Holmes also gave Williams explicit instructions on how to prompt Smisky to name the arsonist. "I'll sleep on all this and give you my report tomorrow before suppertime, Mr. Holmes," Hobo Willie vowed.

Holmes arrived back at Baker Street in the wee hours of the morning and devoted much of the time thereafter poring over his Index of criminals or pacing the floor of our sitting-room in his purple dressing gown, smoking his bent-billiard, briar-root pipe.

I awoke at dawn to the sound of his brewing the strong coffee that he favoured, which gave off a pleasant aroma that circulated upstairs to my bedroom. Groggy, I stumbled down to the table and helped myself to a cup while Holmes was sipping his as he scribbled a long message to Inspector Lestrade of Scotland Yard.

"Watson," he muttered without looking up from the stationery, "I have deduced the identity of the arsonist and will receive confirmation of my finding today from my informant, Gunther Williams, if he follows my script." Then, staring into my bleary eyes, Holmes warned: "Tonight will be a dangerous time. I must be off now to bait the trap."

While he was gone, Williams was fulfilling his commitment to Holmes, rapping on the door to Smisky's coin shop about eight o'clock to roust him out of bed in a back room. Drowsy from a deep slumber and in a foul mood, Smisky unlocked the door and opened it a crack. "Well, Hobo Willie, what do you want at this ungodly hour?" he sneered.

"Let me in, Joe, I have something to sell," Williams pleaded.

Opening the door wider and motioning with his head for his visitor to come inside, Smisky greeted him with an insult. "Something to sell? From one of your sticky finger endeavours?"

"No, Joe, it's information I'm pitching," came the answer.

"I'm not buying. I have all the information I can use," Smisky growled.

"This is about you and your future in the labour camp, or maybe even at the end of a rope," Williams enticed.

"What's that worth to you?"

"It's not worth one pence so far. Are you out of your mind?" Smisky, now curious, said to lead Hobo Willie on. "I see you're all spruced up, shaved, hair trimmed, and in a new suit of clothes. Come into some money, have you?"

"Yes, I've been working, and these are my working clothes," Williams lied.

"Working at what, you tramp?" Smisky cackled.

"I've been working with Sherlock Holmes, the renowned detective, and he has the goods on you, Joe," Williams revealed.

"Has the goods on me? For what?" Smisky clamoured.

"That's what I have for sale, the whole picture," Williams professed. "I can give you information that will save your bacon."

"You're doing your pandering behind Holmes's back, then, for a bit of extra cash?" Smisky wanted to learn.

"You could say that, Joe, but it's more like I'm sharing what I know with a friend," Williams continued.

"Let me hear what you have to tell, and then I'll decide if you get anything from me for it," Smisky specified.

"Doesn't happen that way, Joe. First, you make an offer, and, second, I make the decision if the price is right," Williams bargained.

"Ten shillings, then, is that enough?" Smisky acquiesced.

"Not for what I have," Williams spouted.

"How much do you want, you little crook?" Smisky smirked.

"A five-pound note will buy everything you need to know," Williams boldly stated.

"Five pounds! Do you think I'm made of money?" Smisky protested, his face flushing.

"That's my price, take it or leave it," Williams countered.

"I'll take it, but this better be good, you blackmailing bastard," Smisky cursed.

"Good. By the way, Joe, this is extortion, not blackmail. There is a distinction in the law. Put the money where I can see it and I'll not touch it until you're satisfied I sang like a bird," said Williams confidently.

Smisky, moaning, went into the back room and emerged with a five pound note, which he laid on the counter between himself and Hobo Willie. "Now sing your song," he demanded.

"I'll start with how you cooked your own goose yesterday," Williams began. "The young woman who came here with rare coins to sell was in league with Sherlock Holmes. All they wanted was for you to show them you knew a 1707 crown was a phony. You did just that, which made the case against you for transacting in counterfeit. That'll probably get you a three or four-year stretch. Now for the bad news.

Holmes has tracked down the party who burned your building in the East End, and the man has confessed, with the prospect of escaping the gallows if he testifies against you and the others who paid him to set fires. He told Holmes how he did them all, by rigging the gas valves. Now if he goes to court and fingers you, that could mean you'll swing from Old Bailey."

"I don't believe it," Smisky bellowed. "Frank Kiefer is smarter than any private detective. He wouldn't spill his guts if his life depended on it."

"His life did depend on it, Joe," Williams argued. "Sherlock Holmes caught him in the act of doing another job."

"T-t-this is terrible," Smisky stammered. "Has he gone to the police with his evidence?"

"Not yet, because he hasn't wrapped up the package in a neat bundle, at least not until he persuades you to confess, too," Williams informed Smisky. "Besides, he isn't working for the police. His client is an insurance company."

"I have some time, then. I can still do something about this meddlesome busybody," Smisky surmised. "Where can I find him?"

"He's pounding the bricks, he's on the street right now," Williams advised. "But I know where he'll be at seven o'clock tonight – having dinner at Simpson's in the Strand with a witness on another case."

"What's he look like?" Smisky questioned. "I think I'll have dinner with him."

Hobo Willie described Holmes down to the clothing he would be wearing that day, picked up the five-pound note, wished Smisky good luck, and departed in a jolly frame of mind, mission accomplished. He would make his report of a successful effort to Holmes at Baker Street in the afternoon, as he had prophesied.

Meantime, Holmes was experiencing success as well. He had traced Frank Kiefer to a brothel and opium den he owned in the sleazy Limehouse district.

"Frank, I am a friend of Joe Smisky, who says you can make gravel burn," Holmes exaggerated by way of introduction. "My name is Matthew McKinney, and I am a businessman from Baker Street, where my haberdashery is located. I have lost all my savings on the poker tables and I am in debt to the gamblers. I need you to arrange a gas leak."

"I can do that easily enough, but the cost to you will be severe," Kiefer foretold. "Joe had to triple the coverage on his apartment building to accommodate me and make a tidy profit at the same time. He was pleased with the results, though. The job turned out beautiful. What a sight it was! Oooo, the flames were magnificent. Too bad so many people had to die and get hurt, but, like Joe said, they were the scum of the earth. How much insurance do you have?"

"Ten thousand pounds. How much do you want for the job?" Holmes asked.

"Ten thousand is my price," Kiefer allowed. "You'll have to do the same thing Joe did, double or triple the coverage, depending on how much you owe the sharks. What kind of building is it – what's it made of?"

"It's brick on the ground floor and wood frame on the floor above," Holmes related.

"Brick, you say?" Kiefer said hesitantly. "That will add a thousand pounds to the price. Brick needs a powerful blast. I'll come take a look at it tomorrow afternoon – be there at two o'clock. What's the address?"

"It's 221 Baker Street in the West End," Holmes told him. "Will you come alone?"

"My understudy, Donald Bonsal, will be with me," Kiefer disclosed. "He is my right arm, ever since I lost mine in an explosion three years ago. I was chopping holes in the roof of a club for ventilation when my ax struck a steel beam and created a spark. That was enough to ignite the gas. The vapors are volatile. I charge a lot of money for my work because it is so hazardous. But I guarantee the results and leave the coppers scratching their heads. When Frank Kiefer finishes a job, they can't prove a thing."

Stunned by Kiefer's callous attitude, Holmes made an excuse to exit after declining the arsonist's invitation to stay for a smoke in his opium room. Upon his return to our diggings, Holmes rubbed his sinewy hands together and fished half a cigar from the coal scuttle, lit it, inhaled, and repeated for me the incriminating chat he had with Kiefer.

"He is an amoral slouch with a haughty indifference toward the lives of the impoverished, as is Smisky," said Holmes to preface his rendition of the dialogue. "Society will be better off with those two reprobates in their graves. And I have the material to put them there."

Just as he completed his version of the event, Mrs. Hudson appeared on our threshold to announce that a Gunther Williams was in the foyer asking for Mr. Sherlock Holmes.

"Send him up with dispatch, Mrs. Hudson," Holmes directed her

"It's uncanny, Mr. Holmes, but you were on target with what you said would happen," Williams praised. "He fell for it hook, line, and sinker. The name of the arsonist is –"

"Let me guess, Gunther, it's Frank Kiefer," Holmes butted in.

"If you knew that, why did you put me through –" the informant went on.

"I am sorry, but it was because I needed confirmation, Gunther," Holmes apologised. "I only had a suspicion it was Kiefer when I read in my Index at four o'clock this morning about the one-armed arsonist who was an expert with the properties of natural coal gas. Tell me more of your encounter, Gunther."

"Well, Smisky is planning something, probably to harm you fatally," Williams postulated. "Like you told me to say, I mentioned that you would be having dinner at seven o'clock at Simpson's. He asked me to describe you and said he might join you."

"Excellent, Gunther!" Holmes extolled. "Here are three guineas for your trouble. Let us fix you a ham and cheese sandwich, for I am certain you've had no lunch."

"Oh, thank you, Mr. Holmes, I am awfully hungry," Hobo Willie admitted. "I'll take it with me and eat it on the way home – in a cab, no less, now that I have the fare."

"Wait! Before you leave, Gunther," Holmes boomed with concern, "I feel obligated to warn you to keep a low profile for a day or so – don't patronise your usual haunts, don't follow your usual pattern. Smisky is sharp and he could smell a rat, meaning you. He is capable of violence against you, too."

"He is an idiot and a weasel, Mr. Holmes, and he'll never think to suspect me," Williams quarreled. "He is the least of my worries."

As Williams left, devouring the sandwich, an incensed Joseph Smisky was standing at the entrance to Frank Kiefer's brothel and opium den in the Limehouse district, summoning up the courage to do what he had come to do: eliminate the threat of a hardened criminal testifying against him at a trial that surely would spell his doom. He would silence Kiefer before he had the chance to speak under oath the words that would sway a jury to find the coin dealer guilty and send him to the gallows.

Smisky burst through the door and was immediately

confronted by a Chinese attendant, who asked him in broken English if he wanted a girl, a smoking room, or both.

"I'm here to see Frank, that's all," Smisky barked..

"I fetch Master Frank, you sit," ordered the Chinaman, sensing an altercation. He climbed a stairway and opened a door.

"Master Frank, angry man downstairs to see you, very mad," said the agitated Chinaman.

Kiefer retrieved a six-shot revolver from a drawer and leveled it at his waist, then went to the bottom of the staircase and saw Smisky stewing on the sofa.

"Joe!" he hollered. "Yung-se says you're upset. Excuse the pistol. What's the matter?"

"I came here to choke you to death, Frank," Smisky acknowledged. "What's this I hear about you cooperating with Sherlock Holmes?"

"With who? Never met the man," Kiefer insisted. "But I did meet a friend of yours today, Matthew McKinney, who wants me to pulverise his haberdashery."

"A friend of mine? I don't know the name. What did he say about me?" Smisky queried.

"He said you recommended me to him. He knew I took care of business for you," Kiefer informed a puzzled Smisky.

"What did this McKinney look like?" Smisky asked.

"He was tall, skinny, a bird's beak for a nose, piercing eyes, with dark hair that was perfectly combed," Kiefer recalled.

"That was no Matthew McKinney. That was Sherlock Holmes," Smisky wailed.

"Who is Sherlock Holmes anyway?" Kiefer wanted to know.

"He's a beastly private detective who is investigating us for the fire," Smisky said to enlighten him.

"That evil rodent! Let's take care of him before he can do us in!" Kiefer roared.

"He'll be at Simpson's in the Strand at seven o'clock.

We'll kill him there," Smisky agreed. "We'll make minced meat of him. But there's somebody I want to dust before him, Hobo Willie. He set me up for Holmes. Lend me a gun and twelve rounds of ammunition."

Smisky and Kiefer made plans for the murder at Simpson's, then Smisky left to hunt down Gunther Williams.

Finding him at the same cafe where Holmes ran across him, Smisky sneaked up behind him as he drank coffee on a stool, knocked the cup out of his hand, pointed the muzzle of the weapon in his pocket at Williams's ample belly, and coldly instructed him to walk outside. From there he escourted the victim to an alley, where he accused him of a double-cross.

"You are a traitor, and traitors are shot!" Smisky howled, then pulled the trigger six times, pumping Hobo Willie full of lead even after he was dead. "Let that be a final lesson to you, you maggot," Smisky seethed with abject bitterness, hovering over the corpse, "I'll see you in hell."

Word of Gunther Williams's demise would not reach Holmes that day, for the newspapers already had published their late afternoon editions, and the body was not discovered by constables until their evening rounds.

Holmes was pensive, fiddling with his chemicals at the deal-top table, stroking his violin aimlessly, checking the firearm in his shoulder holster to make sure it was loaded, asking me twice if I had examined mine, talking idly about the theatre and concerts, and, ultimately, about what Smisky might be intending and how. The minutes until seven o'clock ticked away.

When the timepiece on the mantel struck six-thirty, we donned our jackets, ventured casually out the door past Mrs. Hudson in the kitchen – "Enjoy your night out," she called to us – and stepped onto the pavement to flag down a hansom at the corner.

"Where to?" the driver sputtered, and Holmes gave him a light-hearted answer: "Simpson's in the Strand beckons us for a delightful meal." I boarded the vehicle first, and Holmes, ever vigilant, glanced in all directions before following me up into the seat. The horse moved forward and trotted through Cavendish Square, then beyond Regent Street near the intersection of Oxford Street, where Holmes raised up and surveyed the avenue behind us to determine if we were being stalked. "It looks clear, save for one cab about 50 yards to the rear," he observed, almost under his breath.

When we reached the Strand, my careful friend told the driver to pull to the curb around a bend in the road. "We'll walk the rest of the way," he apprised the driver. "Here is an extra two shillings if you continue on to Simpson's and stop in front for a minute until the cab behind us passes you by."

"Will do, guv'nor, whatever you say. Appreciate the tip," the driver concurred.

We strolled briskly toward the restaurant past the familiar shops and hotels until we were within sight of our destination. I checked my pocket watch and noted to Holmes that the time was 6:50. "Avert the front door, Watson – we'll go in through the back and into the kitchen,"

Holmes advised. "Keep your eyes peeled, Watson. Remember, he's the stout fellow with a handlebar moustache."

"I would never forget that face, be certain," I assured my companion.

We emerged from the busy kitchen and into the crowded dining area, where an astonished *maître-de,* Oswald, excitedly encountered us. "Good gracious, Mr. Holmes, Dr. Watson, I never expected an entrance like this!" he cried. "Nonetheless, your table is ready."

We trailed after him to a setting in the centre of the room, seated ourselves, and scoured the faces of the patrons to see if the assassin had already arrived. There was no sign of Smisky, so we asked the waiter to bring us two glasses of dry sherry. It was seven o'clock.

Our drinks were served and Holmes proposed a toast. "May the dinner be succulent, uneventful, and safe," he prayed, "and may Joe Smisky be all bravado with no nerve."

Suddenly, two men with hoods covering their heads, their handguns thrust outward, appeared inside the front door, the weapons scanning the dining area as if searching for a target. One by one, the clientele noticed the intruders. The sounds of a vibrant atmosphere became eerily silent. One of the hooded figures trained his revolver on our table and a voice cracked the motionless air. "Holmes, you monster! Prepare to meet your Maker!"

With that, four other men at a scattering of tables flashed weapons that were aimed at the two assailants. One of those men spoke authoritatively and loudly. "Drop the guns or we'll fire. I am Inspector Lestrade of Scotland Yard and you are both under arrest for attempted murder."

"Murder it will be, then!" the second hooded man bawled, squeezing off two rounds in the direction of the lawmen, missing them and sending the bullets over the scalps of the diners into the wall. The four officers cut him down with a volley of shots as the hooded man closest to Holmes wheeled and tried to escape. He was accosted by two more members of Lestrade's squad and engaged them in battle, killing one before the other policeman emptied his revolver into the belligerent's chest and abdomen.

The odour of sulfur penetrated the dining room, and the customers, especially the ladies, shrieked in horror before the pandemonium dissipated.

The officials removed the hoods from the heads of the deceased assassins and Holmes informed Lestrade that their names were Smisky and Kiefer.

"When I received your message this morning," Lestrade remarked, "I thought it was another of your wild goose chases. But I couldn't be certain, so I came, anticipating nothing of this sort."

"You should know better by now, Lestrade, that when

I humble myself to ask for your assistance, I am certain," Holmes scolded. "This outcome was predictable. I told you as much."

The next morning, after reading the account of the gunplay in the *Times,* Holmes saw a separate article, a small item, about the death of an ex-convict, Gunther Williams, also known as Hobo Willie. The newspaper said the police reported he was gunned down by an unknown attacker in an alley behind the Southpointe Cafe in Pope's Court.

The writer speculated that the killing was an act of revenge perpetrated by an enemy who also had been an inmate at Dartmoor Penitentiary. "Leave it to the naïve press, Watson, to jump to such a conclusion without having the data to support it," Holmes groused. "I shall make a contribution to the orphanage in Gunther's honour."

The Saviour of Cripplegate Square

by Bert Coules

This play was commissioned by the BBC as the fifth episode in the first series of The Further Adventures of Sherlock Holmes, 16 pastiche mysteries based on some of the throwaway references to other cases which Conan Doyle scattered throughout the Canon. The shows followed the earlier dramatisations of all 56 short stories and four novels, the first time it had ever been done in any medium. Clive Merrison repeated his Holmes in the sequels, with Andrew Sachs taking over as Watson after the untimely death of Michael Williams.

If you have the original broadcast, either on CD or as a download, and try following the script as you listen along, you'll notice a few minor differences. Things almost always get changed during the recording: cuts for time, clarifications of plot points, smoothing out of lines that have proved unexpectedly tricky to say, and so on.

Readers unaccustomed to radio scripts are sometimes surprised by the presence of detailed directions for movement and business, especially if they've imagined the studio sessions as a group of performers sitting round a table and acting to a single microphone. In fact, the process is a very physical one: there are sets with practical doors, windows, staircases, and furniture which the cast can roam around, and most directors choreograph a scene in much the same way as they would for a stage, film or TV production. Action, even something as simple as crossing a room to open a door, is valuable for preventing a static feel, and even a gesture or the position of the head changes the voice and makes for aural variety as well as dramatic realism.

INT and EXT in the scene headings stand for Interior and Exterior, distinctions achieved not only by the addition of appropriate background effects but also by recording in different acoustics: purpose-built radio drama studios are divided into areas with contrasting wall, floor and ceiling treatments which radically affect the sound.

A note on dates: In general, I was careful not to be too specific about the dating of any of the Further Adventures. Not only was I well aware that we had a loyal audience of extremely knowledgeable Holmesians eager to pounce happily (and good-naturedly) on any inadvertent inconsistencies with the canon – Conan Doyle is himself often vague or completely silent on the subject of dates – so I was following in the best possible footsteps. But having said that, this particular story's mood of reminiscence and revelation seems to sit nicely with the time of Holmes's reappearance from his wanderings and Watson's return to the old Baker Street rooms, twin events which in this instance Sir Arthur pins down exactly; so 1894 let it be.

The case at the heart of the story though took place long before. It happened shortly after Holmes's arrival in London following his years at university, when, as it says in the script, he would have been in his early twenties. And I'm happy to leave things at that.

Finally, a playscript isn't as easy to read as a story: the experience can feel disjointed as the eye and the brain moves from scene heading to character name to dialogue and directions. Any initial awkwardness usually disappears as the pages succeed each other and, with luck, as the world of the drama begins to form in the reader's imagination. I hope this happens for you, and you find yourself transported back to a stormy Victorian night with the rain beating against the windows, the wind howling in the chimney, the fire crackling in the grate and Sherlock Holmes in the mood to tell a dark tale of his earliest days as a detective.

This script is protected by copyright. For permission to

reproduce it in any way or to perform it in any medium, please apply to the author's agent. Contact details can be found at www.bertcoules.co.uk.

THE CAST
in order of speaking

SMITH – Nathaniel Collington Smith, librarian at the British Museum. Mildly eccentric, soft-spoken, widely experienced and very wise in an unconventional sort of way: a mentor to the young Sherlock Holmes. Sixties or older.

WATSON – Doctor John Watson.

HOLMES – Sherlock Holmes.

JENNY – Jenny Snell, a working class cleaner and general household servant. Early teens.

GUTTRIDGE – A working class East Ender. Forties.

LANDLADY – Ruler of a rough working class pub in the East End of London.

WOMAN – A young working class mother. East End Londoner.

MRS. GUTTRIDGE – An East Ender from the upper ranges of the working class. Forties or older.

DOCTOR – Working in one of the most desperate and poor areas of the East End.

MAN – An East End local.

Plus a noisy bunch of REGULARS in the Landlady's pub

TEASER. INT. THE READING ROOM, THE BRITISH MUSEUM.

Huge, echoey. Very quiet atmosphere, occasional distant footsteps, the odd cough and similar. After a few moments, close and quiet:

SMITH: Look around you, my young friend. A library is a perfect reflection of the ideal world. Every single volume in my care has its allotted place in the great scheme of things. Move one, even by an infinitesimal degree, and you diminish its value.
What use is information if one cannot instantly obtain it, or see precisely how it fits into the universe as a whole? Nothing exists in isolation. It is the relationships between facts which give them their meaning. These connections may be subtle, they may be hidden, they may be...unexpected. But if you are to master the world of knowledge, it is these links which you must seek out and understand. However well concealed, the truth is always there to be...detected.
At least, that is my view – and I should like to think that you agree with me...Mr. Holmes.

Music: the opening sig.
Opening announcements.
The music fades into:

SCENE 1. INT. THE SITTING ROOM, 221b BAKER STREET.

It is the winter of 1894.

An almighty thunderclap right overhead. Rain lashes, wind howls. Watson is off at a window, looking out.

WATSON: What a filthy night.

He pulls the heavy curtains shut. The sound of the wind and rain becomes more muted.

(Approaching) God only knows what's going on under cover of that.

We become aware of the open fire crackling away.

HOLMES: Crime, you mean?

WATSON: (Sitting) Of course. (He flexes his injured shoulder) Damn weather.

HOLMES: Not much, I'd wager. How's the old war wound?

WATSON: Making its presence felt. What do you mean, not much?

HOLMES: It's fog that's the criminal's friend. On a night like this, most self-respecting villains are safely tucked up with a drink and a good smoke.

WATSON: Both of which they probably stole from some honest, hard- working citizen.

HOLMES: No doubt.

WATSON: Brandy?

HOLMES: Thank you.

The brandy is close at hand. Watson pours two glasses. As he does so, Holmes idly picks up his violin and prepares to play, quietly checking the tuning. He breaks off.
You don't mind?

WATSON: Of course not. Take my mind off my damn shoulder.

HOLMES: I'll do my best.

A moment as he composes himself.
Then he begins to play: a slow plaintive melody: The Shepherd's Lament from Wagner's Tristan and Isolde. After a few bars he breaks off.

WATSON: Don't stop.

HOLMES: Not too depressing for a cold winter's night?

WATSON: I wouldn't have called it depressing. Plaintive, yes.

HOLMES: Plaintive. The very word.

He starts again. As he plays:

A dying man lies alone, helplessly waiting for the woman he loves. For her sake, he's turned his back on everything: his friends, his country, his hopes for the future. And now he waits for her...and she does not appear.

WATSON: What's it from?

HOLMES: Tristan and Isolde. A hymn to love and death.

He stops playing.

WATSON: He had a pretty bleak view of love, your Wagner. HOLMES: It's a bleak emotion.

WATSON: Oh, come on.

HOLMES: The Elizabethans had the right idea. To them, love was a disease. If you caught it, you were doomed.

WATSON: I'll stick to my definition, thank you. Here.

He passes Holmes his brandy.

HOLMES: Thank you. Love is a positive force for good? Love brings out the best in man?

WATSON: I think so.

HOLMES: You should have met Tobias and Emily Guttridge.

WATSON: Who the devil were they?

HOLMES: The Guttridges of Cripplegate Square. They caught the disease.

WATSON: You mean they were in love.

HOLMES: It goes somewhat further than that.

WATSON: One of your cases?

HOLMES: Yes, before you and I met. WATSON: Is it a...good story?

HOLMES: (A smile) Come on, Watson. If you want to hear it, say so.

WATSON: (A smile) Of course I want to hear it.

HOLMES: A dark tale for a dark night. Very well, Doctor. Keep the brandy to hand, light up a cigar and let me shatter your illusions about love.

Music: the Tristan tune, this time as heard in the actual opera – the haunting, atmospheric sound of a solo flute.

The music takes us into Holmes's tale. It runs under:

SCENE 2. INT. THE READING ROOM, THE BRITISH MUSEUM.

Nathaniel Collington Smith is checking a pile of books. Holmes is in his early twenties.

SMITH: The Annals of Crime. Police Review. Criminals and Their Characteristics. A Survey of Delinquent Behaviour. Your books, Mr. Holmes.

HOLMES: Thank you, Mr. Smith.

Smith slides the books across a counter.
The music disappears as we cut back to:

SCENE 3. INT. THE SITTING ROOM AT 221b, BAKER STREET.

HOLMES: I don't believe I've ever mentioned Collington Smith.

WATSON: Never.

HOLMES: Nathaniel Collington Smith. He worked in the library at the British Museum. When I came down from university I spent a good deal of time there reading up on various subjects.

WATSON: Like the history of crime?

HOLMES: It's an essential study for a detective. If they'd put in a book collection down at Scotland Yard, their success rate would soar.

WATSON: Only if you persuaded them actually to read the books.

HOLMES: Smith could have persuaded them. He had that rare combination: he not only possessed knowledge, he was able to enthuse others with the thirst for it.

Cut to:

SCENE 4. INT. THE READING ROOM, THE BRITISH MUSEUM.

SMITH: If I might make a small comment...

HOLMES: Of course.

SMITH: Criminals and Their Characteristics. It is perhaps a trifle...unsound.

HOLMES: You've read it?

SMITH: Oh dear me no. Librarians don't read books, Mr. Holmes. They simply know about them.

HOLMES: (Chuckles. Then:) Unsound?

SMITH: That is the general opinion. Sloppily argued from

some highly dubious data.

HOLMES: Then please take it back.

SMITH: Why?

HOLMES: I've no wish to clutter my mind with useless information.

SMITH: My dear sir. Your mind may not have elastic walls but it does at least possess both an entrance and an exit. Read the book. Decide for yourself what to retain. One can learn from the unsound as well as the sound, you know. Surely they taught you that, up at the university?

HOLMES: Mr. Smith, anyone foolish enough to have voiced that sentiment would have been rapidly removed from the building and confined as a lunatic.

SMITH: Really? Fascinating. What a good job I never went there.

HOLMES: (A vocal smile)

Cut to:

SCENE 5. INT. THE SITTING ROOM, 221b BAKER STREET.

HOLMES: He was a remarkable man.

WATSON: He sounds it.

HOLMES: I learned a good deal in that reading room, and by no means all of it from the books.

Cut to:

SCENE 6. INT. A GALLERY, THE BRITISH MUSEUM.

No-one is around.
Holmes and Smith approach, deep in conversation.

SMITH: This is the finest place in the capital to study one's fellow man.

In the course of a single morning here you can observe more characteristics than in a week outside. Only the other day – (I noticed a man...)

Holmes interrupts, stopping their progress.

HOLMES: What was that?

SMITH: I heard nothing.

HOLMES: I was sure...Yes. Listen.

They listen.
For the first time, we hear:

JENNY: (Off, muffled) (Crying)

SMITH: That's a woman crying.

HOLMES: I thought I was right. Probably one of the cleaning staff. I'm sorry, you were saying?

SMITH: Mr. Holmes, you disappoint me.

HOLMES: In what way?

SMITH: I believe it's emanating from that store-room. (Moving off) Come with me.

Cut to:

SCENE 7. INT. A SMALL STORE ROOM, THE BRITISH MUSEUM.

The door opens.

JENNY: (Stifles her tears)

SMITH: My dear child, what are you doing in here?

JENNY: Sorry sir. It won't happen again, sir. I'll get back to work.

SMITH: You'll do nothing of the sort.

JENNY: Sir?

Cut to:

SCENE 8. INT. SMITH'S OFFICE, THE BRITISH MUSEUM.

Small, homely. Perhaps an unobtrusive clock ticks, sedately. Smith is pouring a cup of tea.

SMITH: Sugar?

JENNY: Sir?

SMITH: Do you take sugar?

JENNY: No, sir, no thank you.

SMITH: Very well. Mr. Holmes, kindly pass over that plate of biscuits, would you?

Holmes is a little nonplussed by all of this. It makes him uncomfortable.

HOLMES: Yes, of course. Here.

He passes over the plate.
I should be going.

SMITH: No, I think perhaps you should stay.

Something in Smith's voice makes Holmes change his mind.

HOLMES: Very well.

SMITH: Excellent. Now – I am Nathaniel Collington Smith and this gentleman is Mr. Sherlock Holmes. And you are...?

JENNY: Jenny, sir. Jenny Snell.

SMITH: Drink your tea, Miss Snell.

JENNY: I shouldn't be in here. If Miss McCarthy finds out...

SMITH: You may safely leave Miss McCarthy to me. Drink your tea, then Mr. Holmes will pour you some more and you can tell us what's wrong.

JENNY: (Relaxing) Yes sir. Thank you, sir.

She drinks, gratefully.

Cut to:

SCENE 9. INT. THE SITTING ROOM, 221b BAKER STREET.

HOLMES: That was typical of the man. She wasn't a servant to him, just a soul in distress.

WATSON: What was the matter with the girl? Obviously, it was nothing trivial.

HOLMES: How do you know that?

WATSON: If it were, you would hardly be telling me about it, would you? When do we get to the Guttridges of Cripplegate Square?

HOLMES: Patience, Doctor. Let the tale unfold at its own pace.

Cut to:

SCENE 10. INT. SMITH'S OFFICE, THE BRITISH MUSEUM.

Jenny takes another gulp of her tea. She puts down the cup.

SMITH: That's better. Now, Miss Snell. What is it that's so upset you?

JENNY: I...can't tell you.

HOLMES: Is it something to do with your other job?

JENNY: How did you know about that?

HOLMES: I've observed you once or twice arriving here

in the evenings as I was leaving. You always come wearing some sort of uniform.
Obviously, you have other employment during the day.

JENNY: I'm a nursemaid. Well, not really a nursemaid. Just a sort of cleaner really. Like here. (Panicky again) Look, I've got to go.

She stands.

SMITH: Miss Smith, please try to stay calm.

JENNY: If anyone finds out...

SMITH: No-one will learn anything from me. And my young friend here is the very soul of discretion. Do you know what a detective is?

JENNY: I think so, sir.

SMITH: Well you're looking at one. Guardian of secrets, seeker out of truths.

JENNY: Oh.

SMITH: Now please – sit down, compose yourself and tell us what's wrong. You must not fear.

Cut to:

SCENE 11. INT. THE SITTING ROOM, 221b BAKER STREET.

HOLMES: He had an almost hypnotic way with her. I'd never seen anything like it before.

WATSON: What was her story?

HOLMES: At first it seemed nothing. Just an oversensitive reaction.

Cut to:

SCENE 12. INT. SMITH'S OFFICE, THE BRITISH MUSEUM

JENNY: During the day I work at Guttridge's Private Orphanage in Clerkenwell. Have you heard of it?

SMITH: No.

JENNY: Mrs. Guttridge she's the owner. She takes in babies.

HOLMES: Orphans, presumably.

JENNY: No, sir, not orphans though most of them might as well be.

HOLMES: Then what?

SMITH: Unwanted children, Mr. Holmes.

HOLMES: Unwanted? For what reason?

SMITH: There are many. Cost, space, social stigma, general encumbrance.

HOLMES: Good God.

SMITH: Something else they didn't teach you at university?

HOLMES: (Absorbing the idea) Yes...

JENNY: Anyway, the women bring their babies to Mrs. Guttridge, and she takes them in.

HOLMES: So she's a philanthropist.

SMITH: I think you'll find that money changes hands.

HOLMES: Ah.

Cut to:

SCENE 13. INT. THE SITTING ROOM, 221b BAKER STREET.

WATSON: (Distaste) Baby-farming. You're talking about baby- farming.

HOLMES: The concept was totally new to me then. It was quite a shock.

WATSON: It's a shocking practice.

HOLMES: No, I mean it was a shock realising how little I actually knew of life. A valuable lesson.

WATSON: Yes, I'm sure it must have been. (A moment) So – this girl Jenny worked for a baby–farmer.

HOLMES: Yes.

Cut to:

SCENE 14. INT. SMITH'S OFFICE, THE BRITISH MUSEUM.

JENNY: The women pay so much a week. Or sometimes,

they just make one...donation.

HOLMES: And what happens to the children?

JENNY: Mrs. Guttridge looks after them until they're older. Then she finds people to take them.

HOLMES: I see. And something has happened to upset this arrangement?

JENNY: Yes sir.

SMITH: Something connected with Mrs. Guttridge?

JENNY: No, sir, not her. It's her husband. He's a nasty piece of work, sir, though I shouldn't say so.

Cut to:

SCENE 15. INT. THE MEDICINE ROOM, THE GUTTRIDGE HOUSE.

GUTTRIDGE: (Very sharp) Get out of here, girl. You've no business in here.

JENNY: Please sir, Mrs. Guttridge sent me to fetch some iodine, sir.

GUTTRIDGE: Iodine?

JENNY: Yes sir.

GUTTRIDGE: Very well.

Glass bottles clink as he takes one from a shelf.

You fetched this yourself, do you understand? I was not here.

He hands it over.

JENNY: Very good sir. Thank you sir.

GUTTRIDGE: Tell her otherwise and I'll see you're dismissed. Now go.

Jenny rustles away. Cut to:

SCENE 16. INT. SMITH'S OFFICE, THE BRITISH MUSEUM.

HOLMES: Where did this conversation take place?

JENNY: In one of the store rooms, sir. Where the medicines and things are kept.

HOLMES: Interesting.

SMITH: Go on with your story, Jenny. Surely you're not so upset just because someone told you off?

JENNY: If I was, I'd always be crying, sir. No, it's more than that.

HOLMES: Give us the facts.

JENNY: Well...I'm not sure I can. Not real facts, like.

HOLMES: Without the facts, how can we help you?

JENNY: Well...(She trails off)

SMITH: There's more to life than cold facts, Mr. Holmes. Jenny, suppose you tell us this in your own way?

JENNY: Yes, sir. Well, there's something wrong in that house. Something very wrong. If it was just Mrs. Guttridge, everything would be so different...

HOLMES: But it's her husband who causes you this alarm. JENNY: He hates them, sir. The poor little babies. He hates them!

Cut to:

SCENE 17. INT. THE PARLOUR, THE GUTTRIDGE HOUSE.

From a nearby room, three babies cry, noisily, insistently.

GUTTRIDGE: (Wearily) For the love of God. Can't you shut them up?

JENNY: Some of them are sick, sir.

GUTTRIDGE: Again?

JENNY: Mistress says they'll be over it soon.

GUTTRIDGE: Why she has to devote her life to this, I cannot tell.

JENNY: She says they need her, sir. They need her.

Cut to:

SCENE 18. INT. THE SITTING ROOM, 221b BAKER STREET.

WATSON: She was a rare woman. Most of them are only interested in the money. The babies come a very poor second.

HOLMES: You speak from experience?

WATSON: Indirectly. These people are supposed to be registered. Local doctors carry out regular checks. The stories I've heard...

HOLMES: Perhaps this one will be different. WATSON: I hope it is.

Cut to:

SCENE 19. INT. SMITH'S OFFICE, THE BRITISH MUSEUM.

JENNY: Mr. Guttridge's always complaining about the children, about his wife, everything.

HOLMES: And yet he helps her run the orphanage?

JENNY: Yes, sir. In some ways...in some ways he's just a quiet little man. He does whatever his wife tells him to. He only moans about things when she isn't there. (She realises how relaxed she's become) I shouldn't be talking about him like this. Promise me you won't tell! Please!

SMITH: We've already promised. Have no fears.

JENNY: I'll try, sir.

SMITH: That's the way. Well, Jenny – a husband who complains about his wife. I'm afraid that's something that goes on in a good few households, West End as well as East. Something else has happened, hasn't it? Something more serious.

JENNY: Yes. Yes it has.

Cut to:

SCENE 20. INT. A BEDROOM, THE GUTTRIDGE HOUSE.

A large room with many cots.

The babies are quiet. Gentle snores, snuffles, sleeping–noises. Jenny is checking one particular cot.

JENNY: (Approaching) There, that's good. That's nice. (Very low) He'll have nothing to moan about now, will he, the old misery? (Closer) Feeling better, now, are you? Are you?

The baby is not moving. A long moment.

Oh no. No. Please, no...

She runs out. Cut to:

SCENE 21. INT. SMITH'S OFFICE, THE BRITISH MUSEUM.

HOLMES: (Matter–of–factly) How many of them were dead?

JENNY: (Very upset) Three. The three who'd been sick. And sir – (low) This was the day after I saw Mr. Guttridge messing about with the medicines. The very next day.

SMITH: Ah.

JENNY: As God's in his heaven, sirs. I...I think he killed them.

Cut to:

SCENE 22. INT. THE SITTING ROOM, 221b BAKER STREET.

WATSON: It wouldn't be the first time, I'm afraid. Were the babies insured?

HOLMES: As usual, you cut straight to the heart of the matter. Yes, they were.

WATSON: Was there a doctor's report?

HOLMES: Mrs. Guttridge did everything by the letter of the law. The doctor was sent for straight away.

WATSON: And?

HOLMES: No obvious cause of death.

WATSON: It may not have been the most rigorous examination. Those East End practices are desperately overworked.

HOLMES: And some of the doctors there are not above taking money to turn a blind eye.

WATSON: That is a disgusting suggestion.

HOLMES: Which you know full well to be true. Every barrel has its rotten apples, Watson. It will always be so.

WATSON: (Reluctantly) Yes, I'm afraid you're right. (A moment) I take it you investigated this Guttridge man, then? Was it your first murder case?

HOLMES: Actually, I was reluctant to get involved.

Cut to:

SCENE 23. INT. SMITH'S OFFICE, THE BRITISH MUSEUM.

HOLMES: You must go to the police.

JENNY: The police! I can't! Don't you know what happens to servants who criticise their masters, sir? I'd be out on my ear and no character. Then what would happen to me?

HOLMES: You have your job here.

JENNY: Four hours work at fivepence a night? Could you live on that?

SMITH: No, he couldn't. I understand your problem, my dear.

JENNY: (Very fearful) There's something else, sir. Something I haven't said.

SMITH: And what is that?

HOLMES: She's afraid that Guttridge knows of her suspicions.

JENNY: That's it, sir. He knows I saw him doing it – whatever it was. With the medicines.

HOLMES: When was this?

JENNY: Five days ago.

SMITH: Have you been in to work there since?

JENNY: Every day. I'd get the elbow otherwise.

HOLMES: You are a very brave young woman.

JENNY: Brave? Not me, sir. I've been terrified, I tell you straight.

HOLMES: Has Mr. Guttridge said anything to you? Or done anything suspicious?

JENNY: No. But I've kept away from him best I could.

SMITH: Very sensible of you. (A moment) My young friend here will look into the matter.

JENNY: (Gratefully) Oh, sir...

HOLMES: Smith?

JENNY: I'm ever so grateful, sir. I had to tell someone – I'm glad it was you.

Cut to:

SCENE 24. EXT. OUTSIDE THE BRITISH MUSEUM. NIGHT.

Quiet traffic, pedestrians.

SMITH: (Deep breath) Another fine night.

HOLMES: Why did you say that to the girl?

SMITH: My dear Mr. Holmes, surely you found the story... interesting?

HOLMES: Of course. The girl is observant and intelligent, and her suspicions are probably correct.

SMITH: And she appears to have great faith in your ability to help her. Which I share.

HOLMES: Thank you. But the fact remains I don't see what on earth I can do.

SMITH: You can stir yourself out from behind your books and look into the real world for a change. What sort of detective turns his back on a possible murder case?

HOLMES: I can hardly march up to this woman's... establishment and tell her I'm investigating three suspicious deaths.

SMITH: Of course you can't. But there are other ways. Put that brain of yours to use.

Cut to:

SCENE 25. INT. AN EAST END PUB.

Full, raucous and a bit frightening. Conversations, arguments, laughter.

Glass breaks. An ironic cheer goes up.

Closer, some of the regulars react to an incongruous sight...

REGULARS: Look what the cat dragged home / Slumming it, are you dearie? / Gordon Bennett, it's champagne Charlie hisself...
The object of their attention makes it unscathed to the bar.

LANDLADY: Good evening sir. What's your pleasure?

HOLMES: Whisky, please. And have one yourself.

LANDLADY: Thank you sir. (Louder, pointedly) Pleasure to encounter a real gent, for a change.

REGULARS: (Good–natured jeers)

Holmes fishes out coins as the landlady pours his drink.

LANDLADY: There. Best in the house.

HOLMES: Thank you.

LANDLADY: (Lower) Now sir, what tickles your fancy? Big, skinny, ripe for the plucking, what're you after?

HOLMES: What I'm after is information.

LANDLADY: (Suddenly cagey) What sort of information?

HOLMES: Do you know a man called Guttridge?

Cut to:

SCENE 26. INT. THE SITTING ROOM, 221b BAKER STREET.

HOLMES: It was a mistake, of course. She shut her mouth

and didn't open it again.

WATSON: They're very suspicious of strangers in those parts. Especially ones from up west.

HOLMES: Yes, so I discovered. It was a stupid miscalculation.

Cut to:

SCENE 27. INT. THE READING ROOM, THE BRITISH MUSEUM.

SMITH: Don't berate yourself. The basic idea was perfectly sound.

HOLMES: If you want the local gossip go to the local pub.
(Ruefully)
Just don't go dressed for the opera.

SMITH: I trust you didn't give up the quest quite that easily.

HOLMES: Of course not. I waited until it was full dark and went round to the house itself.

Cut to:

SCENE 28. EXT. OUTSIDE THE GUTTRIDGE HOUSE. NIGHT.

Cripplegate Square is not in a salubrious neighbourhood. Distant raised voices, dogs, perhaps even a muffled scream from well in the distance.

HOLMES (over): The area wasn't...pleasant. Guttridge's Private Orphanage was a rambling old building set back from the street. It must have been quite a place in its day.

WATSON (over): Didn't you feel even more conspicuous there than in the pub?

HOLMES (over): Oddly enough, no I didn't. Evening wear is ideally suited to hiding in the undergrowth. Every burglar should invest in a set of tails.

In the scene, the front door opens. Two women emerge.

WOMAN: (Sobbing)

MRS. GUTTRIDGE: Easy now. Easy. She'll be safe and well–cared for.

And you can come and visit her whenever you want, I've told you that.

WOMAN: I don't think I could bear it. I really don't.

MRS. GUTTRIDGE: I understand. But if you change your mind, there's always a welcome for you here.

WOMAN: You're so kind. Without you, I...I'd have had to...

MRS. GUTTRIDGE: Now there's no sense dwelling on might–have–beens. Will you be all right going home?

WOMAN: It's not far. I'll be quite safe. Oh...

With a final rush of emotion, she hugs Mrs. Guttridge.

MRS. GUTTRIDGE: There, there child. It's mended. Everything's all right now.

Cut to:

SCENE 29. INT. SMITH'S OFFICE, THE BRITISH MUSEUM.

HOLMES: It was immensely frustrating. I could see in the front door, but I couldn't learn anything of use. And there was no sign of Mr. Guttridge at all. If I'm going to see this thing through, I need to get inside.

SMITH: And how exactly do you propose to do that?

HOLMES: I don't know yet.

SMITH: If I might make a small suggestion?

HOLMES: Please do.

SMITH: This could be an ideal opportunity to put some of that expensive university experience to good use.

HOLMES: Applied chemistry?

SMITH: That wasn't what I had in mind, no. Try to think in something other than straight lines.

Cut to:

SCENE 30. INT. THE SITTING ROOM, 221b BAKER STREET.

WATSON: So that's where you got it from.

HOLMES: Watson, you're interrupting my flow. Got what from?

WATSON: That infuriating expression. How many times have you told me to stop thinking in straight lines?

HOLMES: It's very good advice.

WATSON: Well, did it work?

HOLMES: Actually, yes, it did.

Cut to:

SCENE 31. EXT. AN EAST END STREET. DAY.

Holmes is in disguise. He's a market supervisor – working class but not the lowest rung.

HOLMES: 'Scuse me, mate.

MAN: Yeah?

HOLMES: I'm looking for Guttridge's Orphanage. D'you know it?

Cut to:

SCENE 32. INT. THE SITTING ROOM, 221b BAKER STREET.

WATSON: Are you really saying – (that was the first time...)

Holmes is annoyed at yet another interruption.

HOLMES: Watson.

WATSON: Sorry. But this is fascinating. You're saying that was the very first time you ever used a disguise?

HOLMES: Exactly so. Thinking sideways, you see? What did I do at university apart from study – I acted.

WATSON: You've never told me that.

HOLMES: You've never asked me. May I continue?

WATSON: No more interruptions, I promise. What did you find when you got to the orphanage?

HOLMES: What I expected to find. My primary suspect.

Cut to:

SCENE 33. EXT. THE FRONT PORCH, THE GUTTRIDGE HOUSE. DAY.

Holmes is still in character.

GUTTRIDGE: Yes?

HOLMES: I want to see Mrs. Guttridge.

GUTTRIDGE: What makes you think she's here?

HOLMES: Look, mate, don't mess me about. This is Guttridge's Private Orphanage, right? Where else is she going to be?

GUTTRIDGE: (Very suspicious) Who are you?

HOLMES: (Less aggressively) I'm someone who wants to see the...proprietor. Look, please.

MRS. GUTTRIDGE: (Off, inside) Who is it, Toby?

GUTTRIDGE: Someone for you.

MRS. GUTTRIDGE: (Approaching) Then why didn't you send Jenny to find me? (She sees Holmes. A moment) Good afternoon.

HOLMES: Mrs. Guttridge? I was told...Look...

A moment.

MRS. GUTTRIDGE: It's a chilly day. We'll be more comfortable inside.

Cut to:

SCENE 34. INT. THE PARLOUR, THE GUTTRIDGE HOUSE.

Mrs. Guttridge and Holmes sit.

MRS. GUTTRIDGE: That's better. Now, I expect you'd like some tea.

She rings a small handbell.

HOLMES: (Hastily) No, that's all right. Don't bother on my account.

MRS. GUTTRIDGE: It's no bother.

She rings again.

Where is that girl?

HOLMES: Look, really...

The door opens. It's Jenny.

JENNY: Yes, ma'am?

MRS. GUTTRIDGE: Tea please, Jenny. And some of the cherry cake.

JENNY: Ma'am.

Cut to:

SCENE 35. INT. THE SITTING ROOM, 221b BAKER STREET.

WATSON: Did she recognise you?

HOLMES: I was sure she would. But no, she didn't. Quite a boost to my confidence, I can tell you.

WATSON: It's not easy to imagine your confidence ever needing a boost.

HOLMES: It was a long time ago.

Cut to:

SCENE 36. INT. THE PARLOUR, THE GUTTRIDGE HOUSE.

Mrs. Guttridge is pouring the tea.

MRS. GUTTRIDGE: Now, Mr...?

HOLMES: Hawkins, ma'am. Albert Hawkins.

MRS. GUTTRIDGE: Now, Mr. Hawkins. You drink your tea

and I'll tell you why you've come to me.

HOLMES: Ma'am?

MRS. GUTTRIDGE: There.

She passes him the tea.

Both in and out of character, Holmes is a touch nonplussed.

HOLMES: Thanks. What do you mean, ma'am? You'll tell me?

MRS. GUTTRIDGE: My dear Mr. Hawkins, people only come here for one reason. The details vary, but the basic facts are always the same. Now let me see... You're in work, yes?

HOLMES: Market supervisor.

MRS. GUTTRIDGE: Decent enough pay but not enough to feed one more mouth. Am I right?

HOLMES: We've got five already. Look, no offence and all, but if there was any other way I wouldn't be here.

MRS. GUTTRIDGE: You're not alone, Mr. Hawkins. Oh no, you're definitely not alone. At least you're not contemplating something more...drastic.

HOLMES: I'll have nothing to do with that! And no more will my Elsie. I've seen what those butchers do.

MRS. GUTTRIDGE: And so have I, I'm sorry to say. We shan't mention it again. Does your wife know you're here?

HOLMES: Oh yes.

MRS. GUTTRIDGE: Good. Well, we do have space at the moment. Would you like to see round the house?

HOLMES: I wouldn't mind. Put my mind at rest, like.

MRS. GUTTRIDGE: Of course. Drink up your tea and I'll give you a tour.

Cut to:

SCENE 37. INT. A BEDROOM, THE GUTTRIDGE HOUSE.

The babies are asleep. Odd noises.

MRS. GUTTRIDGE: (Low) You've made a good choice, Mr. Hawkins. I never take in more babies than I can cope with, unlike some, I'm sorry to say.

HOLMES: (Low) We have heard stories, my Else and me.

MRS. GUTTRIDGE: And some of them are undoubtedly true, I'm afraid.

HOLMES: What happens if they get sick?

MRS. GUTTRIDGE: I can care for most common illnesses myself. And of course we're registered with a local doctor.

HOLMES: Good. That's good...And they do look all right, like. Look at 'em sleeping so peaceful. Happy, and that...(He can't continue, overcome with emotion)

MRS. GUTTRIDGE: Oh, my dear young man. I realize how hard this must be for you.

HOLMES: Hard? Hard's not the half of it.

MRS. GUTTRIDGE: Of course it's not. And nothing I can say to you will ease the pain. But look around you, Mr. Hawkins. These babies are clean and well–fed and content. If I can give your little one those blessings, well, isn't that better than the life he'll face outside these walls?

HOLMES: Yeah. Yeah, it is. Course it is. (A moment) So – I suppose all I need to know now...Well...(He trails off)

MRS. GUTTRIDGE: I think there's still some cherry cake downstairs. We can discuss the practicalities over some more tea. Come along.

Cut to:

SCENE 38. INT. THE SITTING ROOM, 221b BAKER STREET.

HOLMES: "The practicalities" turned out to be three-pence a day or a single payment of five pounds.

WATSON: (A whistle)

HOLMES: Yes, it was certainly more than the going rate, I checked. But it was a superior establishment.

WATSON: How many working class women could afford five pounds?

HOLMES: Well, when you consider the alternatives...

WATSON: I'm afraid the alternatives are the only way for most people in that position. Something's going to have to be done, you know.
Sooner or later.

HOLMES: I agree. But we are straying somewhat from the story.

WATSON: Sorry. Did you manage to see that medicine store room?

HOLMES: It would have been too out of character, I'm afraid. But I did at least succeed in getting another look at the alleged child–killer. He was summoned to show me out.

Cut to:

SCENE 39. INT. THE HALLWAY, THE GUTTRIDGE HOUSE.

Holmes and Guttridge approach.

HOLMES: Your wife's a wonderful woman, Mr. Guttridge.

GUTTRIDGE: So I'm constantly being told.

HOLMES: You must be proud of her.

GUTTRIDGE: There are perhaps...nobler ways to make a living.

HOLMES: I can't think of any. She's a real Godsend, she is.

Guttridge opens the front door.

GUTTRIDGE: Do you say so.

HOLMES: (Leaving) I do, sir. God bless her – and you too.

GUTTRIDGE: Good day to you, Mr. Hawkins.

He shuts the door. (Breathes deeply) Cut to:

SCENE 40. INT. SMITH'S OFFICE, THE BRITISH MUSEUM.

HOLMES: There's a definite undercurrent of...I'm not sure – hate, possibly. Weariness, distaste...But I'm not prepared to brand him as a murderer on the strength of it.

SMITH: I'm pleased to hear it.

HOLMES: I have to know what's in that medicine store.

SMITH: And how do you propose to find out?

HOLMES: I've thought of two separate ways. Neither of them is ideal. One is positively illegal.

SMITH: And the other?

Cut to:

SCENE 41. INT. A GALLERY, THE BRITISH MUSEUM.

Open and echoing.

JENNY: No! I can't!

HOLMES: Jenny...

JENNY: Suppose he catches me?

HOLMES: I'll make sure he's out of the way.

JENNY: But I wouldn't know what to look for.

HOLMES: I'll give you a list.

JENNY: A list? Oh, sir...What good's a list to me?

HOLMES: (Realising) You can't read.

JENNY: Nor write. No, sir, I can't.

Cut to:

SCENE 42. INT. THE SITTING ROOM, 221b BAKER STREET.

WATSON: Thank God for it. Holmes, what the devil were you thinking of?

HOLMES: Collington Smith used exactly those words.

WATSON: Good for him. To put that child into danger...

HOLMES: I had a perfectly foolproof diversion worked out.

WATSON: Did you?

HOLMES: (A sigh) As I said, it was a long time ago. I wouldn't do it now.

WATSON: Unless there was no other way.

HOLMES: The point is academic. I had to fall back on my second plan of attack.

WATSON: The illegal one.

HOLMES: Quite.

WATSON: I know exactly what it was.

HOLMES: Of course you do.

Cut to:

SCENE 43. EXT. REAR GARDEN, THE GUTTRIDGE HOUSE. NIGHT.

Very quiet and still.

Close, a glass–cutter does its stuff.

It stops. Tap...Tap...Tap...and part of a pane of glass comes away.

Suddenly, not far off, a dog barks.

HOLMES: (Catches his breath)

He freezes. But then a cat screeches and the barking and squealing recede together as the animals run off.

It was a coincidence. A moment of calm.

(Breathes again)

He reaches through the hole in the window and opens the latch.

(Sotto, smug) Ha. Elementary.

Cut to:

SCENE 44. INT. SMITH'S OFFICE, THE BRITISH MUSEUM.

SMITH: My dear Mr. Holmes. I cannot condone such blatantly criminal activity. (A moment) Unless of course it yielded the desired result.

HOLMES: Arsenic. He's been concentrating pure arsenic and storing it in unmarked bottles in a locked cupboard.

SMITH: Then young Miss Snell was quite correct.

HOLMES: It looks like it.

SMITH: What will you do now?

HOLMES: There's one more piece of evidence I need. Then my case will be complete.

Cut to:

SCENE 45. INT. THE SITTING ROOM, 221b BAKER STREET.

WATSON: I presume you were talking about the doctor.

HOLMES: Yes, I was. I had to be sure that the infants had died from arsenical poisoning. ["arse–EN–icle"]

WATSON: What about your theory that the doctor was in league with the murderer?

HOLMES: I was never said he was, Watson. I said he might have been. I had to hope that seeing him face-to-face would enable me to decide.

Cut to:

SCENE 46. INT. A DOCTOR'S SURGERY, THE EAST END.

Small, cramped, and with a lot of patients-in-waiting noise filtering in from the next room.

DOCTOR: A detective? Do you mean from Scotland Yard?

HOLMES: A private detective.

DOCTOR: Are you sick? Injured?

HOLMES: No.

DOCTOR: Sir, I have a room full of patients out there and a 100 more waiting to take their place. I don't mean to be rude, but I have no time to play games.

HOLMES: This is no game. You are the official medical examiner for Guttridge's Orphanage, are you not?

DOCTOR: What about it?

HOLMES: I have been commissioned to investigate the recent deaths of three infants.

DOCTOR: Mr...

HOLMES: Holmes. Sherlock Holmes.

DOCTOR: Mr. Holmes, when you leave my rooms look around you. Look at the filth and the squalour and the hunger. And ask yourself which is the stranger – that children die or that they manage to live. Have you seen inside Mrs. Guttridge's establishment? Have you met the lady herself?

HOLMES: Yes, I have.

DOCTOR: Then you'll know that the children there live like royalty compared to most. I've seen Mrs. Guttridge take in babies who were more bone than flesh. If some of them don't survive, then look outside that house for the cause, sir, not inside it. (A moment) Now if you don't mind, I have to do my best to help these people.

HOLMES: Will you answer just two questions?

DOCTOR: If you will agree to ask them and then leave.

HOLMES: I agree.

DOCTOR: Then ask me your questions.

HOLMES: Did you conduct a thorough examination of the dead babies?

DOCTOR: As thorough as my time and my resources permitted, yes I did.

HOLMES: And did you detect any signs at all of arsenical poisoning?

DOCTOR: (Taken aback) Arsenic? Good God no. Not a trace.

Cut to:

SCENE 47. INT. THE SITTING ROOM, 221b BAKER STREET.

WATSON: You believed him.

HOLMES: I was impressed with him. I've said to you before now that when a doctor goes wrong he makes a formidable criminal.

WATSON: Yes, you have. I can't say I was flattered.

HOLMES: Then perhaps this will redress the balance. In all my life I've not met many people who were thoroughly decent, uncomplicated, good men. And of the ones I have met – several of them were doctors.

Cut to:

SCENE 48. INT. SMITH'S OFFICE, THE BRITISH MUSEUM.

SMITH: You appear to have arrived at something of an impasse, my friend.

HOLMES: Why else is arsenic there, if not to kill those children?

SMITH: Rats?

HOLMES: You can buy poison for vermin over the counter at any chemist's shop. If I read the evidence aright, that arsenic was being produced in secret, then hidden away.

SMITH: Then what do you propose to do now?

HOLMES: I suppose it could be nothing more than a coincidence...I have to talk to the girl again.

Cut to:

SCENE 49. INT. A GALLERY, THE BRITISH MUSEUM.

After closing time.
Jenny is mopping the floor, absorbed in what she is doing.

HOLMES: (Close) Jenny.

JENNY: (Starts)

HOLMES: I'm sorry. I didn't mean to startle you.

JENNY: It's not you, sir, it's me. I'm just frightened at any little noise, now. (A sudden thought) You're not going to ask me to spy on him again?

HOLMES: No, no. And...I'm sorry about asking you before. It was wrong. Please forgive me.

JENNY: Forgive you? Forgive...(She starts to cry)

HOLMES: My dear Miss Snell...Please stop crying...

JENNY: Sorry, sir. I'm really...(She trails off)

HOLMES: What's wrong?

JENNY: Nothing's wrong. It's just...Well, people like me don't get apologised to, that's all.

HOLMES: Ah. Then you do forgive me.

JENNY: Course I do, sir. You was only trying to help me, after all.

HOLMES: Thank you.

JENNY: So – what do you want this time?

HOLMES: I want to ask you this. When you surprised Mr. Guttridge with the medicines – can you remember what he was doing. Exactly what he was doing?

JENNY: Well...(She trails off)

HOLMES: It might help if you tell me what he was working with. Do you remember?

JENNY: I'm not sure...

HOLMES: Recall the scene. Mrs. Guttridge asked you to get some iodine.

JENNY: That's right.

HOLMES: So you had to stop what you were doing. What was that?

JENNY: I was washing the sheets. I'd just put the clean ones on the beds, and I was washing the old ones.

HOLMES: Very good. So you had to stop washing the sheets and you went to the medicine store. Was the door open or shut?

JENNY: (Slowly remembering) Shut. It was shut.

HOLMES: Excellent. You pushed open the door – and you saw Mr. Guttridge. Was he facing you?

JENNY: No he had his back to the door. That's right – he was bending over the table. He turned round...And he had...(puzzled) flypapers. He was holding flypapers.

Cut to:

SCENE 50. INT. THE SITTING ROOM, 221b BAKER STREET.

WATSON: Flypapers.

HOLMES: Made by impregnating a strip of paper with a weak solution of...

WATSON:...arsenic. Soak the paper in water, boil the solution dry, and what's left is pure concentrated poison. Pretty damning.

HOLMES: Conclusive.

Cut to:

SCENE 51. INT. A GALLERY, THE BRITISH MUSEUM.

HOLMES: Excellent, Jenny. You've done well.

JENNY: Have I, sir?

HOLMES: Very well indeed. I fancy that what you saw was the very poison being prepared.

JENNY: No! That's so horrible.

HOLMES: I need to you do something else for me, now.

JENNY: I'll do anything I can, sir.

HOLMES: Continue to keep your eyes and your ears open. There's more to be discovered. If you see or hear anything else that might be important – anything at all – let me know at once. Do you understand?

JENNY: Oh yes, sir. I understand.

Cut to:

SCENE 52. INT. A SMALL ROOM, THE GUTTRIDGE HOUSE.

Jenny is bottle–feeding a baby. It produces rhythmical sucking noises.

JENNY: There you are...Oh, not too fast, now. Good...

MRS. GUTTRIDGE: When you've finished here Jenny, collect up the bottles and leave them to soak.

JENNY: Yes ma'am.

MRS. GUTTRIDGE: (Going) I'll be in the scullery if you need me.

JENNY: Ma'am.

Mrs. Guttridge has gone. The baby continues to drink.

JENNY: Yes you like that, don't you? Course you do. That's the way...

GUTTRIDGE: (From nowhere) You, girl.

JENNY: (Starts, very frightened) Sir?

GUTTRIDGE: Stop that and come with me. I want to talk to you.

Cut to:

SCENE 53. INT. THE MEDICINE ROOM, THE GUTTRIDGE HOUSE.

Guttridge and Jenny approach from the corridor.

GUTTRIDGE: Get in there.

JENNY: No. No!

GUTTRIDGE: Quiet, girl. Go in, I say.

He pushes her in, follows her...and closes and locks the door.

JENNY: (Fights for breath, very scared)

GUTTRIDGE: Stop that and listen to me. I want to know exactly what you saw in here the other day. You understand? Exactly.

Cut to:

SCENE 54. INT. SMITH'S OFFICE, THE BRITISH MUSEUM.

SMITH: I'm afraid I have some disturbing news.

HOLMES: What news?

SMITH: I've been speaking to the cleaning supervisor. Jenny Snell hasn't come into work for the past four nights.

Cut to:

SCENE 55. INT. THE SITTING ROOM, 221b BAKER STREET.

WATSON: Oh, God.

HOLMES: No, it didn't look good.

WATSON: What did you do?

HOLMES: I trusted that my disguise really had taken them in, and went round to Guttridge's Orphanage as myself.

WATSON: Quite a risk.

HOLMES: It had to be done.

Cut to:

SCENE 56. EXT. FRONT DOOR, THE GUTTRIDGE HOUSE. DAY.

HOLMES: Good afternoon. My name is Sherlock Holmes. I'm here to enquire about Miss Jennifer Snell.

A moment.

GUTTRIDGE: Then you'd better come in.

Cut to:

SCENE 57. INT. SMITH'S OFFICE, THE BRITISH MUSEUM.

SMITH: What happened?

HOLMES: I was presented with this. Here.

He produces a folded piece of paper.

Cut to:

SCENE 58. INT. THE SITTING ROOM, 221b BAKER STREET.

WATSON: But surely...

HOLMES: Exactly. A fatal error.

WATSON: But what did it mean? Had he killed her, too?

HOLMES: The girl had been silenced. I'm afraid I could see no other explanation.

WATSON: What did you do?

HOLMES: To be honest – I wasn't sure what to do.

Cut to:

SCENE 59. INT. SMITH'S OFFICE, THE BRITISH MUSEUM.

HOLMES: I want to ask your advice.

SMITH: My advice? My dear sir, I'm just a tired old librarian, too rapidly approaching an unwilling retirement. What can you possible wish to ask me?

HOLMES: If I should go to the police with what I know, or confront the murderer myself.

Cut to:

SCENE 60. INT. THE SITTING ROOM, 221b BAKER STREET.

WATSON: What was Smith's advice?

HOLMES: To do neither.

WATSON: Neither? Why on earth not?

HOLMES: For a very good reason, which I'd completely overlooked.

Cut to:

SCENE 61. INT. SMITH'S OFFICE, THE BRITISH MUSEUM.

SMITH: You're too eager to show off your cleverness. A calculating criminal has made a slip and Sherlock Holmes has detected it. Am I correct?

HOLMES: Well, yes, I suppose you are. But if I'm right and the girl has been done away with...

SMITH: Then justice must be done. Of course. But it seems to me, Mr. Holmes, that you're proposing to confront your villain with only half a case. You may have solved the new crime – but what of the old one?

Cut to:

SCENE 62. INT. THE SITTING ROOM, 221b BAKER STREET.

WATSON: The dead babies.

HOLMES: He was quite right, of course. I had nothing to link the three dead infants with the secret store of arsenic. No evidence whatsoever of foul play.

WATSON: What did you do?

HOLMES: Something you've seen me do many times. I just sat and smoked and thought. And eventually, I saw the truth. And then I knew exactly what course I should take.

Cut to:

SCENE 63. INT. THE PARLOUR, THE GUTTRIDGE HOUSE.

MRS. GUTTRIDGE: Mr. Holmes, I fail to see how I can help you further. I've given you Jenny's home address, I suggest you contact her at her father's.

HOLMES: I doubt if I should find her there.

GUTTRIDGE: What do you mean by that?

HOLMES: But I am not here solely about Miss Snell. I am investigating the recent deaths of three babies in your care, Mrs. Guttridge.

MRS. GUTTRIDGE: Those children died of natural causes,

God rest their souls. I have the doctor's certificates.

HOLMES: I'm well aware of that.

MRS. GUTTRIDGE: Then what is there to investigate?

HOLMES: A very great deal. For instance – I know that your medicine store contains a hidden supply of concentrated arsenic.

MRS. GUTTRIDGE: What?

HOLMES: And I know that the arsenic was used to kill those infants.

MRS. GUTTRIDGE: But there was no trace of poison – (in them...)

GUTTRIDGE: (To Holmes) You know that?

HOLMES: Oh yes. And finally, I know that Jenny Snell was unfortunate enough to stumble on to what was happening. And was killed, to keep her silent.

MRS. GUTTRIDGE: Jenny's dead?

HOLMES: Unfortunately for her killer, she came to me first.

MRS. GUTTRIDGE: She can't be dead. It's a lie. Toby, tell him.

GUTTRIDGE: I already have. She had to leave unexpected.

HOLMES: Oh yes.

He produces his sheet of paper.

"My Mum died sudden I have to go home"...

MRS. GUTTRIDGE: There you are.

Holmes examines the paper.

HOLMES: Actually, it's quite well done. Except for one rather significant detail.

GUTTRIDGE: What are you on about?

HOLMES: Next time you forge a farewell letter, Guttridge, I suggest you first make sure that your victim knows how to write.

A long moment.

MRS. GUTTRIDGE: Tobias, tell me this isn't true.

HOLMES: What did you do with the body, Guttridge? There's newly- turned earth in the back garden – shall we go and dig it up?

MRS. GUTTRIDGE: Oh dear God.

HOLMES: I have you, Guttridge. There's no sense in denying it.

A long moment.

GUTTRIDGE: I'm not going to deny it.

MRS. GUTTRIDGE: Oh dear God. Oh dear Lord. How could you do it? Why?

HOLMES: Well? Will you tell her, or shall I?

A long moment. Guttridge reaches a decision.

GUTTRIDGE: I had to shut her up. She knew I killed those babies.

MRS. GUTTRIDGE: Toby!

GUTTRIDGE: Don't say nothing, Emily.

HOLMES: You admit it? You killed Jennifer Snell?

GUTTRIDGE: I said so, yes.

HOLMES: And the three children?

GUTTRIDGE: Yes.

MRS. GUTTRIDGE: Oh, Toby...

HOLMES: How?

GUTTRIDGE: What do you mean, how?

HOLMES: It was brilliantly done. Not a trace of poison in their systems. Tell me how you did it. (A long moment) Very well then, tell me why.

Guttridge says nothing.

Perhaps it was for the insurance money.

GUTTRIDGE: Yes! Yes, that's it. The insurance.

HOLMES: The insurance money goes to your wife. I checked. I ask you again: just how were the murders done? (A long moment) You don't know. Of course you don't know – because you were not the killer.

GUTTRIDGE: I tell you I was.

HOLMES: You found the evidence. You knew there had been foul play even though you didn't know the method – and since then, you've done everything in your power to protect the real murderer. To protect your wife.

No–one speaks. A long moment.

Only she handles the children. Only she supervises their food and their medicines. And only she stands to benefit from their deaths.

GUTTRIDGE: No!

MRS. GUTTRIDGE: (Moving off) I've had enough of this.

HOLMES: Please remain exactly where you are. Thank you. Since one of you can't explain and the other won't, permit me. It's been done on adults before now, but never on children – so I congratulate you on a totally original crime. You start with the smallest of amounts – almost infinitesimal, I suppose, on an infant. Then you build up the dose, a fraction of a grain by a fraction of a grain, day by day – until you have a child hopelessly addicted to arsenic. Keep administering the drug

and the child lives. Withhold it – and the result is death. And not a trace of anything harmful to be detected. Clever – and diabolical.

A long moment.

MRS. GUTTRIDGE: You've got no proof.

HOLMES: I have abundant proof. It's here, in this house.

GUTTRIDGE: You'll find no arsenic here.

HOLMES: Of course I won't. You've destroyed it all, just as you destroyed that innocent young girl, and for the same reason – a perverted desire to protect your wife.

MRS. GUTTRIDGE: Toby, my dear...

GUTTRIDGE: Don't say anything, Emily. You're right. He's got no proof.

HOLMES: Tell him, Mrs. Guttridge.

GUTTRIDGE: What? Tell me what?

HOLMES: Tell him the rest. Tell him that three wasn't going to be enough.

GUTTRIDGE: What?

HOLMES: Tell him that every single one of the babies in this house is already a drug addict – waiting to be casually snuffed out, the next time you felt the whim or the need for power or some ready cash. Tell him!

A long moment.

MRS. GUTTRIDGE: You are so wrong.

HOLMES: I don't think so.

MRS. GUTTRIDGE: A whim? Power? Money? (A long moment. She sighs) That's not why I do it.

GUTTRIDGE: Emily...

MRS. GUTTRIDGE: Do you know what my babies have to look forward to, Mr. Holmes? Do you know about the factories and the workhouses and the filth and the squalour? Have you seen the children begging and stealing? Have you seen them selling their bodies on the streets for a penny a time?

HOLMES: I've seen them.

MRS. GUTTRIDGE: Well, before it comes to that – for a time – for a tiny, fleeting time – I can give them warmth and comfort...and love. And then...Then, I can make sure the world doesn't get them and soil them and wear them down and finally destroy them like animals. And don't you tell me that what I do is wrong. It's the world that's wrong, sir. Forget about me, I don't matter. Do something about the world out there – if you can.

A long moment.

GUTTRIDGE: What are you going do with us?

HOLMES: Take you to the police.

MRS. GUTTRIDGE: And then it'll be the courts. And then the hangman.

HOLMES: I imagine so.

MRS. GUTTRIDGE: Then tell me this, Mr. Holmes: what will happen to my babies now? You tell me that.

Holmes has no answer. A long moment.

Then cut to:

SCENE 64. INT. SMITH'S OFFICE, THE BRITISH MUSEUM.

SMITH: (Sighs)

HOLMES: I didn't know what to say.

A moment.

SMITH: I have one question.

HOLMES: What is it?

SMITH: The evidence of the other children – were you sure? Or was it just a bluff on your part?

HOLMES: It wasn't a bluff. One of the side-effects of progressive arsenic addiction is unnatural lethargy and calm, especially in the young. I'd seen the signs when she showed me round the house on my first visit. I just didn't recognize them for what they were until later.

SMITH: So – all the children are due for the same fate. Dear God.

HOLMES: The doctor thinks they can be slowly weaned off the stuff.
They might live. If you can call the world that's waiting for them a life.

SMITH: Come now, Mr. Holmes. Whatever our experiences may suggest, I like to think that the world is basically a good place. There's still tolerance and warmth and humanity out there. Don't you believe that?

A long moment. Cut to:

SCENE 65. INT. THE SITTING ROOM, 221b BAKER STREET.

WATSON: I'd very much like to meet that man.

HOLMES: I'm afraid that's not possible. He died, early last year.

WATSON: Oh. I'm...sorry.

A moment. Holmes doesn't like acknowledging an emotional bond to anyone. But eventually:

HOLMES: Thank you.

A moment. Watson deliberately breaks it.

WATSON: Why didn't the doctor recognise the symptoms in the other children?

HOLMES: I dare say I was lot more familiar with the signs of poisoning than he was. Besides, he had no reason to look for them. He saw clean sheets and good care and was grateful for it.

A moment.

WATSON: So – that was your story about love.

HOLMES: It was. Guttridge loved his wife, murderer or no. He loved her so much that he was willing to take her guilt on himself – and to kill to protect her. And she loved the children – and so she murdered them. Do you still insist that love is a positive force for good?

WATSON: Yes, of course I do. You can't argue from the particular to the general like that. It's...it's thinking in straight lines.

HOLMES: Touché, Doctor. A palpable hit.

A moment. The fire crackles.

WATSON: What a sordid business. Poor Jenny Snell.

HOLMES: The wrong place at the wrong time – she must have walked in on Guttridge at the very moment he discovered the arsenic.

WATSON: How can a young girl's life hang on such a slender thread?

HOLMES: How, indeed?

Wearily, he gets up.

(Moving off) (An exhausted sigh)

Distant, echoing, not in the scene, a solo violin plays the Tristan theme.

Holmes has moved to the window. He pulls aside the curtain and looks out into the darkness. A long moment.

Was Smith right, do you think? Is the world basically a good place?

WATSON: I believe so. Don't you?

HOLMES: I wish I could, my friend. I wish I could. (A long moment) I think the rain's stopped. (He peers out) Yes, it has.

A moment. The fire crackles.
Perhaps a not-too-obtrusive hansom cab clops by outside.

The music becomes the closing sig.
Closing announcements.
The music ends.
The End.

A Study in Abstruse Detail

by Wendy C. Fries

"Good heavens, Watson, out with it already!"

It is a mark of my state of mind that at first I didn't hear my friend Sherlock Holmes, instead interpreting those words as my own frustrated thoughts.

It wasn't until a lean shadow cast itself over my work, and I looked up to see his scowling face looking down, that I realised he'd spoken.

I glanced at the papers in my lap, most with but a few notes, then scowled back at my companion. The January evening was cold, the fire burnt low, and I – too aware of Holmes's opinion on my record of his exploits – was in no mood to be chivvied again for my devotion to these "fairytales."

"I'm out of sorts and mumbling to myself. It's nothing."

Holmes collapsed into the chair across from me, peered over his steepled fingers. "My dear fellow, you've tapped out and recharged your unlighted pipe twice in thirty minutes, hoisted an empty brandy glass three times, and, most tellingly, taken four deep breaths and held them for long seconds at a time."

Already discontent, I took nothing of my usual delight in Holmes's attentions, so I'm afraid my reply was snappish. "And what of it? The surgery was dull, I don't much care for my new tobacco, and all this snow has given me a chill."

Holmes patted his chair and then himself, eventually unearthing a packet of shag, which he tossed to me. "You're writing, Watson," he accused. "Or rather, those are your tells when you're not."

Despite what my friend might say, I do see and observe, so I've both seen Holmes pick up my accounts of his adventures, and observed his frown as he scans the prose. I tossed the shag back to him and was about to make a bad thing worse, arguing for the sheer distraction of it, when Holmes stood again.

He moved with the quick and economic stride he so frequently uses to cover a crime scene, but that energy was this time expended in refilling our glasses with brandy. He glanced at my papers as he handed me mine. "Those are your notes for the Smith-Mortimer succession. What will you call this escapade?"

I recognised his solicitous tone. It was the same one he uses to relax over-excited clients, and I was resentful in the face of it. "That's just it! It wasn't an escapade at all, you barely rose from your chair or finished that terrible brew Scotland Yard has the nerve to call coffee!"

As I ranted, Holmes wandered to our dining table, peering at an experiment that looked to me like an effort to grow dirt.

"True enough, it was a very simple matter, even more so than that business with the Harpsichord Widow – really, who wouldn't have noticed the woman had no stoop? I expected more from Inspector Gregson. I don't know why I'm forever surprised by the incompetence of London's detective class." Holmes poked at the loamy black culture with his finger, then jerked it away at the sound of a faint hiss. With a pencil he pushed the vicious flora into the bin. "Present company excepted."

I recognised this solicitous tone, as well. It was the same one my companion uses when he's bored and wants distraction. I was about to take him to task for this obvious manipulation when I realised the bin was on fire.

"Holmes, the bin is on fire."

Before my companion could answer, I rose and upended my half cup of cold tea over the small blaze; a puff of smoke followed. I watched the grey cloud drift and felt sure I was about to channel its darkness, taking Holmes to task for his carelessness, when instead we both broke into gales of laughter.

Minutes later we were in repose again, me with my papers, Holmes slumped like a discontented idler in his chair. When possessed by his nearly-frantic energy, Sherlock Holmes's limbs are a whirlwind and it is all I can do to stay at his heels. When the torpor is on him, I have more than once given in to the impulse to see if he is breathing. By his splay- legged slouch, I knew an east wind of such discontent was coming, so decided my trifling problems could provide us both suitable distraction.

"If you've nothing pressing, I'll tell you what I have so far."

I gestured to Holmes for his tobacco pouch, which he dutifully sailed my way. "I seem to have accidentally murdered my black mould, and it'll be a few hours yet before the Mayflies hatch, so my schedule is yours. Share with me your fairytale, dear Watson, and I'll do my best to supply it with a few cold, hard facts."

Holmes hoisted his glass and I read aloud my evening's endeavours. "Ah ha!' cried Holmes.

I relit my pipe and waited.

Holmes gestured for the tobacco, which I tossed back to him. He smiled sly as he refreshed his briar. "Well done, you've pared back from your usual florid embellishments."

Rejecting the bait, I continued. "The problem as I see it, is that the case itself was solved so quickly that there's really nothing to it, yet I've been often asked about your involvement in this one, due to the famous lady involved."

Holmes waved his spent match, tossed it into the fire.

"The morbid curiosity of gossips who feel ever justified in hounding the exceptional."

I won't go into whether Holmes's bitterness came from knowing this truth, for indeed the ordinary often think they have 'a right to know' about the lives of the extraordinary – and Miss Mortimer was certainly that – or if his rancour was more personal.

"If you'd rather I not share these curious cases and how they highlight your talents, I promise you I'll cease this instant." I rose with my papers and stepped to the fire.

I have mentioned that Sherlock Holmes is sensitive to flattery, and he himself admits how much he enjoys the attention when a case affords the occasional dramatic moment, so I wasn't surprised when he waved his hand in the air.

"Oh, sit back down and stop encouraging my vanity. I understand why you share some of our adventures, adventures which might show the ease with which even the complex can be understood, but why this particular case? If I recall, we were at that same time sorting out the much more interesting problem of the Hammersmith Wonder."

While Holmes aimed blue smoke ceiling-ward I again took my chair. "Yes, but Mr. Vigor was neither rich, famous, nor a legendary beauty. Miss Mortimer was all three and was followed by many behind-the-hand whispers in her day. Your readers – "

"Your readers," Holmes corrected airily.

"My readers of your adventures have more than once taken me to task for mentioning but not detailing some of your more abstruse cases. And the many I don't mention at all are themselves mentioned by the press. For their absence I'm also lectured."

"An ungrateful public is a terrible thing," said Holmes, grinning. "Laugh, but you can't deny it, if left to your own devices these two words – " I waved the small sheaf, " – would be the only colour in your report of Miss Mortimer's case. Yet what you call my florid embellishments are often nothing more than your method made clear."

Holmes swirled a long finger through a lazy cloud of smoke. I noted that his inflammatory mould had left a chemical burn and rose to fetch my bag.

"Then forget the Smith-Mortimer problem. That was the matter of noticing one or two abstruse details, as you say. How about 'The Affair of the Shooting Star' or 'The Conk-Singleton Forgery'?" he asked when I returned to treat his blistered finger.

"You know perfectly well that publishing anything of the first would lose a Lord his parliamentary seat, and an account of the second would take even less time to tell than Miss Mortimer's story. You solved that when Mr. Singleton said his watch had stopped at 1300 and not at one pm. You're being no help."

Holmes conceded every fact with an insouciant shrug. "There's that matter of the Venomous Lizard. A fascinating array of chemicals in lizard venom," he said, inspecting his neatly-dressed wound.

"Really now! A murderously toxic creature that turned out instead to be perfectly harmless, unmasked in seconds when you tickled it with a feather."

Holmes chuckled, as if he himself had been poked with a bit of plumage. "I knew a herpetologist in Soho and once did a rather unsystematic study of her menagerie, which consisted of 57 distinct species, including both the highly-toxic Gila monster and the beaded lizard. Each creature has a forked tongue, so it was but a matter to tickle the accused in this particular case and get it to stick out its blue, bulbous one at us."

Holmes sighed dramatically, as if unfairly put upon. "Oh, you're right as always, Watson. Sit down again and we'll craft things so that the Smith-Mortimer Succession offers a moment of distraction to your readership. Now refresh my mind on the case, would you? This January blizzard's wiped away its particulars completely."

Whether Holmes was truthful in his forgetfulness, "my" readers no doubt remember the extensive press given this case at the time, involving as it did a distinguished family and the right of succession to their family fortune.

The last of the Smith-Mortimer line, Miss Mariam Penelope Caroline Mortimer, was once a familiar name to every reader of The London Leader and the Illustrated Courier, both of which followed the young lady's world-travelling exploits, frequently spangling their pages with her elegant, cool-eyed image. That is, until Miss Mortimer disappeared from the City's social whirl under mysterious circumstance.

The lady's departure from the public eye of course aroused speculation and suspicion, from a love affair gone wrong, to behaviours too shameful to gossip about in polite company.

And then the poor woman was found dead in her large and lonely home, sitting in her favourite wingback chair, dressed for dinner and clutching new pearls. At first, foul play was suspected and once again Miss Mortimer was in every paper. It was soon discovered that criminal trespass had not cut the young lady's life short at thirty-two, but a sadly weak heart, legacy of the Smith side of her clan.

Soon after, it was discovered that this last scion of a proud family had no family after her and, despite an extensive search for cousins, nephews or nieces, none were found. Aunts and uncles, parents of parents, all had long since passed. Hope of a successor was thought lost, and within a month a new beauty captured public attention.

Then, not quite two years after, Dr. Lealand Bentham, the Smith-Mortimer's old family physician, sat nursing a gin at Simpson's long bar and let slip a very interesting fact to a very interested man.

The fact given away was this: Young Miss Mariam had been deaf upon her passing. Her hearing loss had begun soon after her thirtieth birthday, the garrulous physician told the obliging man buying his expensive drinks, and it was this early-onset deafness – a legacy of the Mortimer side of her line – that had lead the young lady to withdraw from society.

That was when the interested man, he called himself Stephen Smith Larkyns, devised a plan: He would pose as a lost member of the Smith-Mortimer clan. He knew he bore a striking resemblance to Miss Mariam herself, a fact that acquaintances had more than once remarked upon. As a matter of fact, over years of reading newspaper accounts of the family, and once exchanging a word with its matriarch, Larkyns had become more than half-convinced he must be related, and so was justified in succeeding Miss Mortimer to the family's fortune.

"Nothing gives a lie the varnish of truth quite like self-delusion, eh Watson? I remember the case now. Larkyns did indeed bear a striking resemblance to young Miss Mortimer, yet of course that wouldn't have been proof enough. He couldn't very well manifest the bad heart of the Smiths, but at all of 26 he did seem to suffer the early deafness of the Mortimers."

"The executors of the estate suspected he was lying, as did Gregson," I said. "They wanted only for a bit of proof, which you provided in seconds."

Holmes's small smile belied his words. "You give me too much credit, as usual. It was Inspector Lestrade who solved this particular case."

"I'm sure he'd be surprised to hear you say so."

"It's true. You may have noticed the good inspector is quite tone deaf, and yet often amuses himself by humming, whistling, and turning perfectly serene environments into music halls."

"He's even more bombastic when he thinks he has one up on Gregson!"

"Just so. Which explains why the inspector was lurking

that day, whistling away. He was sure Gregson was about to blunder and wanted to be near when he did. Of course it was Mr. Larkyns, alias Stephan Plum, Hampton Bishop piano teacher, who did the blundering."

Holmes tapped out his pipe, placed it on the table beside him, then brushed stray ash from his dressing gown. After his housekeeping, he looked briefly thoughtful, then slumped in his chair, eyes closed, fingers laced over his heart, looking for all the world like a man settling down for a doze.

I checked my watch. It was only a bit past eight. As I've said, the winter night was cold and neither Holmes's mood nor mine were at their highest. Yet, we'd lived long enough together to learn how to cope with one another's fuss and foibles, so I knew that, with little more to do than wait for his Mayflies, Holmes craved distraction as much as I craved a good tale to tell.

I waved my papers until the rattling opened my friend's eyes. "I was there, I've written down the climax of that blunder perfectly. Ah ha!' You unmasked the man easily, but I'm still not sure how."

Holmes pretended for a moment longer that he preferred a catnap to clarification, then he straightened slightly in his chair.

"It was the E-flat, Watson! You remember that Mr. Larkyns insisted that, though deaf, he could read lips well. You saw after our initial written introductions that we spoke face-to-face? As it will, this put us in fairly close proximity. While he busily insisted on his veracity, Inspector Lestrade lurked in the background, repeatedly hitting an F-sharp in the popular ditty he was whistling, instead of the E-flat for which he should have been aiming. Each time he did this and only when he did this, Mr. Plum's right ear shifted a fraction. It was after observing this that I realised how to prove our man could indeed hear. I quickly arranged what I needed, and then knew I need only depend on human reflex."

"Well, Mr. Plum seemed to lack at least one of those. I've never seen a man with no startle reflex."

I proved I had one when Holmes stood abruptly, shouting, "Agaricus gardneri!" No sooner had he risen than Holmes fell to his knees.

"Watson, move your knees!"

I bounded from my chair and Holmes immediately stuck his head under its skirting. He shouted, "My tea!" then reached out a long arm.

I handed him his half-empty cup, heard a triumphant crow, and then he emerged, smiling. "I was afraid my mushrooms had succumbed, but it seems luminous Agaricus gardneris is far more resistant to neglect than Mrs. Hudson."

Now, it's not uncommon for Sherlock Holmes to inform a room of his final deduction before he's granted us knowledge of his first, but often I can belatedly follow his logic. This was not one of those times. "Mrs. Hudson?"

Holmes dusted his knees, handed me his empty tea cup, then sprawled languid into his armchair again. "Haven't you noticed? When the clock went eight, our dear landlady started muttering. By a quarter past she began banging pots. By half eight her pique was so great she over-roasted the potatoes, which has only increased the muttering and the pots. Watson, we've again neglected to inform Mrs. Hudson when we want dinner."

The kitchen noises were indeed much louder than usual, and I hastened to go apologise to our landlady, when Holmes waved a hand.

"Sit, sit, she'll be up shortly and we can beg forgiveness then. We could no more prevent the dear lady from feeding us than we could hope to outwit every criminal in London."

"Lord knows you keep trying to achieve both," I said. While my friend laughed, I hesitantly approached my chair.

"It's all right. I moistened the mushrooms with my tea. It'll be interesting to see if a bit of milk fat fattens up the spores. Soon I'll be able to add an even dozen Agaricus gardneri to the Kew herbarium's sparse collection."

I resisted the urge to peek under my chair and took my seat, jotting Agaricus gardneri in the margin of my notes, never sure when just such abstruse detail might be useful later. "So, you were about to tell me how human reflex gave that imposter Plum away."

"I take it you thought it unusual that the man didn't startle when Constable Margola snuck up behind him, dropping that weighty book on the floor?"

"I know how powerfully the human body will protect itself. The instinct to snatch your hand from a candle flame or jump at an unexpected noise is all but impossible to resist."

Holmes tapped out his pipe, began cleaning the stem with a bit of wire. "'Unexpected' being the key! Constable Margola is an 18 stone man. To be sure he moves with a rare grace, but you cannot be that large without affecting the things around you, even the air. Why do you think I became a consulting detective, Watson?"

Trusting this sudden deviation was driving a point home, I said, "Because you're very good at it."

"Precisely! My skill is for noticing small things, and for recognising when those things add up to something larger. The same goes for a man like Mr. Plum, who probably learnt early on that he had an exceedingly fine-tuned ear, that he could hear things others did not. Such as a student's misstep on the keys of a piano, the stealthy tread of a heavy man, or the slight gust of air as a large book falls to the floor. In short, Plum was prepared for the sound, which is why he did not startle."

"And this betrayed him?"

Holmes was now sitting fully upright. "A deaf man would have felt the vibration of that weighty tome striking the floor just behind him and turned – that same protective reflex of which you spoke. That Plum did not was all I needed. After I crowed 'Ah ha!' the man realised his error. His immediate and simple human reflex was guilt – which was the same as an admission."

I sighed. "Of course! He could have passed off his error if he'd simply maintained his charade. It's always so simple when you explain, and I'm surprised that that still surprises me."

"Another human reflex, I expect," said Holmes, who then took up his position of a half-hour previous, peering at me over the tips of his fingers. "Now you have your account drawn up, all it needs are the romantic embellishments."

A harsh wind rattled the windowpanes and again the snow was falling thickly. I rifled through the notes in my lap. "On its own, the Smith-Mortimer Succession may be a bit short, perhaps we can flesh it out with another one of your small cases. What of that incident last week with the Grosvenor Square furniture van?"

Holmes slumped in his chair again. "Oh, Watson, I'm no help with these! That was so obvious, even the greengrocer suspected. I've no idea why the duchess came to me, though I was happy to pocket the fee. Barium of Baryta does not come cheap."

"Well, what about the Account of the Red Room? The problem of the Marques of Breadalbane? The Case of the Misplaced Gavel? How about – "

When Holmes scowled and slumped further in his chair I knew he was moments from a serious brood that might have him reaching for a particular diversion for which I have no fondness. "You once mentioned the case of Vamberry, the wine merchant. I recently asked Inspector Lestrade about it."

Holmes straightened in his chair the smallest bit, eyes narrowed. "Pray tell, what did the inspector say?"

"He said you solved the case because Vamberry was vain."

Holmes sat straight up in his chair. "As ever the inspector does not see what's in front of him waving the equivalent of semaphore flags! It was the smell of tar!"

As if that were that Holmes slumped again, and it was at this time Mrs. Hudson came in with a tray and pointedly did not look at either of us. She put a pot of tea on the crowded dining table, laying around it a Scandinavian repast of small plates. Beef, roast potatoes, bread, horseradish, pickled onions, sliced gherkins. She did this in silence, and in silence Holmes and I rose and came to the table. While I took my seat and made apologies for our neglect regarding supper, Holmes opened one of the innumerable drawers in his card cabinet and extracted a long packet, loosely wrapped in a pretty pale tissue paper.

"You are far more patient than we deserve, Mrs. Hudson," he said, holding the packet toward her, "We've been saving these for just such a moment. Please consider them one of many future apologies for our being such trying tenants."

Mrs. Hudson looked at Holmes and then at myself. I mirrored Holmes's expression. There was nothing else I could do. I had no clue what was in the package.

Mrs. Hudson looked at the thin packet with a wary eye, then unwrapped it. "Oh, Mr. Holmes, Dr. Watson!" she said, face quickly spangled in smiles. Pushing newspapers, magazines, and dinner plates out of the way, Mrs. Hudson spread the contents of the packet on the table. Those contents were these: Feathers. Dozens of gleaming feathers from chaffinches, siskins, kingfishers, herons, and peacocks.

Suddenly I remember what I had seen but not quite observed on upward of 20 journeys to and from crime scenes: Holmes snatching something up from ground or a shrub, then pocketing it. Feathers. For months he had been collecting feathers.

"We hope these will suit your millinery efforts dear lady, and have assurances from the veterinarian at Holland Park that when the white peacock drops his finery he will save that bounty for you."

Mrs. Hudson looked from Holmes to myself again, then walked to the window. Shortly she buffed away a nonexistent smudge on the glass, sniffing softly. After a few moments she nodded at us, collected her avian finery, said, "I already know just what to do with the chaffinch," and left.

As we settled down to our dinner Holmes said, "I sometimes think that good human relations are like detective work. If you observe but the smallest thing about someone and then perform a kindness related to it, most people are touched out of all proportion to your efforts."

As usual, Holmes seemed to underestimate the magnitude of his gifts. Instead of saying this, I thanked him for including me in his considerations to our dear landlady.

"Ah, but that's a small apology offered to you as well, Watson, for not only am I a trying tenant, I'm aware I'm not the most common of flatmates," my friend said, waving as if by example to the unseen mushrooms beneath my chair.

I did not tell Holmes it was just such small excitements that added the grace of colour to an often-dreary world.

"Pass the horseradish if you would Watson, and let's hear more of Lestrade's version of this story."

I did as asked, claimed the gherkins, and continued retelling the tale of Vamberry the wine merchant, just as I would tell it to you, dear readers.

"Vamberry was the Spanish Infanta's wine merchant, Mr. Holmes, reported to be her most loyal servant, above reproach, or so they thought until he scarpered with her small pleasure craft and only enough gold coin as he hoped would go unmissed!"

Sherlock Holmes stopped dead in the doorway of Scotland Yard. "Sorry sir," said Inspector Lestrade, hastening forward, "I didn't mean to jump right in. We're a bit eager to have a solution to this mess. You know how things stand with Foria."

Sherlock Holmes followed Lestrade through Scotland Yard's busy corridors. "Strained as always. The Forian royal family seem to find the rest of humanity a disappointment, just so many idlers and dilettantes."

Lestrade gestured to a chair across from his desk, signaled a passing constable for coffee. Only once the steaming cups arrived did the men take a seat.

"I don't know much about that, but I do know this mess might make a mess of diplomatic relations. We've promised to not only find out why Vamberry fled, but why to England."

Holmes eyebrows rose and he replaced his cup upon its saucer. "Most interesting. The Infanta, like the Borgias from whom she descends, is famous for both her superb capacity to rule and her lack of sentiment to those who betray her. With a little effort, perhaps we can give the lady the answers she craves."

"Well you'd be the man for that, Mr. Holmes." Lestrade leaned across his desk, dropped his voice. "You may have noticed some of my men have a roughness about them. You employ softer ways, put people at their ease, and I'm afraid you will need that, as Mr. Vamberry is exceedingly tight-lipped. To be perfectly honest, I think we'd get more from a stone. Or at least another go at his boat."

Holmes steepled his fingers. "Tell me about it."

Lestrade shrugged, "The boat? Not much to tell. It's one of those new-fangled vessels that can be sailed by one man, though roomy enough for two. A pretty thing, all full of gilt and carved follies. Apparently the Infanta once let Vamberry take his boy and hers out on it."

"Interesting," said Holmes, leaning forward in his chair.

Lestrade placed his hands on his knees, ready to respond to a sudden burst of energy. Certainly Mr. Holmes would ask to see the boat now, or the suspect, perhaps someone's left shoe. It was never entirely clear where Sherlock Holmes would start an investigation, and so Lestrade had learned to expect anything.

What he got was nothing.

Instead of bounding to his feet, Sherlock Holmes leaned back, crossed his legs, and reached for the coffee that Lestrade had himself made – truly it was the only way to get a good cup.

While Lestrade is often startled by Mr. Holmes's tendencies to dash about a crime scene, falling upon his belly and looking beneath carriage wheels, this precise opposite of his usual behaviour was frankly disappointing. However, Lestrade is not an inspector at Scotland Yard for nothing. He's keen of eye and so he knew Sherlock Holmes was – Holmes paused in pursuing a gherkin with his fork. "Did he call himself keen-eyed, Watson? Did he really?"

Even in her pique Mrs. Hudson makes a fine roast potato. I finished mine with relish, sipped some port. "Oh, he did indeed, as his retelling of the case advanced, both you and he gained ever-greater powers of cunning and deduction."

Holmes laughed and then looked at me side-eyed. Suddenly it was I who did the deducing. "Yes, Holmes, be glad Inspector Lestrade is not your biographer, for by the end of any story he told, I suspect you'd be able to fly, and he the wind beneath your wings!"

Eventually we'd finished with our supper and our laughter. Port in hand, we again settled by the fire. Holmes doffed a hat he wasn't wearing, "I find myself grateful for a restraint I never realised you show, dear biographer. Do please continue."

"Well, Mr. Holmes, don't you want to see the boat?" Lestrade asked. "As I said, we've gone over the craft carefully and found nothing."

"Soon. Tell me, what do you think of the Infanta's wine merchant?" The inspector leaned over his desk again, keen to share his finely- observed opinions. "He will not look at any one of us, much less talk. I think there's something sinister about Mr. Vamberry."

"Why?"

"He's arrogant! Not once has he addressed me by title or name, he simply says 'you.' He's what I suspect you'd call imperious. He twice told me to fetch him tea. He's treated my men as if they are here to buff his shoes. And when I told him we'd called you and who you are, he said you'd be no better than a dancing bear at finding what he never took."

Holmes laughed, "That might prove quite true, one never knows."

"Don't be hard on yourself, Mr. Holmes. He doesn't know how well regarded you are here. Anyway, you might form your own opinion, as they're bringing the man himself through now. Mr. Holmes, this is Constable Hynes and Mr. Vamberry."

Sherlock Holmes stood to find standing before him two small, dark men. Only one looked off in the middle distance as if he were alone in the room.

It was to this one Holmes addressed himself. "Mr. Vamberry, I am Sherlock Holmes. I'm delighted to meet a member of the distinguished Infanta's household. I hope you'll answer a question or two for me."

Vamberry looked in the very opposite direction from Holmes. To no one in particular, he said in perfect English, "I still await my pomegranate tea."

Lestrade looked in exasperation at Holmes, at Hynes, at the same spot in the distance at which Vamberry stared. "I have told you Mr. Vamberry, we can offer you as much plain tea as you like. I really don't know where a man would find pomegranate tea in London."

Holmes interrupted me with a laugh. "Oh, it's a shame you weren't there then, Watson. You could have laid bare London's tea underbelly, you who has found in our city's byways shops to not only satisfy your taste for Afghan and Egyptian teas, but also located that awful sea salt brew you like from Ullapool."

Here Holmes shivered in memory at accidentally taking a sip of this north Scotland specialty when I had left my steaming cup near his microscope.

As if to wash away the memory, Holmes delicately sipped at his port, smacking his lips with relish. Momentarily he nodded at me in apology. "I'm sorry, do go on."

After his pronouncement regarding tea, Vamberry fell silent, ignoring any and all questions no matter from whom they came.

Holmes observed all of this in keen silence, and then said, "The Infanta is quite angry, sir."

For but a moment, Vamberry frowned then cleared his expression, blinking slowly as if bored.

"Perhaps if we could share with her why such a trusted servant has done this unthinkable thing, she would find within her mercy."

Another fiercer frown, this one chased away by a haughty lift of the chin.

"If you and the noble lady fall out, I'm sure her son and your fine boy will grieve."

At this all expression washed from Vamberry's face. And it was this response that helped Sherlock Holmes solve the mystery.

With a sigh I rose to refill my port glass. At the extended silence, my friend cracked open one fire-dozy eye.

"I'm afraid the inspector stopped the story there," I said, returning to my chair. "He quite belatedly said it was not his story to tell. Diplomatic secrets."

Holmes straightened in his chair, lifted his own glass. "Mr. Lestrade has unexpected wells of reserve, though tardy. He told you more than enough to un-secret this diplomatic secret. Ah, well."

At that, Mrs. Hudson quietly entered, and began serenely collecting our dinner plates. As we thanked her for the fine meal – I suspect we laid it on a trifle thick – my gaze went repeatedly to Holmes. When our landlady withdrew I leaned close, "Well, what happened? Why did Vamberry's lack of reaction to your remark about his son solve the case?"

"That last is the good inspector quoting something I said later and it's overstating the matter. I did not solve the case then. However, as with Plum, it was Mr. Vamberry's opposite response to the expected one – even greater arrogance – that told me we were close to his nest, so to speak.

"You must understand Watson, to Vamberry I was certainly no better than any other detective in that station – worse, in fact, as I'd been suddenly called from home that day after a fussy experiment left me with yellow-stained fingers, a singed collar, and a small plaster on my cheek. I looked disreputable. My discussing his royal employer in familiar terms rankled a man that class proud. The lack of his response when I was even more familiar in talking about his son – that told me this issue might be about his son. Following a brief viewing of his boat, it was then the case was solved."

Suddenly my friend bolted restless from his chair, then grousingly began pacing the sitting room, pushing aside rumpled dressing gowns, sheet music, and newspapers, careless of where they landed.

"I've told Mrs. Hudson I have a method and that her tidying – ah, here it is!" Tossing aside a bird's wing and a magazine on its belly, Holmes snatched up a blue waistcoat. Mumbling something about the secret pocket he'd only half-installed inside the snug silk, he settled again across from me with needle, thread, and thimble.

"So sorry, Watson, where was I? Ah yes, it was then that our small party of four decamped to the sailing vessel Ayng.

"Once onboard, there were two things of note. The first was the deplorable mess left by the police search. The narrow mattresses had been turned up, the dish cupboards ransacked, a child's small bucket been overturned, and its wet sand pawed through. Despite the disarray, I was assured no stolen coins had been found.

"The other thing of note was the familiar scent of tar. The very commonality of this odour is what likely prevented the good Inspector from perceiving it, or that the scent of it was especially strong. Yet, as Lestrade had mentioned, the boat was new. It was also a royal vessel, so no doubt kept in prime condition. So why had it been so freshly tarred the scent was strong?

"I'm afraid I then did that thing which seems to so alarm the tidy mentalities of Scotland Yard. I began climbing over the interior furniture of the little boat, and was quickly rewarded with what I sought: a fine black seam of tar at the bow. I dug into it with my thumbnail and within a few seconds had unearthed edge-on a gold coin, a bit more effort revealed a second.

"The inspector was jubilant, Vamberry unmoved, and here is where one of the more abstruse bits of deduction comes to the fore Watson. You must always remember that, though you've found what you're looking for, keep looking.

"While Lestrade went about the messy business of prying gold coins out of stiffening tar, I went about my business: I continued searching the boat. After a while I located in the hull near the stern another tar seam, this one better hidden and even thinner than the first. Two seams perpendicular to it also gave in to my nail. I knocked against the hull; the sound was hollow – and followed by a small-voiced whimper.

"Then, quoting Poe at his most grimly poetic, it was like 'a hideous dropping off of the veil.' All was clear, and I knew why this proud and trusted man had risked so much when he seemed to want for so little."

Holmes paused here to put on his freshly-tailored waistcoat. He spun in a slow circle, arms akimbo. Only after I assured him that I couldn't spy the location of the newly-installed secret pocket did my friend settle in his chair again and this time complete his story.

"I returned to the wine merchant. Mr. Vamberry, please allow us to help you. Still the man said nothing, and so I said, Then I'm afraid we shall have to burn your boat."

"At the bow of the boat, Lestrade stopped buffing gold on his trouser leg. Beg pardon, Mr. Holmes?"

"'The criminal is in hand Lestrade, and we have found the missing treasure. The Ayng is taking up valuable space in a dock already short of it. If I recall today's headlines, the 2nd Earl of Westfriars has requested berth in this same snug harbour and been denied. I say burn Mr. Vamberry's boat."

"It was then Vamberry's iron spine crumbled. For the love of God, no! he cried."

"Why, Holmes?" I cried, starting forward in my chair. "Why?"

"I didn't make the nest analogy lightly, Watson. Like a mother bird who flaps on the ground as if wounded, leading a predator away from her chicks, once Vamberry knew he was caught – and for diplomatic reasons Scotland Yard announced their intention of boarding his craft a full half hour before doing so – Vamberry flapped us away from his nest. He hid the coins at the bow, in sight of the observant, while at the stern he more carefully covered the seams of the hidden door cut into the Ayng's hull, and behind which lay his ill son."

"No!"

"Yes. Vamberry's child was desperately sick, and the wine merchant with not enough resources to help the poor boy. Vamberry's brother, a physician, lives in London, and so in desperation the Infanta's pleasure craft and a pittance of her gold were stolen, the boy secreted on board, and Vamberry sought safe haven for both of them here. When he knew he would be boarded, he hid his young son in what any diplomatic vessel holds: A hiding spot.

"Vamberry's failing in all of this was pride, Watson, which made him both blind and rash. Though it is true that the Infanta and her kin do not much truck with weakness, any good ruler understands mercy. Not only had this never occurred to Vamberry, but he, who hews so strictly to lines of class, did not believe the Infanta could hold him or his family in tender regard, so he simply never thought to ask for her help. Fortunately all ended well. Father, child, and boat were returned to Spain, and after a time the boy was made well. As a matter of fact, both Vamberry's son and the

Infanta's son made the papers recently, together starting University at Oxford."

With a faint smile, Holmes nestled further in his chair. "And so you see, simple cases hinging on a few abstruse details. I hope they suit your needs, Watson?"

I agreed that they gave me more than enough to while away the rest of the cold winter evening.

And so it was, while Holmes dozed contentedly in his chair, I crafted the heart of each missive you've read here. It was a bit past midnight, and as I was banking the fire, that my friend woke with a start and shouted.

"The Mayflies will be hatching!"

Sherlock Holmes rose and ran to his water-filled jars lined upon the window sill and began to tut-tut at an experiment that would take him busily through the night.

For my part, I took down an encyclopaedia and began reading up on Mayflies.

The Adventure of St. Nicholas the Elephant

by Christopher Redmond

It was a mild day near the end of March, in the year 1895, when Mr. Thomas Sexton appeared at the Baker Street rooms which I shared with my friend Mr. Sherlock Holmes. Holmes and I were lingering over one of the fine breakfasts provided by our landlady, whose imposing figure as she appeared in the doorway of our sitting-room to announce our visitor was promptly followed by the much smaller figure of Mr. Sexton himself. There was something a little comic about his old-fashioned and threadbare black suit, the jacket and waistcoat stretched to contain his rotund belly, with a smear of some greasy substance near the cuff of his right sleeve, while the firm jaw and solemn countenance above his double chin gave warning that, although he might be small of stature, he expected to be treated with some deference. And yet he was clearly in the grip of an intense agitation, as his writhing hands made evident.

"Come in, come in," said Holmes at once. "Pray have a seat, and perhaps your nerves will be no worse for a cup of Mrs. Hudson's not unsatisfactory coffee. What can be amiss in the affairs of the church to bring you out so early on a Saturday morning, Mr. – ?"

"Sexton, sir, Thomas Sexton. But how do you know I come from the church? I've heard of your wonderful guesses, Mr. Holmes, as we all have, but I have not said a word yet about the church – St. Nicholas the Elephant it is, sir, out in Lambeth, past Elephant and Castle. How could you guess that I was a churchman?"

"I did not guess," said Holmes. "When the available data justify no more than a guess, I remain silent and I observe. In this case, Mr. Sexton, I have observed a spot of what must be candle-wax on the sleeve of your coat. Your attire is otherwise immaculate, so that the stain has come there very recently, and you would hardly have been lighting and extinguishing candles for any household purpose on so bright a morning. Further, I recognize the distinctive if somewhat dull typography of the Church Times on the sheaf of paper protruding from your pocket. I conclude that you have been in church this morning, and that your name reflects your calling: that you are, in fact, a sexton."

"It's true enough," our caller replied, gratefully sipping the coffee that Mrs. Hudson had brought for him, "although the word sexton is one I don't care to have used, if it's all the same to you, Mr. Holmes. Church-officer is the right name nowadays, and church-officer at St. Nicholas is what I have the honour to be. Still, it's true that my grandfather and his fathers before him called themselves sexton. I dare say that may be why my family bears the name it does. Church-officer I have been at St. Nicholas for 19 years this Whitsun, and never have I seen anything like what has happened this week. Witchcraft, I call it, witchcraft!"

"Tut, man, you call it nothing of the sort," said Holmes. "If you believed that it was witchcraft, you would hardly be here in Baker Street. You would be seeking help within the church itself, from the bishop's chaplain, or whatever the proper dignitary is called. You know very well that whatever has happened is the result of human agency, and so you rightly turn your steps to Baker Street. Or rather, not your steps, but the wheels of the Metropolitan Railway, if your journey is from far-off Lambeth. And so I ask you again: what is amiss, and what have you to tell that might be of interest to me?"

"Well, it may not be witchcraft in the end, but Mrs. Brickward calls it witchcraft," the little man replied, "and what else might anyone call it, with blood on the very steps of the church, and a page of the Bible burned there on the stone beside it?"

"Beside what, Mr. Sexton?" I interjected. "Beside the bloodstain?" "Beside the body, sir!" he shot back. "Beside the body, there on the pavement. A page taken from the church's own Bible, that sits on the lectern for Mr. Brickward to read each Sunday. Now if there is no witchcraft in it, why would somebody have burned a Bible page, and a chapter of the Holy Gospel at that?"

Sherlock Holmes, who had shown some impatience when our visitor began to describe his problem, was now leaning forward in his chair, his long bony fingers rubbing together rapidly. "Why indeed, Mr. Sexton," he said. "Why indeed. I could suggest six, no, seven possible reasons at once, but without data I can hardly be expected to choose one. But you interest me much more when you speak of a body. What body?"

"That's just it," was the reply. "A body, a young woman, lying there dead, at the side door of St. Nicholas, in Moss Road. We didn't know who she was, not any of us, and nor did the police."

"Ah, the police?" said Holmes. "Of course, they would take an interest in the matter. For all the deficiencies that the police sometimes demonstrate, they can at least be relied upon to take note of a woman's body found at the door of a suburban church. Found when, Mr. Sexton?"

"On Sunday last, at twelve o'clock. We were coming out of Matins and we found it. Mrs. Brickward found it first, as she went round into Moss Street on the way to the rectory, and Mr. and Mrs. Wallace said she was crying and weeping beside it when they saw her. Mrs. Wallace was the first to see the Bible page there, burned so that all you could read were a few words at the bottom of the page. 'Cometh in his glory' it said, and that's all that was left that wasn't blackened, 'cometh in his glory'."

"I see," said Holmes, "and this Mrs. Wallace no doubt summoned the police? But no, she will have been fully occupied with comforting Mrs. Brickward – I take it that is the rector's wife? – and doubtless it fell to Mr. Wallace to go in search of a constable."

"Exactly."

"And when the constable came?"

"Well, Mr. Holmes, he told all the people to go home, all the people who had gathered round I mean, and he sent a messenger for an inspector to come. I waited to see if I could be of any assistance, but there were enough police to do everything, and after they took the body away in a waggon I locked up the church as I always do, and I went home to my dinner."

"Where, no doubt, Mrs. Sexton was all agog to hear every detail of the affair?" I put in.

"I am sorry to say that there is no Mrs. Sexton," said the little man quietly. "She died last year of a fever."

"A careful observer could have seen as much from a glance at our visitor," said Holmes. "I will not insult you, Watson, by mentioning the clues that you might have seen, had you only looked for them. Tell me, Mr. Sexton, as you waited in case your assistance might be required, what did you in turn observe?"

"Observe, Mr. Holmes?"

"Yes, man, observe! Mark, learn, and inwardly digest, to put it in words you must often have read in your Bible. What did you see? There was blood – was there a wound? How was the girl dressed? What did she look like?"

"As to that, I can't rightly say," was the response. "She seemed a fair enough girl, and dressed well enough. She did have a wound, for certain, for her shoulder and side were all wet with thick blood, such as I never saw but once, when a lumber-waggon overturned in Moss Road and there was a man crushed to death."

"Just so," said my friend. "If this woman's death on Sunday last made such an impression upon you, why have you waited until Saturday and then come in such haste to see me?"

"It was the Bible, Mr. Holmes. When we saw the burned page beside the body, we all knew it was from a Bible, of course, but it was only today, when I went into the church to make the candles ready for tomorrow and do my other Saturday tasks, that I glanced at the Bible on the lectern and saw the page had been torn from there. Of course I went straight to the rectory to tell Mr. Brickward, and Mrs. Brickward screamed out that it was witchcraft. When I came away and thought it over a little, I determined to come and see you at once."

"Hmph," said Holmes. "Well, Mr. Sexton, your story is an interesting one, and I do not object to looking into it briefly, for I am rather at loose ends since we put old Carstairs and his not-so- prepossessing son behind bars. Tell me, and then I will detain you no longer: what was the name of the police inspector who took charge of the case?"

"Hopkins, sir," said Sexton, and Holmes gave a brief nod of satisfaction, for I knew that he esteemed Stanley Hopkins more highly than any of the other official detectives. Thus I was not surprised when, as soon as our pompous little visitor had taken his leave, he rang for the pageboy and scribbled a telegram to be sent to Scotland Yard.

"Hopkins will not object to dropping round," he said, "and it may be that he can offer us transportation to south Lambeth this afternoon, as well as the benefit of whatever information the police have failed to overlook. We can at least be confident, I think, that they will have a better theory than witchcraft to explain matters – although, sad to say, little explanation may be needed, for a body at the side door of a church on a Sunday morning is the natural consequence of a quarrel or attack outside some nearby public house on the Saturday evening."

"But the Bible page?" I asked.

"I admit that is a little out of the ordinary," said Holmes. "What do you make of it, Doctor?"

I was flattered that my friend, who had spoken slightingly of my deductive skills just a few minutes earlier, was now eager to hear any suggestion I might be able to make. "I suppose," I said judiciously, "that we may disregard the words left visible at the bottom of the page, since whoever took the page and set it alight cannot have been able to guarantee how much would remain unburnt. 'Cometh in his glory' is hardly a very illuminating message in any case. But might the whole page be some sort of message? It should not be difficult to find out what else should have appeared there."

"Indeed," said Holmes. "Then your theory would be that someone wished to point out a connection between the dead woman, or perhaps the reason for her death, and some incident or moral in Holy Writ? I have known something of the sort once or twice before. The difficulty in this case is the burning. If you seek to leave a written message, Watson, do you generally set fire to it and watch it shrivel to ash before it can be read? No, I think the explanation must be a little different – although I do agree that a message was sent, and indeed received."

He would say no more, and I was left to turn the matter over in my mind, and to occupy myself as best I could, while Holmes leafed through the day's newspapers and cut out two or three items with his black, long- bladed scissors, for later pasting into his steadily growing commonplace - books. I glanced at the cuttings later, but could make nothing of them: one was a report on glue manufacturing in some Midlands town, while another discussed the anticipated marriage of a Member of Parliament to the daughter of a Professor of Poetry.

Shortly after luncheon, however, Stanley Hopkins was announced, and both Holmes and I greeted him as the old friend he had become through a succession of odd and once or twice dangerous adventures together. "So it's the Lambeth case, is it?" said the inspector with a smile, as he sat easily in the chair where we had seen him so often before. "Well, you won't find much in your line this time, Mr. Holmes. A dead girl in south Lambeth is nothing so unusual, you know. I say a 'girl' by habit, for so many of those we find dead on the streets are very young, as you know, but this one can't have been less than 30."

"The girls you find dead on the streets are not so often on the doorsteps of churches, or marked by torn pages from a Bible," Holmes observed. "And I note that you speak of this particular girl as 'the Lambeth case', although there is, as you say, never any lack of cases in Lambeth."

"You have me there," Hopkins grinned. "As a matter of fact, the matter has been on my mind all this week, although I have not been able to spare so much as a constable to look into it since Sunday afternoon. There was something just a trifle odd about the matter."

"The lack of a weapon, for example?"

"I see you know a little about it already," said the inspector. "That was certainly a striking feature, although it may mean nothing, for a knife is a valuable thing to some of the roughs who can be found on the streets thereabouts. I have a little time to spare this afternoon; would you care to ride down to Lambeth with me and see the place for yourself? I can't offer to show you the body itself, for we had it buried on Wednesday in the usual way."

Holmes and I accepted the offer with alacrity, and as we rode through London and across Westminster Bridge, Hopkins gave us, in response to my friend's request, a brief sketch of the personalities at the church of St. Nicholas the Elephant, apart from the church-officer, our caller of a few hours earlier. Ambrose Wallace, the churchwarden,

Hopkins dismissed as an elderly busybody, and his wife as a nonentity. "The rector and his wife are another thing altogether," he said, "and I gather that there has been a good deal of talk about them, although it may be no more than the usual gossip in any church, or any pub for that matter, when a young man comes to take the place of an old one. Mr. Brickward is no more than 25 and 26, fresh from the theological college up in Durham, and of course a London parish is a difficult place for a man from the north. Then his wife is a northerner too, and she is said to be a sulky young woman, with a dark eye and a hot temper, who has been slow to seek friends and slower to find them. If Mrs. Wallace had not been nearby to take a motherly interest, she would be entirely without female company."

"An admirable thumbnail sketch," said Holmes. "And she is the one who discovered the body, our client told us. I should be very glad to meet Mrs. Brickward."

However, when the carriage stopped in Moss Road and we rang the bell at the rectory, it was the Rev. Mr. Brickward himself who answered the door. I wondered at the lack of a maidservant, but Hopkins murmured to me that the girl who had been employed at the rectory had left the previous week with Mrs. Brickward's screams of fury ringing in her ears. "A matter of burnt toast, I was told," he added.

"I may have a question or two for you, and also for your wife if she is at home," Holmes told the rector, "but first, it would be a great kindness if you would allow us to see the interior of the church. I dare say these modern bricks conceal stonework and woodwork of some real antiquity and artistic merit, do they not?"

Mr. Brickward, who at first had appeared far from gracious, brightened at once, and in a moment had snatched up a key and was escorting us to the north door of the church, chattering all the way about mediaeval tracery, Elizabethan carvings, and Georgian re-pointing. Inside the building it was so dark, even on a bright spring afternoon, that my eye could distinguish little, and when Mr. Brickward pointed into the gloom and spoke ecstatically about the foliated rood-screen, I nodded mutely. Holmes made even less pretence of taking an interest in the architecture, but made a beeline for the brass-and-oak lectern, where he pulled out his thick magnifying lens, struck a match, lit a stub of candle, and bent to peer closely at the great Bible which lay there. As he moved the flame from side to side, then up and down the open page of the book, I heard a gasp from the back of the church, and realized that the church- officer, our client, had joined us. I chuckled at his anxiety, knowing the care with which Holmes avoided so much as touching, let alone scorching, anything that might yield a clue to his extraordinarily keen eye.

"Thank you, I think that will do," he called, joining us again near the doorway. "Now if Mrs. Brickward can spare us a moment, her clarification of one or two points might be most illuminating."

Mr. Brickward led us back along the path we had taken from the rectory, stepping carefully to avoid the stone flag on which I could still detect a pale brown stain that doubtless represented the dead woman's blood. "Jennie!" he called as we entered the rectory. "Jennie, these gentlemen would like a word with you."

We took seats a little awkwardly in the parlour, all of us save Holmes, who propped his lean frame against a bulging bookcase beside the mantel and surveyed the heavily furnished little room with a keen eye. In a moment, the rector's wife appeared before us: a slight, dark woman, as Hopkins had said, neatly though inexpensively dressed in a pale blue costume. Dark shadows beneath her eyes reminded me of the strain this mysterious bloodshed, with the curious and even sinister desecration that had accompanied it, must be imposing on a young couple not yet much tried in the fires of life. It crossed my mind that the young rector, through his ecclesiastical training and no doubt an innately religious cast of mind, must have resources for facing the proximity of death that were not available to his more delicate wife. Seated together on a horsehair sofa, her little hand resting gently on her husband's arm, they seemed a picture of courage in time of sorrow.

Hopkins introduced us, Thomas Sexton adding with a note of pride in his voice that as church-officer he had taken the responsibility of asking Mr. Holmes to look into the affair. Holmes murmured a soothing word or two to Mrs. Brickward, then asked her to tell how she had found the body on Sunday morning.

"I had slipped out of church during the last hymn," she explained. "I know it seems dreadful of me, and I always do stay long enough to listen to John preach, but I do feel so alone in the middle of the congregation sometimes, and suddenly I thought, 'I can't bear to listen to Alleluia! Alleluia! one more time. I'll just leave quietly and have a few things started for luncheon before Mr. and Mrs. Wallace arrive, since I don't have Mary Ann to help me any longer.' So I did that, and when I came round the side of the church to the rectory path, I saw the woman lying there on the stone step, with the blood splashed out around her like – oh, like a red cape!"

Her low voice rose in pitch and her dark eyes seemed wider than ever; I saw her husband's protective arm reach around her. "Mr. Holmes," he said, "I hope you will forgive me if I say that my wife is overwrought; she is really not able to discuss this dreadful affair."

"I have only one other question of importance to ask," said Holmes. "Mrs. Brickward, when did you first recognize Ellie?"

The rector's young wife stared at Holmes in horror, rose to her feet, gave a little shriek and crumpled to the floor.

"It was obvious from the first that someone closely connected to St. Nicholas had killed the young woman," Holmes explained as he, Hopkins and I rattled homeward in the inspector's cab. "If you will forgive me for saying so, friend Hopkins, street brawls that end in sordid bloodshed are most unlikely to take place on a Sunday morning, when the public houses are closed and their denizens asleep in their lodgings or under Lambeth Bridge. As soon as I saw the place, I recognized that if there had been a body in Moss Road before the service began, someone among the good people of St. Nicholas would certainly have seen it, perhaps the diligent Mr. Sexton himself. It followed that the murder was committed during the time of the service itself.

"The most important indication, however, was the page from the church's Bible. We may dismiss witchcraft – a suggestion which, I strongly suspect, Mrs. Brickward put forward as a desperate attempt at misdirection. Likewise it was apparent from the beginning that there must be an excellent reason for someone to have ripped a page from the great Bible in the church itself, when so many other copies of scripture are easily at hand.

"You spoke, Watson, of a message being conveyed by the page. Indeed it was, but through no work of the printer or any divine hand. Asking myself why that particular page was torn from the volume, I looked in the volume itself to see what remained, and in the margins of the next page after the torn stub, my candle revealed deep and irregular impressions. It was not difficult to tell that words had been scrawled on the missing page, and I was able to read them: 'John, I have returned. Meet me in Moss Road after the service ends. Ellie.'

"Evidently it was a message for Mr. Brickward, which he was to find when he looked at the Bible during the service on Sunday. The writer, this Ellie, cannot have anticipated that he would find it beforehand, presumably when he came in to see that all was in readiness for Sunday morning, or that he would tear it out, for fear that others might see it – still less that he would confide in his wife. On the contrary, she must have assumed that he would keep his wife in darkness, and even abandon her for the sake of the one who had 'returned'.

"Of course we do not yet know exactly what had been the relations between Mr. Brickward and this woman, but it is clear that despite her husband's remarkable willingness to show her the letter, Mrs. Brickward perceived Ellie as a serious threat and was prepared to take drastic action to keep her from ever meeting her husband.

"Taking the page from the Bible is not, of course, the same thing as murder, but the one led to the other. Again, the opportunity to be in Moss Road during the service is the vital indication. Mr. Brickward himself was, if I may say so, under close observation by the entire congregation throughout the service. Much the same must be true of Mr. Sexton, the church-officer.

"Mrs. Brickward says that she left the service early, and that in itself might have given her the opportunity to find Ellie. It must have taken some little time, however, to have words with her, stab her dead, and conceal the knife somewhere. I dare say, your constables will find it in the cellar or kitchen-garden about the rectory if they take the trouble to search. More than that, however, she also needed a moment to burn the Bible page beside Ellie's body."

"I cannot see why she took the trouble to do that," Hopkins remarked.

"I should think," said Holmes, "that she intended her husband to recognize the remains of paper and to realize what had happened. Her heart told her that he would feel himself as much to blame as she, and the secret of Ellie's death would bind them close together. Burning the page, of course, would also ensure that no stranger could read the pencilled message.

"Doing all these things must have taken more than the few seconds by which Mrs. Brickward preceded other churchgoers into Moss Road, and for a moment or two I wondered whether the young woman had, in fact, been killed earlier than I thought. But then Mrs. Brickward herself gave us the explanation. You will recall her remark that the service had included the words 'Alleluia! Alleluia!' again and again.

"It is many years since I was compelled to attend Sunday School classes as a boy, but I do recall being told with determination, as a matter of great importance in the mind of the maiden lady who instructed me, that in the austere season of Lent, those words are never used in the liturgy. Here we are in March, a fortnight before Easter, and so it is Lent. Mrs. Brickward cannot have heard the congregation repeating Alleluia! this Sunday morning – because the prayer book told them not to say it, and because she was not in church at all. I knew that she was not telling the truth, and the matter was settled. Unnoticed by the other churchgoers, for she had no friends to look for her, she was not in the church, but in Moss Road, where she waited for Ellie, killed her, and burned her last message to John Brickward."

"It seems very straightforward as you set it out," said Hopkins. "If only I had had a few minutes to consider the case, I should have come to the same conclusion on Monday last, and you need not have been troubled."

"Ah," laughed Holmes, "and so my hours have made good your minutes. It was a trivial matter, certainly, and yet not without interest, particularly for the novelty of the message written on a leaf of the Bible. Watson, I recall hearing that some device of the sort was used in one of the romance novels of your friend James Barrie. I must look into it one of these days, although I understand that his works are written in a Scots dialect which is perhaps more congenial to you than it is to me."

The Lady on the Bridge

by Mike Hogan

Sherlock Holmes pushed back his chair, stood, and laid his napkin on the table. "Settle up, would you, old chap? I have a small errand to run." He weaved among the tables of the restaurant and disappeared through the main entrance doors.

I pulled out my pocket book and sighed. Our finances, as often at the end of the month, were at a low ebb, but at Holmes's insistence we had travelled from Baker Street to Sydenham on a blustery afternoon to take an early dinner at a fine French restaurant in the Byzantine court at the Crystal Palace. The decor was as highly stylised as the menu prices were highly inflated.

And Holmes's attention had not been on the food. Even as we were ushered into the room, his eyes had flickered around as if looking for someone, and between courses he had glanced at his pocket watch as if gauging whether he had time to make a rendezvous.

I requested the bill and peered at a note in tiny print explaining that the charge had been calculated according to a Continental system by which a seven-percent gratuity had been added. It occurred to me as I received my change from the sharp-eyed waiter that a gratuity should be precisely what the word suggested, a token of appreciation from a satisfied customer, not a levy. However, under the supercilious gaze of the waiter and with the maître d'hôtel, hovering with an elderly couple anxious to possess our table, I made a swift mental calculation and left an appropriate amount in the saucer as a 'tip'. The waiter peered at the thru'pence coin and its ha'penny companion with disdain, the maître d'hôtel sadly shook his head, and the gentleman waiting for our table shared a condescending half-smile with his lady companion. Undaunted, I stood and marched to the entrance of the restaurant, where I found Holmes leaning against an iron pillar deep in his Evening News.

He folded the newspaper and tucked it under his arm. "Nothing yet, but there is still the final edition."

I frowned. "What are you expecting?"

"Did you take the receipt?" he asked.

I handed it to him. "The price included a seven-percent charge for service. It was clear from the attitude of the restaurant staff that a further amount was expected as a tip."

Holmes considered. "Fourpence three-farthings would have been an adequate addition to the charge to make it consistent with your usual practice. Come."

I followed him out of the restaurant, counting surreptitiously on my fingers, and into one of the huge galleries in the iron-framed glass building. A crystal fountain glistened in the sunlight streaming through the tremendous glass walls and curved ceiling high above us, and I stood in awe as I gazed at the long vista before me. Tall trees brushed the ceiling of the central nave, and massive monuments from antiquity and gigantic engines from the present day occupied the aisles and transepts.

I looked for Holmes and found him reading his paper in the shade of a palm tree in what was clearly a Roman or Greek themed exhibition. A dozen ladies sat before a row of plaster statues of naked, ivy-leaved young males, while a spade-bearded gentleman discoursed on features of ancient sculpture. One young lady seated at the end of the row of students flicked her eyes along the line of sculptures and then past them to me. I blinked at her, and she smiled. It would have been boorish in the extreme not to return such a charming smile, however inappropriately offered, and I – "

"Watson?"

"The Palace is a virtual university," I said as Holmes led me away. "A very useful institution, especially for young ladies of artistic inclinations."

Desiring to smoke after our meal, Holmes and I strolled the extensive gardens on what had become a balmy, early spring evening and found a bench where we sat, lit our pipes, and watched the Palace come alive with glittering electric lights.

The sky darkened and Holmes looked at his watch, tapped out his pipe and stood. He led me to a gate to one of the special garden exhibits, where he displayed our restaurant receipt to an attendant and we were waved in, gratis.

A newspaper boy ran up to Holmes holding out a copy of the Evening News late edition. Holmes grabbed it from him and flicked through the pages in the light of a gas lamp, humming softly to himself. He folded the newspaper in half and held his hand out to me. "Pencil?"

I reluctantly gave Holmes my propelling pencil and peered at the boy. On one invasion of our rooms by Holmes's band of ragamuffins, his Baker Street Irregulars, I had lost not only my propelling pencil, but a signed score of The Lost Chord by Sir Arthur Sullivan. I was understandably wary of nefarious activity by any boy under Holmes's direction.

Holmes ringed a paragraph in the paper and handed it to me, then he leaned down and fixed the newspaper boy with his steady gaze. "You know what to do?" he asked.

The boy grinned up at Holmes, turned and sped away.

"In the Personals," I said, holding out my hand for my pencil. "To Ajax. 'Seven is impossible – Tower Bridge at nine; agent must wear red carnation and carry a newspaper. One Fearfully Wronged'."

I shook my head. "What silly names; she (we must assume a she) is loquacious, even when paying by the word."

I was talking to thin air; Holmes was on the move. "Come," he called back. "It's ten minutes to seven."

I scurried after him. "We'll not get across London to the Tower in time, Holmes, it must be several miles. It is a physical impossibility, unless you have engaged a private balloon!"

Holmes skirted an ornamental fountain and came to a stop at a magnificent floral display. He plucked a red carnation bloom and slipped its stalk through my button hole.

"I say, old chap," I remonstrated.

He handed me his Evening News and propelled me into a large grassy enclosure, the principal feature of which was an artificial lake crossed by a bridge illuminated with coloured electric globes.

I recalled that some years previously, the promoters of the hideous Tower Bridge across the Thames had built a wood and plaster, quarter-scale model of the structure in the gardens of the Crystal Palace, no doubt hoping that the public would get used to a Gothic monstrosity almost as uncouth as the ridiculous iron tower that defiled the centre of Paris. The model had proved a popular attraction, especially when illuminated on spring and summer evenings. Young couples perambulated the lake and crossed the bridge, no doubt focussed on each other and oblivious to their less than scenic surroundings.

I followed Holmes to the arch that marked the start of the bridge walkway. Close to, the model was sadly dilapidated. Bare wood showed through the paintwork, and the suspension wires hanging from the twin towers were visibly bent and frayed, and it was with trepidation that I followed Holmes onto the creaking deck and we joined the crowd crossing and re-crossing the structure. A police constable stood by one of the towers, but he seemed content to chat with a flower seller rather than enforce any rule of the road. Holmes and I took the leftmost tack as having fewer people walking against our direction.

"Keep an eye out," he enjoined me in a murmur. "What for?"

My question was immediately answered. Coming towards me against the flow and at a stately pace was an oddly-dressed figure, a lady, who, despite the mildness of the evening, was wrapped in a voluminous grey cape. On her head she wore a grey, flowery hat and her face was hidden, veiled in net. She stopped before me and slipped a hand into her reticule.

I blinked at her, started at a huge bang, and looked up as a firework bloomed high above me in the shape of a bright red carnation.

Holmes stepped between the lady and me and took her arm. "Madame," he said softly. "I urge you not to take such a foolhardy step."

More fireworks thundered over us as Holmes drew the lady to the side of the bridge. He made no move to bid me join them, and I stood uncertainly and in a state of utmost confusion as the crowd swirled past me staring up, mouths agape. An instinct of delicacy drew me away from my friend and the lady, and I took a position on the opposite side of the bridge against the balustrade and out of the flow of pedestrians. I could only glimpse Holmes and his companion through gaps in the passing throng and in the bursts of light from the fireworks as if in a jerky, slow-motion Kinematograph. Holmes bent towards the veiled lady and spoke most earnestly, emphasising his words with sharp gestures.

A thickening of the crowd hid them from me for a few seconds, and Holmes was beside me and the lady gone.

"Holmes," I exclaimed. "You arranged a rendezvous for me with that lady!"

The newspaper boy reappeared, handed Holmes a rolled

up newspaper, and disappeared into the crowd.

"In a manner of speaking." Holmes unrolled the newspaper and disclosed a pocket pistol. "She intended to assassinate you." He smiled. "Come, let's take the train home and smoke a pipe or two in the safety of our comfortable den in Baker Street." He took me by the arm and steered me towards the station.

"Miss Berthoud said that she was sorry to have bothered you, but she cannot see very well without her spectacles, especially through her veil and in the glare of the electric lamps and pyrotechnics, and your luxurious moustache is very like that of her oppressor. I advised her to go home and lay the matter before us in the morning."

I dropped both newspaper and boutonniere into a bin. "Bothered, Holmes?" I said, somewhat sharply. "Yes, I dare say a bullet through the breastbone might have been bothersome."

Holmes kept his counsel during our ride home, over late supper, and for the rest of the evening, and I went to bed with no more idea of why I had been targeted by the veiled lady than I had on the bridge.

I came down to breakfast the next morning and found Holmes in his dressing gown, reclining on the sofa, puffing on his morning pipe, and sipping coffee. A newspaper-wrapped parcel lay on the floor beside him.

"I feel that I am owed an explanation, Holmes," I said as I poured my coffee.

"I am sure you do, old man," he answered amicably. He leaned towards me and held out his cup for a refill.

"I think it only right that I should know what the devil is going on," I said stiffly. "Oh, good morning, Mrs. Hudson."

"Language, Doctor," our landlady said as she placed fresh dishes of scrambled eggs, bacon, and kidneys before me on the table. "Naming calls. Billy will bring your toast, hot-and-hot."

"I expect Murchison did what I should have done in

his circumstances," Holmes said as the door closed behind her. "He bribed the boot boy (or boot girl as Miss Berthoud resides in an exclusive ladies' hotel in Bayswater) to slip a note under her bedroom door. The note referred her to the Evening News Personals and gave the gentleman's nom de plume, Ajax."

The bell rang in the hall downstairs.

"Who is this Murchison," I asked. "And how did you become involved in the matter?"

Billy appeared at the door as I was about to tuck into my bacon and eggs.

"Where's the toast?" I asked.

"Which, I didn't bring it, Doctor, on account of the lady in the waiting room come to see Mr. Holmes."

"But, what about breakfast?" I exclaimed.

Holmes jumped up. "Clear the table, Billy, then show her up."

"I am a wronged woman," Miss Berthoud said in a charmingly French-lilted English. "I was harried from my home, driven from my position as a nanny with a titled family, and hounded and threatened by a fiend who will stop at nothing to ruin me."

Our visitor was a fresh-faced young lady of 20 or so, again in grey, but she had exchanged her cape and veil for a well-fitting, tailored ensemble in the latest fashion, and on her head was a tiny grey and pale yellow hat that clung to her tightly coiled hair like a budgerigar to its perch. She refused refreshment and took Holmes's place on the sofa while he and I sat in our usual chairs before the empty grate.

She folded her hands in her lap. "There are moments, gentlemen, when one has to choose between living one's own life, fully, entirely, completely – or dragging out some false, shallow, degrading existence that the world in its hypocrisy demands. I grasped that moment yesterday when I saw you on the bridge, Doctor. I was determined to destroy he who stands between my dear Alfie and me."

Holmes sniffed. "But, you must consider, Miss Berthoud, that you would undoubtedly have been apprehended. Your costume, although admirably conceived for hiding your identity, was too voluminous for speedy escape, and a constable was at hand. You must have been caught and inevitably hanged for murder."

Miss Berthoud seemed about to contradict Holmes, but he overrode her. "I see you frown. Although your English is excellent, I deduce from your accent (and your name) that you are French by birth, and you may not be aware that on this side of the Channel the courts do not have the option of excusing a murder as a crime passionel. Our Judiciary is not known for its Romantic conceptions; no, no, it would have meant the rope."

"I say, Holmes – " I interjected.

"If I might accept your offer of refreshment, Doctor?" Miss Berthoud asked softly.

"Of course, tea or coffee?" I asked.

"A reviving brandy and soda for our guest, Watson," Holmes said firmly. "And a whisky for me while you're at the Tantalus."

I poured the drinks, handed them and helped myself to a whisky. "Tell me more of the target of your assassination attempt," Holmes requested. "This Reverend Murchison."

"Your oppressor is a clergyman?" I asked. "Not of the established church, I trust."

"Of the Church of Scotland," Miss Berthoud answered. "He retired to Boulogne, as do many of his countrymen, particularly professional gentlemen."

She took a dainty sip of brandy. "Although my family was of aristocratic status, we lost everything in the turmoil at the end of the last century. My great-grandfather opposed the tyrant Napoleon, and our family was proscribed. After the death of my father, my mother was obliged to sell what remained of our property and set up a lodging house in Boulogne. A very genteel establishment, you understand, catering to elderly ladies and retired gentlemen, several of them from Britain, as the town has a reputation as a welcoming place for such people: we have an English bookshop, several tea rooms, and a subscription library with the latest newspapers and periodicals from London. I left school in order to assist my mother in the business."

"Your English is most remarkable, Miss Berthoud," I said.

She bowed. "In France, I received a typical education for a girl of my class and background, but I had the good fortune to make the acquaintance of an English lady who boarded with us. She took me under her wing and tutored me in your language."

Her voice took on a more severe quality as she continued. "My life changed forever when an elderly man in clerical hat and clothes appeared at our door enquiring whether we had rooms. He rented the second floor front bedroom, with the use of the necessary facilities on that floor and freedom of the downstairs sitting room where my mother and I spent our quiet evenings, sewing or reading improving literature."

She sighed a most affecting sigh. "From the moment Reverend Murchison entered our household, I had not a moment's peace. At first, he dined with the other lodgers, but soon he was invited to share our supper en famille, and he ate with my mother and me every night, without fail. During meals, he did not take his eyes from me."

Miss Berthoud leaned across and grasped my hand. "I was a caged bird, Doctor!"

I squeezed her hand in a reassuring gesture as she continued. "I must explain that in Boulogne, the English men who reside or holiday there are considered prime matches for young girls of the town; the gentlemen are usually elderly and are thought to be wealthy (at least in comparison the local ouvriers). My mother forced the man upon me. I had nowhere to go, and no funds of my own, but I knew that I could not endure being Reverend Murchison's wife."

"Ouvriers," said Holmes, "labourers." I frowned at him.

"I represented to my mother that the reverend gentleman was of a certain age and an ungenerous disposition, and that I was but 19,"

Miss Berthoud continued with a long sigh. "But she would hear nothing against him. She even sought occasions when she might leave us alone together, and I was obliged to endure his vile advances."

I stood and stroked my moustache. "He did not, ah – "

Miss Berthoud pursed her lips. "Reverend Murchison did not force himself upon me, no. But in every other way, he bound me to him with chains of iron. He visited our sitting room morning and afternoon, visibly annoyed if other persons, such as our neighbours, Monsieur Sublier and his wife, or other lodgers were present."

"You made your escape," Holmes suggested.

"With the help of that kind English lady, since Passed Over, who knew of my travails and offered her wise counsel. I replied to an advertisement in an English newspaper, offering the position of nanny to a young lady of good character who could teach French. As you were kind enough to remark, my English was good (it has improved in the two years I have worked here). My benefactor provided a letter of introduction to Lord and Lady Muntley (for that is the name of my erstwhile employers) that served in lieu of an employment reference, and I happily accepted the position on adequate terms and conditions. I fled Boulogne for my safe haven in the town of Frome, in Wiltshire."

Miss Berthoud blinked sadly at me, and I offered her another glass of medicinal brandy, which she reluctantly accepted.

"I will not say that my life was idyllic," she continued, "although Frome is a pleasant location, and my employers were kind, but – " She sighed. "I hope that you will not judge me too harshly, gentlemen, when I admit that I am not one of those women who dote on children; in fact, I found no charming traits whatsoever in the baby boy in my care, or in the twin girls, his older sisters."

"Reverend Murchison sought you?" Holmes asked.

"He somehow found me out and settled at an inn in the town. He followed me whenever I left the house, even to church on Sunday. He plagued me with bouquets of meadow flowers and boxes of inferior chocolates."

"The hound," I said.

"Frome is a small town, gentlemen, a village really, and Reverend's Millward's activities were noticed." Miss Berthoud frowned down at the clenched hands in her lap. "He wrote to me, often daily."

"The fiend!" I cried.

"I think we might accept Reverend Murchison's villainy as a given, Watson," Holmes said, turning to me, "requiring no further expostulation."

I sniffed and sipped my whisky in a decided manner.

"One day," Miss Berthoud continued, "earlier in the summer, the youngest child of the family was out of sorts, and our physician in Frome recommended the waters of Bath. We took lodgings there."

Miss Berthoud seemed lost in thought for a long moment. "And?" Holmes asked sharply.

She looked up. "I met Lieutenant Lord Alfred Bartholomew by chance in a small park where he played at quoits with some of his brother officers from HMS Atropos, his armoured cruiser. She is in the second rate of that class, but Alfie and I are convinced that she is the most effectively armed of her sisters, as she has no less than five six-inch quick firers, all Armstrong guns. He is Third Officer."

Miss Berthoud smiled at me, and Holmes tut-tutted for her to continue.

"Alfie proposed, but I hesitated. I did not care to exchange one kind of domestic slavery for another; to become an officer's wife living at the admiral's manor house while my husband was in China or the Cape, with my contentment dependent on the goodwill of my mother-in-law. No, no, that would never do. But my beloved convinced me that the Navy is quite different from the Army, in that wives may follow their husbands to foreign stations and set up a home, if they have sufficient means."

She took a sip of brandy and smiled again. "Admiral Lord Charles Bartholomew is very well situated, and Alfie has high expectations."

"Reverend Murchison discovered your attachment to Lieutenant Bartholomew?" Holmes asked.

"He did. My tormentor followed me as I wheeled Baby to the park in his perambulator. I refused to enter into communication with him, but he sent me messages through the Personal Columns in which he avers in veiled terms that he will do everything in his power to sever relations between Alfie and me. If I will not be his, he is determined that I shall have no future with another, that I shall die an old maid."

"The brute!" I exclaimed, and Holmes gave me a reproving look. "He is determined to ruin my happiness," Miss Berthoud said, sobbing into her hands. "The wedding is on Saturday at ten in the morning at the church in Rowland's Castle, a village in Hampshire close to Admiral Bartholomew's estates. Reverend Murchison requires me to submit to him within 48 hours or he will write to the admiral and acquaint him with his prior claim to my hand."

"Very well," said Holmes, rubbing his palms together in what I thought a rather callous gesture. "I must now ask if there is anything known to Murchison that might cause unease if it were relayed to the admiral."

"Nothing! He will make something up. He is the Devil incarnate. Alfie's father would instantly forbid the match if he detected any taint of impropriety. Lady Bartholomew is of a frail disposition of mind. I fear for her sanity if any shadow of scandal adhered to the family name."

"I must press you, Miss Berthoud," Holmes said coldly. "If I am to help you in this matter, I must know everything."

Miss Berthoud looked down and wrung her hands. "You must understand that I was very young, Reverend Murchison was very persistent, my mother entreated me, and I could conceive of no alternative to accepting his proposal."

"You did so?" Holmes asked. "In a manner of speaking."

"There is written proof of your acceptance of Reverend Murchison's offer?"

"There were certain allusions in one short note I wrote to Reverend Murchison," she answered. "Nothing untoward, you understand, but they might be taken as a statement of assent."

"To marriage with him?"

Miss Berthoud nodded unhappily.

Holmes stood. "We have but two days before the deadline and four before the nuptials. We must act. Watson?"

I stood.

"Perhaps you might see Miss Berthoud to her conveyance."

I offered Miss Berthoud my arm and accompanied her downstairs and to the omnibus stop.

I returned to our sitting room, and found Holmes leaning against the mantel smoking a cigar from my packet and undoing the string on the parcel I'd seen earlier.

"An interesting lady," I suggested, "who mixes the delicacy of her sex with an admirable streak of determination; think on the pistol."

"She is One Cruelly Used," Holmes exclaimed, throwing his arms up in a melodramatic gesture.

"Are you quite well, Holmes?"

"We could visit the fellow as friends of Miss Berthoud and warn him that his behaviour is intolerable," I suggested later in the day as we rumbled towards the West End in a four-wheeler. Holmes was dressed in the uniform of a district messenger. On my knees was a picnic hamper.

"Reverend Murchison is already in a paroxysm of jealousy

over the naval lieutenant," Holmes answered. "I fear that his Scots intransigence would meet your own well-documented pugnacity and lead to fisticuffs. He boards at the Langham Hotel in Portland Square, a genteel establishment whose staff might look askance if violence (however justified) were offered to one of their guests. No, we must adopt a more circumspect approach."

"How did you come across the correspondence in the Evening News, Holmes?" I asked.

"You know that the Personal Column is the first I turn to in every paper. The thread of messages between Ajax and One Cruelly Wronged intrigued me. She refused to countenance a face-to-face meeting with Ajax to discuss the matter between them. He suggested instead a rendezvous on the bridge with a go-between. Miss Berthoud accepted, and I intervened and sent a message to Ajax putting the meeting back and signing it – "

"One Cruelly Wronged."

"Exactly." Holmes sniffed. "I believe Miss Berthoud saw through Reverend Murchison's ploy of confidential agents and knew that the reverend himself would accost her on the bridge. She was prepared to end the matter there and then."

"Would she have shot her adversary?"

"French women are unencumbered by notions of propriety." I frowned.

"There was no danger, my dear fellow; everything was under my control," Holmes said. "On my orders, the newspaper boy at the Palace contacted a local band of pickpockets and gave them a commission to dip the lady's reticule as she stepped onto the bridge." He smiled. "Two hours later, the same band accosted a gentleman carrying a folded Evening News and wearing a carnation buttonhole," Holmes continued. "The newspaper boy delivered a parcel early this morning in exchange for twelve-and-six from our contingency fund, plus omnibus fare and refreshments."

Holmes displayed a silver pocket watch, a spectacle case,

an empty wallet, a bill for accommodation at the Langham Hotel at the clergy rate, and an unopened, unstamped letter addressed to Admiral Bartholomew, care of the Railway Hotel, Rowland's Castle, Hampshire.

"So, we not only have the reverend's address, we have the letter he intended to give to Miss Berthoud to show that he was in earnest." Holmes slit the envelope open with a pocket knife.

"I say, old man, you can't just – "

"The envelope is not franked; it is unprotected by law."

I muttered something about the inviolability of private property while Holmes held the letter to the light from the cab window. He offered it to me, but I waved it away.

He shrugged. "It is as vile as we might expect. Miss Berthoud, however circumspect she has been with the truth, is under threat from this man."

"Will Reverend Murchison not take precautions after his things were stolen?"

"No, no," Holmes answered. "He was prey to a band of ragamuffins who will throw the letter away, take the cash, and sell the empty wallet, spectacles and watch."

The cab turned off Regent Street and halted in Portland Place "We must return Reverend Murchison's possessions," I said. "And pray that no more contingencies occur this month."

We stepped down from the cab, and I sat on a bench under a tall plane tree just across from the grand entrance to the Langham Hotel.

"I expected you to infiltrate the hotel in the guise of an aged clergyman," I said as I peered into the hamper, but Holmes was already out of earshot and halfway to the cab stand on the corner. I poured myself a cup of wine and sipped it as I watched Holmes chatting with the drivers in his guise as district messenger. He nodded farewell to them and climbed the steps to the hotel entrance.

"The task before us may be divided into several stages,"

Holmes said when he returned to the bench some minutes later. "The first is already accomplished: we have the address and room number of our mark and, after a moderate distribution of silver to the cab stand and the hotel door and boot boys, we will soon note his routines. The second stage is the letter he threatens to send to the groom's father and how we may prevent it reaching its recipient."

Holmes accepted a chicken leg and a cup of wine. "Word from the cab drivers is that the reverend gentleman is of a choleric disposition, prefers to travel by omnibus, and frequents Madame La Rout's establishment in Jermyn Street."

I heaved myself up. "And the hound has the effrontery to pursue Miss Berthoud, despite her clear revulsion. I should take a horsewhip to him, reverend or no. He is a disgrace to the Kirk and, and – "

Holmes handed me an apple. "Calm, old man. Let us plan our dispositions."

I subsided onto the bench.

"The letter, then," Holmes said. "According to the door boy, Reverend Murchison is a prolific letter writer. He drops a bundle of envelopes into that letter box before dinner each evening." Holmes indicated an iron post box on the pavement a few yards from the hotel entrance. "He uses no other."

"He does not employ the hotel mail service?" I asked.

Holmes smiled. "Reverend Murchison is clearly a man of frugal habits. If he posts the letters himself, he saves a tip."

"Merely dipping the letter from his pocket will not answer," I said, "as Reverend Murchison will simply write another letter and take better care when he posts it. What other measures may we adopt?"

Holmes considered. "Lead line and plumb, with tar or glue on the plumb bob, dropped into the letter box slit just after he posts the envelope to fish it out. Or fit a bag inside the slit. Or we can just set fire to the letters. Do you want the last boiled egg?"

I listened to Holmes's suggestions with mounting unease. "Set fire to Her Majesty's mails! I say, Holmes."

He shrugged. "Very well. According to the cab drivers, the postman has no less than seven mouths to feed on his wage, and he moonlights as a knocker upper."

"I refuse to countenance bribery of an official of the Crown," I said stiffly. "You speak of criminal activity with the insouciance of a Hoxted costermonger."

"Perhaps you could offer a more benign solution to our problem, Doctor?" Holmes said, taking the last boiled egg. "Miss Bertaud's deadline expires at midnight tonight."

We returned to Portland Place at 11:30, and I sat in a four-wheeler cab parked across the road from the hotel. Holmes, now in the guise of a London postman, was opposite me.

He smiled. "Three-and-six to a specialist firm in Lambeth for rent of the uniform and post box key."

"The expenses in this case are mounting," I said, noting the rental cost on my shirt cuff.

At two minutes to midnight, the hotel door opened and a stooped, elderly man with a thick walrus moustache emerged and paused at the top of the steps, peering around myopically and sniffing the air. He wore clerical weeds and a flat vicar's hat and carried an umbrella. Seemingly satisfied with the balmy weather, he strode down the steps to the pavement, marched to the letter box, and without a moment's hesitation slipped an envelope inside. He turned and sauntered back to the hotel entrance, humming a tune and with his umbrella clicking rhythmically on the steps.

"Pinafore," I murmured, frowning. "Murchison looks nothing like me."

Holmes put his finger to his lips as we watched Reverend Murchison re-enter the hotel lobby. Holmes instantly leapt from the cab, raced to the post box and unlocked it with his key.

I glanced down at my watch. We had met the regular

postman, Mr. Willis, at his local public house earlier in the evening before he started his round. He had blankly failed to comprehend the hints and innuendos that Holmes employed, and Holmes did not dare make a plain offer in case the man informed the authorities. We had fallen back on an alternative plan which required Holmes to retrieve the letter before Willis collected the mail at midnight.

I stiffened as Holmes, kneeling beside the post box, struck a match, but he stood, relocked the box, hurried across to the cab and leapt inside just as a tricycle turned into the square. It stopped beside the post box and Willis emptied the post into his sack.

Holmes tapped on the cab roof with his stick and we set off for home.

"I thought for a moment you were going to set fire to the letters," I said with a soft chuckle.

"I would not dream of interfering with Her Majesty's mails," Holmes answered.

I frowned.

"Reverend Murchison will expect his letter to arrive at the admiral's villa in Hampshire tomorrow," Holmes continued. "The reply, probably by telegraph or express letter, should reach him no later than Friday afternoon, the day before the wedding. If Murchison does not receive that reply, he will gird his financial loins and spring for a telegram."

"He will not use the Langham Hotel telephone service?"

"Too expensive." Holmes smiled. "And I checked the directory.

Admiral Bartholomew does not possess a telephone."

We arrived back at Baker Street and settled in our sitting room. "Take down Bradshaw would you, old man?" Holmes requested. "I want a Portsmouth train stopping at Rowland's Castle not later than 9:30 on Saturday morning. That gives Murchison time to have his breakfast (included in his room charge and not to be missed by our frugal friend), take a 'bus to Waterloo and get to Rowland's Castle before the wedding starts at ten."

Holmes sat at his writing table, took a sheet of notepaper from an envelope, dipped his pen and wrote in silence for a few moments.

He looked up and handed me the note. "I have made an appointment for Reverend Murchison to meet Admiral Bartholomew on the morning of the wedding – that will appeal to the reverend's sense of drama. He will relish his power to destroy the happiness of Miss Berthoud and her naval swain."

"This is The Railway Hotel, Rowland's Castle notepaper, Holmes."

"A touch of authenticity courtesy of Wiggins' Uncle Silas, confidential printer, and purveyor of slush paper to the Quality at tuppence a sheet."

I made a note.

We were on our bench opposite the Langham at 6:30 on Saturday morning.

"Reverend Murchison has checked out," said Holmes. "And, here he is, curtly spurning the offer of a porter to carry his carpet bag and stalking head down towards the omnibus stop."

"He is not as sprightly as he was two nights ago," I remarked as we stood and picked up our bags. "He seems to be in a gruff mood."

"I want Reverend Murchison in a lather," Holmes said, rubbing his hands together. "I did not destroy his letter to Admiral Bartholomew, I merely crossed out the address and marked the envelope 'return to sender'. Oddly, when the letter was returned to the Langham in yesterday's morning post, the admiral's reply came in the same delivery. Reverend Murchison has had a confused night. Come, we will go on ahead to Waterloo by cab."

"What if he takes a Portsmouth train from Victoria Station?" I asked as we crossed the square to the stand.

"He will not. That service does not stop at Rowland's

Castle. He would have to buy a separate ticket from Portsmouth and incur more expense. No, no, we shall wait for him at Waterloo."

Holmes purchased our tickets at the kiosk in Waterloo Station and instantly disappeared into the crowd. I looked about me and started as Reverend Murchison strode purposefully from the arched exit from the omnibus stands, bought a second-class ticket at the kiosk, and headed towards the Departures Board.

Holmes reappeared beside me dressed as a railway porter. "Holmes!" I cried. "He is here. What now?"

He passed me a ticket. "Stick precisely to my plan, of course."

I stalked my prey as he squinted up at the Departures Board and at the station clock hanging from the roof above us.

"What platform for the eight-oh-four to Portsmouth?" I called across Reverend Murchison to Holmes lounging against a porter's trolley.

"Moved to platform seven, sir," Holmes answered.

"Stopping at Rowland's Castle?" Reverend Murchison asked in a gruff tone tinged with Scots.

"Number seven, sir. You'll have to hurry."

Reverend Murchison reached towards his empty watch pocket and frowned. "I will do no such thing. I have 30 minutes or more."

Holmes pulled out a brass pocket watch and checked it with the clock above us. "Five or less, sir. It's just gone eight."

"My watch says eight and a bit," I said truthfully. "We'll have to run!" I hefted my Gladstone bag and raced towards Platform Seven with Reverend Murchison grumbling at my heels.

A group of schoolboys milled about the entrance to the platform with a harassed looking master attempting to bring them to order. I pushed through them and waved my ticket at the attendant guarding the platform entrance. A line of a dozen or so carriages stood behind him with the engine in front hissing and puffing out billows of steam. The attendant glanced at my ticket and indicated with a jerk of his head that I and my clerical companion might proceed.

"Have I time to get a paper?" I asked.

"You have not, sir. She's away any moment."

"Come now, boys," the teacher cried in a shrill voice. "You heard the man, you must come along. The train is leaving."

The gate attendant chuckled. "He'll never get that lot on; he's herding cats."

Reverend Murchison and I pushed through the mass of boys, who seemed to take delight in obstructing us. I lost my stick in the commotion, which was probably just as well as I would have been sorely tempted to use it on the brats. I saw that Reverend Murchison's hat was askew and his umbrella had become unfurled.

At a harsh cry from the teacher, the boys came instantly to attention, and I was able to struggle through to clear ground on the platform beyond with Reverend Murchison close behind, rolling up his umbrella.

"We must make haste," I cried, pointing to the guard with his flags in his hand marching along the side of the train and closing the last few doors. Reverend Murchison and I raced behind a gentleman in a top hat and overcoat also running for the train. We three jumped through the first open door, which the guard slammed behind us. The reverend and I sat on either side of the compartment, he opposite the gentleman, who snapped open his Times and disappeared behind it.

Reverend Murchison nevertheless addressed him, and my heart sank.

"Excuse me, sir, this is the eight-oh-four to Portsmouth, I collect?"

A shrill whistle sounded and the train jerked into motion.

The man put down his paper, stood and smiled at me. "Come, my dear fellow."

Holmes opened the door and we stepped out onto the platform. I closed the door behind us. The train picked up speed, and as it left the station and curved west, a walrus-moustached face squinted from the window of our compartment.

The harassed schoolmaster came up to Holmes with his charges.

"A shilling each boy," Holmes murmured in my ear, "and three bob for the cat herder."

I fumbled in my waistcoat for the necessary coins, paid the master and boys and glared down at one schoolboy who held out my stick.

"Reverend Murchison may have some difficulty with the guard before he arrives in Exeter," Holmes remarked.

"Exeter!" I exclaimed.

"He is on the 738 non-stop to Exeter without his watch and spectacles and with my Times and the wrong ticket." Holmes smiled. "He might go on to the coast in this fine weather."

"I trust you will post his things back to him, or hand them in at the Lost and Found."

"I will post them. I want him to know that Miss Berthoud (soon to be Mrs. Bartholomew) has friends."

I threw my Exeter ticket into a bin, took out my watch and corrected the time. "Where did you find such brats, Holmes? Are they the Crystal Palace gang?"

"No, no. I applied to the nearest Doctor Barnado's Home and borrowed a dozen of their inmates. Before they became Barnado's cherubs, the boys were street Arabs; I am happy to see they have not lost their skills."

I took out my pencil and made a note of our expenses on my shirt cuff, tut-tutting to myself.

Holmes took my arm. "Come, we have 20 minutes before the Portsmouth train." He indicated the railwayman's uniform he wore under his coat. "I must change, and then let us have a celebratory coffee."

I had a sudden thought. "But will Reverend Murchison not pull the communication cord, at the next station and stop the train?"

"And incur a hefty fine?"

Rowland's Castle was a picturesque village nestled around a green, with a Railway Hotel and a church, where I was roped in to give Miss Berthoud away during a short and very simple service. After the requisite photographs at the lynch gate, the groom, Lieutenant Bartholomew, having unaccountably disappeared, I took it upon myself to take the bride's arm and lead the wedding party across the green, where wickets were being set up for a cricket match, to the hotel.

We joined Holmes in a pleasant room adjoining the bar, and the newly minted Mrs. Bartholomew took glasses of Champagne from a waiter and handed one each to Holmes and to me. I proposed a toast to the happy pair, which Mrs. Bartholomew acknowledged with a gracious bow. "I cannot thank you gentlemen enough," she said, tears glistening in her eyes. "I should have been lost without you."

"What are your plans?" I asked.

She smiled as she dabbed her eyes with her handkerchief and regained her composure. "Alfie and I leave immediately on the mail packet for our honeymoon in Grenoble, then to Gibraltar and our new life."

"Grenoble?" Holmes asked in a musing tone. "Not Paris? I thought you might like to revisit your old haunts. The Moulin Rouge is very entertaining, or so I am told."

Mrs. Bartholomew regarded Holmes through narrowed eyes.

"Of course, you will want to put Daisy behind you," Holmes continued. He lifted his glass again. "To a fresh start for you with Lieutenant Lord Alfred Bartholomew and a very happy life together."

Holmes bowed and left us, passing through the front door and onto the village green.

I blinked at Mrs. Bartholomew.

"I will indeed start anew with Alfie," she said stiffly. She considered for a moment, smiled and continued in an accent more reminiscent of Balham than Boulogne. "And I suppose I owe you the truth, Doctor, now that things are all hunky dory, as they say. I met my beloved in Paris, not Bath." She giggled. "Not at the Moulin Rouge neither. No, no, my little establishment was not at that level, 'though we had a show."

Mrs. Bartholomew smiled up at me. "Poses plastiques et tableaux vivants. Alfie visited the house with some other officers. They took a girl each upstairs and left, but Alfie stayed watching the show, and he called me to his table."

She frowned and looked around the room. "Where is he?" She turned to me. "Do you have a cigarette, Doctor?"

I opened my case with a cold gesture and Mrs. Bartholomew took a cigarette and lit it with a match from a passing waiter. "Alfie was polite and handsome, and he wanted to take me out for supper."

She blew out a long stream of smoke. "He saw me home to my lodgings after, with no 'how's your father' expected. On the third evening, he proposed, not only marriage, but a cycling trip through the Camargue. I accepted."

"You went on holiday alone and unchaperoned with a man you had known a bare three days?" I asked.

Mrs. Bartholomew laid a hand on my arm. "What a darling you are, Doctor. Alfie was a perfect English gentleman. You remind me of him."

I smoothed my moustache.

"After a very jolly holiday, he brought me here to London and set me up at a ladies hotel. I provided myself with a suitable wardrobe, and I met Admiral Bartholomew and his dear, but delicate wife at their London home."

She squeezed my arm. "What I told you of Reverend Murchison's unwelcome attentions was true, Doctor. The wretch bombarded me with billets-doux in Paris, wouldn't take no for an answer, and followed me to England. What better way to get him off my back than to persuade the great private detective, Sherlock Holmes, to deal with him? Your stories in the Strand Magazine gave me the idea of hooking Mr. Holmes by insisting that Murchison only contact me through the Personals."

She chuckled. "One Cruelly Used! Ha!" She frowned again. "Where is Alfie? He should be with me, the attentive husband and all." She leaned towards me. "He's been a might skittish today. I suppose he was afraid of a scandal if Murchison turned up. Men are such cowards. They outrage every law of the world and are afraid of the world's tongue."

I sniffed and looked away.

"Oh, Doctor, do not judge me. You don't know what it is to fall into the pit, to be despised, mocked, abandoned, sniffed at!"

Mrs. Bartholomew took a silk handkerchief from the sleeve of her bridal dress and blew her nose. "One pays for one's sin, and then one pays again, and all one's life one pays. But let that pass."

"If Mr. Holmes had not turned up," I asked. "Would you have used your pistol?"

Mrs. Bartholomew looked around with a moue of annoyance. Guests, mostly female, were in small clusters around the room, looking rather nonplussed. "Where the devil has the boy got to?"

I found Holmes on the village green in a deckchair under an umbrella, drinking a pint of ale and watching the cricket match. "Should we not meet the groom and family?" I asked.

Holmes waved me to a chair beside him and ordered a pint of ale from a boy in sailor suit and a bright scarf.

I settled back in my chair. The afternoon was warm, mellowed by a cooling breeze that brought the smell of new mown grass and the scents of spring flowers across the green. There was a thwack of leather on willow, and the ball arched across the cloudless sky and was deftly caught by an elderly gentleman in cover.

"I should have expected a more Naval wedding; an arch of cutlasses and so on," I said as we applauded.

Holmes chuckled. "What a minx it is, Watson."

The boy arrived with my beer, and I paid him, took a sip of deliciously refreshing ale, and frowned. "Miss Berthoud, I mean Mrs. Bartholomew? Have we met her before? Who is this Daisy?"

"You mentioned once that you saw Oscar Wilde's Lady Windemere's Fan a few years ago."

I shrugged. "In '92, if I recall, while you were gadding about Asia. A lot of high flown, airy nonsense, I thought. Very clever, of course, but not my cup of tea."

"Our Daisy Watts was not on the boards that night, but she was in the wings as understudy for the part of Rosalie, the maid. I saw Daisy play the role of Lady Windermere at a private performance in the residence of the Apostolic Nuncio in Montpellier in '94."

"Watts?"

"An East End costermonger family of ancient lineage."

"Not French?"

Holmes laughed. "The taste in the bordellos in Paris, and, I dare say, Boulogne and Montpellier, is for English roses, or Daisies in this case. She crossed the Channel to try her chances, picking up a smattering of the language and the sultry accent she deployed against us. I recognized her purple prose as shadows of passages from the Wilde play, snipped and fitted for her new role as One Cruelly Wronged."

I blinked at my friend, and a new and unpleasant thought struck me. "But what of the wedding, Holmes? Have we not set the young officer up for a terrible fall when he discovers Daisy's true identity?"

Holmes pocketed the cheque. "And we dine at the Amati's tonight." Another crack came from the cricket field and the bails of the nearer batsman's wicket flew apart. Lieutenant Bartholomew waved a languid hand in acknowledgement of the congratulations of his teammates and the crowd's applause. He bowed to the elderly gentleman fielding in cover.

"Admiral Bartholomew," Holmes said. He lifted his glass. "Any man who can forsake his bride on her wedding day to play a taut game of cricket deserves a salute from us. I very much doubt that Daisy knows what she's taken on, but let us wish them both the greatest happiness."

I raised my glass. "The Navy, Holmes!"

"And Daisy," he answered.

He smiled. "You wanted to meet the groom, old chap? There he is."

A lithe young man in cricket whites with a full, imperial beard raced towards his opponent at the far wicket, swung his arm in a blur of motion and let the ball loose. It bounced just before the feet of the batsman, but he was able to deflect it, with a satisfying thwack, across the green towards the church.

"Well played, sir!" I cried. "Both of you, actually."

I turned to Holmes and frowned. "But I just gave Daisy Watts away under the name of Miss Berthoud! Can that marriage be valid? And isn't her impersonation highly illegal and my involvement culpable?"

"Do not fret, my dear fellow; few things in life are what they seem. You were involved in a form of words, a charade for the admiral and his wife. The legal wedding took place sub rosa at dawn this morning in the Library of the Railway Hotel. It was presided over by the chaplain from young Bartholomew's ship and attended by his brother officers."

"How did you – oh, the boot boy."

Holmes smiled. "The only servant up at the time. He was bribed to silence and commandeered to serve the Navy rum in which the officers toasted the happy pair. I re-bribed him to paint the scene in his own words; the ceremony was, by his account, very affecting."

Holmes reached into his pocket and waved a cheque at me. "On Hoare's in the Strand and for a 100 guineas. Lieutenant Bartholomew buttonholed me in the bar of the hotel before the church wedding and congratulated me on keeping Murchison away (he mentioned that he had a horsewhip handy if the reverend had turned up). Ha! Daisy's husband is not quite as easily gulled as she thinks."

The Adventure of the Poison Tea Epidemic

by Carl L. Heifetz

We were residing at the time in furnished lodgings close to a library where Sherlock Holmes was pursuing some laborious researches in Early English charters – researches which led to results so striking that they may be the subject of one of my future narratives.

– The Adventure of the Three Students, April 1895

After the adventure that took place at the onset of the Great War in August 1914, during a quiet time over Scotch and soda, my friend Sherlock Holmes finally gave me the permission to publish the event that brought us to one of England's great universities in a search for clues to another mystery – The Adventure of the Tea Epidemic. The name of the university and its locale must still be concealed due to the fact that some of the principals in the story, published as "The Adventure of the Three Students," are still alive, though elderly. I pray that my readers will forgive my occasional use of spellings and references more appropriate to an American, but my language has been contaminated by my three-year sojourn in Baltimore, Maryland obtaining a fellowship in neurological diseases at Johns Hopkins University School of Medicine.

If I recall, the story that I will name "The Adventure of the Poison Tea Epidemic" began in the early spring of 1895. March had been particularly cold and dry that year, and we were welcoming the anticipated sunshine and warmth of April, only to experience a week of torrential rains. Being alone after the sad occasion of the death of my dear Mary, I had retaken residence in my old home on Baker Street with Mr. Sherlock Holmes. Since most doctors were unavailable after surgery hours, I was often called upon during those times to render emergency medical service. In addition, I was serving two shifts in the neuroscience facility at St. Barts to keep my hand in and to provide additional income for entertainment.

I had been sitting in my favorite chair by the window, although the heavy downpour impeded the light to some extent. I had just finished Lancet, the British Medical Journal, and several treatises on experimental neurosurgery, when I noticed that Holmes had installed his large capacity curved briar into his mouth. This signaled the need to organize his papers, which were strewn into every corner of our sitting room, into his notebooks and files. Unimpeded, after a few hours work, he would have our quarters as neat as a pin. Since this was much to my liking, I thought it best to sneak off of the premises. Otherwise, seeing my presence, he might feel impelled to narrate one of his old adventures instead of completing the organizational task. I glanced at the huge grandfather clock that had been a gift from the King of Scandinavia, and noted that it was past three p.m.

I quietly tip-toed to the door and was approaching the stairs, when glancing back, I saw Holmes remove his pipe after taking a large inhalation. He said, "Have a nice evening." He smiled briefly, as was his custom, and returned to his chores.

As I entered the street, I noticed that the rain had temporarily ceased and the sky was finally clearing. I encountered a messenger and gave him a note to deliver to my old friend Thurston, stating, "Thurston, old man, are you up to a nice dinner at our club, a few drinks, and several rounds of billiards? If so, meet me at our club. I will be there in less than 30 minutes."

After that, I beckoned a hansom cab over, and went on a short, splashy ride to my club. I climbed the flight of stairs, entered the reading room, and ordered a Scotch and soda to while away the time and read the Guardian.

After only a brief interlude, I spotted Thurston wiping his feet at the entrance to the chamber, his hat still dripping from the renewed downpour. After the servant had removed his rain gear, I noticed that my friend was still thin and well built. He looked as if he could still command his platoon as he had done in Afghanistan. His smile revealed bright teeth under his red moustache that was spotted with specks of gray. I ordered a Scotch and soda for him, and he sat next to me.

Picking up the drink from the intervening table, after we shook hands and seated ourselves, he took a sip and said, "Just the thing after a hard day of filing taxes for the lords and ladies of the kingdom. I'm happy to see you for a long savored relaxation." He continued in his deep baritone voice, just slightly showing the deleterious effects of age on its timbre, "I hope that you are ready for a serious match. I haven't played in two weeks, and I'm anxious to deprive you of some of your money."

After downing our cocktails, we were notified that our table was ready for our dinner of rare prime rib with tasty potatoes and vegetables, and a bottle of Bordeaux. Afterwards, satiated, we went up the one flight of old oaken stairs to the beautiful mahogany paneled billiard room. We were enjoying a leisurely game of three cushion billiards and our second aged cognac when a melee burst out at the entrance to the portal.

Our play was interrupted by one of the servants. He made me aware of the fact that the commissionaire, whom I had known for many years, had invaded the facility. Unlike the usually staid demeanor of the former non-commissioned officer in her Majesty's marines, the commissionaire came bursting into the billiard room. Gone was he usual military bearing and stiff upper lip. Instead, he was trembling all over. His usually stern face was red with grief and his eyes flush with tears.

He exclaimed in a loud voice, "My youngest child, Edith, is dying from pneumonia. She is burning with fever and can scarcely breathe. She is shaking all over her little body. My doctor expects her to die by morning."

Obviously, it was my ethical duty to comply with this urgent call to service. I scooped up my bag, said a hasty farewell and apology to my opponent, and rushed down the stairs, following my old commissionaire, whom I had known for many years, and who had always provided faithful service. I dashed out the door to find a four wheeler peopled by the commissionaire, an old woman, and a tiny infant wrapped in woolen blankets. Without a second's delay, I yelled to the cabbie, "Off to St. Barts as fast as you can go. If you make it in 20 minutes you will earn an extra sovereign."

My stethoscope informed me that the female infant was in the last stages of pneumonia. She was barely breathing and her lungs were congested. Also, I didn't need the assistance of a thermometer to determine that she was highly febrile. I knew there was only one chance for her: the new experimental serum being developed at the Serology Institute in the research area of St. Barts. The rabbit antiserum containing antibodies to all three strains of diplococccus was her only hope. When we had entered the new facility, I summoned the colleagues with whom I had researched for several years prior to switching to neurology. They quickly arrived, all five of them, from the areas in which they were working. My medical colleagues and I spent all night ministering to the baby with multiple intravenous injections of serum, an ice bath, and aspirin. Finally, at two in the morning, she reached the expected climax. By God's willing answer to my prayers and the power of the new medication, the fever broke, and she was again spirited and well. Joyfully, I left her and her father in the loving care of the hospital staff. I trudged out into the deep night, after promising to return at noon to see how she was faring. Finally, finding a cab, I made my way back to Baker Street, not recalling how I made it up the stairs and into my bed.

I didn't arise until a quarter past 11 a.m., if you can believe the old grandfather clock that was provided by the King of Scandinavia. I was in desperate need for a cup of hot coffee, and was grateful that the smell of fresh beverage filled the air. However, my ability to obtain this beverage was retarded by my colleague's actions. Now, I may have certain character flaws, but when it comes to plucking out a thick facial hair at the breakfast table, I draw the line. Not only was Sherlock Holmes performing that less-than-elegant act that should have been restricted to the bathroom, but he was using the highly polished coffee pot as his mirror.

"Holmes, if you don't mind, I would like to have the coffee pot. Maybe you could find a mirror in your bedroom for your preening," I said with some asperity.

Holmes turned to me with a smile, handed me the coffee pot, and said, "I see that you made a late night of it. What did you and Thurston do after leaving the club? Did you seek female companionship? I tried to leave a message for you, but my courier could only say that you rushed out."

"Holmes, what did you want me for? You weren't busy when I left for supper and billiards. I'm busy now. I must eat a quick breakfast and hurry off to St. Barts. I have a pneumonia patient," I replied. "When I return, you can tell me why you went to the trouble to summon me."

Holmes replied, "All will be revealed. Here is a sandwich that Mrs. Hudson made for me. Take your coffee with you and eat in the cab."

Grateful to Holmes for the thoughtfulness he occasionally showed when appropriate, I was even more grateful that my miniature patient had now recovered. However, I was shocked the commissionaire had left the facility and the child was being ministered to by the previously seen elderly woman.

"Where is Bracket?" I asked loudly, "and who are you?"

Smiling gently as she stroked the child, the gray haired woman said, "Don't fret doctor, I am Edith's aunt, Teresa. Mr. Bracket is my brother. He rushed off after seeing another doctor. I don't know why or where."

I rushed out to the nurse's station, yelling, "What happened to the commissionaire? What has caused him to leave his daughter, who is just now recovering from pneumonia?"

A beautiful, young, blonde-haired nurse, whom I had often visited for conversation, walked over to me and said, "It's Mr. Bracket's wife and other two children, a boy of two and a girl of five. They seem to be suffering from a severe poisoning. You may find them in the women's ward. Follow me."

I walked behind her, admiring both her figure and her control of the situation. She said, pointing to the left, "Go this way. The doctors are in with them now. Perhaps you would like to take charge of the case, since the men ministering to them are only young interns."

She turned and smiled at me, and then quickly left for her station as I reluctantly watched her go. "Well, another time would be more propitious," I thought.

As I entered the room, I quickly sized up the situation. Bracket was sitting in a chair, his head in his hands. His wife and two children were shaking all over, in an obviously nervous state. The young interns rose to greet me, and then recognizing a senior colleague backed away as if awaiting my orders.

"These people are obviously suffering from a poisoning.

Their moans indicate a state of hallucination. It appears to be some type of food poisoning, since there are no wounds on the bodies or bleeding, as I can tell from your notes. You must clear their bodies as quickly as possible. Pump their stomachs, apply enemas, flush with copious amounts of water, and then administer activated charcoal and very strong tea."

"No tea! It's poison!" yelled Mrs. Bracket, as she sat upright in the bed. Then she quickly fell back to her supine position.

I ordered, "Cancel the tea until further notice. Continue with the other instructions."

Observing the patients more closely, I began to recognize their symptoms as I slowly recalled the lectures I had received many years ago. They had undergone seizures, hallucinations, tremors, and now they expressed that they were nauseous. There was no diarrhea that one would expect from typical food poisoning. I hypothesized that they were suffering from a mild case of ergotism. I turned to my youngest colleague, an Indian, and said, "Mr. Singh, please run to the chemists and bring me amyl nitrite solution. Have the woman inhale 0.3 ml. and give the children 0.1 ml."

Turning to the other two men, I said, "Mr. Riley and Mr. Addison, please watch them carefully and keep me abreast of their progress."

As my young colleagues were ministering to my new patients, I went over to the commissionaire. Kneeling next to him, I asked "What is happening? Why are your wife and children ill and you are not? Did you drink any tea? Did it have a strange taste?"

He responded with a tremulous voice, "We were just sitting down to tea when I had to rush Edith off to the hospital. Thus, I had no tea. When I was at Edith's bedside, talking to my sister, a doctor took me away to see my family in this state. They were yelling and convulsing. No one knew what to do."

"Fortunately, I have neurological training and I recognized signs of chemical poisoning. Has anyone eaten freshly baked rye bread or anything unusual?"

He replied, "No sir. We had eaten nothing until tea was served. I left with Edith and told them to continue the tea service while I rushed to find you. Fortunately, I know where you often go when you are not in Baker Street, and I knew that it was not one of your work nights."

I said, "So it would appear that the tea was contaminated with rye bearing the ergot fungus. That is most unusual and surprising. Please stay here and watch your family. I will ask the nurse to bring you Edith on my way out. Now I must summon Mr. Sherlock Holmes. This sounds like a rare mystery that is beyond my power to discern," I said as I turned to leave.

Running out to the busy street, I spotted my friend, the cabbie Jonathon. Handing him five shillings, I shouted, "Bring Mr. Sherlock Holmes. Tell him that Bracket's family has been poisoned, and such a criminal act requires his immediate attention. Other people may be at risk."

While I awaited Holmes visit, I noticed that the victims were recovering from their attack. Finally, Mrs. Bracket turned to me and said, "Dr. Watson, thank you very much for saving our lives. We must get that tea out of the house before anyone else gets sick."

"Where did you buy the tea? We must retrieve any that they sold or still have in hand, in case there are more poisoned lots. Also, did it taste unusual?"

"Well, Doctor, I didn't purchase the tea. It was a gift from one of my husband's employers, John Alexander. She said that he hadn't bought the tea, but that it was a gift from his employer's neighbor, Sir James Green, who had given it to Mr. Alexander."

"So the tea wasn't originally intended for you. It was originally intended for Mr. Alexander," I stated.

"That is correct, Dr. Watson. But the tea tasted a little

like rye bread. I really didn't like it, but you can't look a gift horse in the mouth."

Just then, Holmes rushed in and took over the scene. He turned to the commissionaire and said, "I have a very important job for you. Get as many men as you can and go to the shop that sells this brand of tea, locate all of the recent customers, and bring all you can find to my lodgings on Baker Street. Here are several shillings to get the necessary cooperation. Tell the proprietor that Sherlock Holmes thinks that they are selling poisoned tea."

Relieved that he now had an important assignment, and that his entire family was recovering and in the hands of medical professionals, Bracket resumed his normal erect stature and bearing, and marched out of the room quickly with precise steps.

Holmes and I made the short carriage ride to Bracket's abode to see if we could find any other evidence that would point to a source of poison or, as I thought, ergot contaminated rye. We arrived at the small lodging, contained on the third floor of a brown brick building in the working class neighborhood housing the workers who served the local hospital and medical offices. Holmes quickly penetrated the building entrance and the door to the apartment without requiring a key, using methods that he had acquired from his more nefarious colleagues. The only thing out of place were the turned over chairs at the kitchen table, some liquid tea drying on the wooden floor, and tea cups containing the dregs of the teas that had not yet been ingested. Otherwise, there was no evidence of foul play. We scoured the two bedrooms, the bath, sitting room, and kitchen without finding anything suspicious. It was obvious that, as good parents, anything hazardous to children was safely under lock and key. We took the used teacups back with us for further examination. Holmes poured the residue of the tea into small glass containers, and secured the opened carton of tea in a canvas bag that he had brought for that purpose.

As we were exiting, Holmes turned to face me and asked, as a teacher does to a student, "You have examined the contents of this abode. Using your powers of observation and deduction, do you think the Bracket was the kind of man that would purposely poison his wife and children?"

I replied, "Not at all, Holmes. His bed was made with military precision. One could bounce a shilling off of it. His children's beds were covered with care and were warmly dressed. Although one wall in his sitting room was decorated with mementos of his military service, the larger bore many images of his family that far exceeded his personal effects. Also, based on my training as a neuroscientist, I would declare that his grief for his toddler's pneumonia, and his reaction to his other family members' illness, was genuine and palpable. Have I missed anything? Do you agree?"

"Watson," he declared with a smile. "You are coming along nicely. You make an excellent detective's associate. I agree with your analysis and trust the commissionaire completely."

As soon as we had arrived at our lodgings, Holmes quickly got to work. First he smelled the package of tea and invited me to do the same.

"It smells like rye bread," I said. "I have never experienced that odour in tea before."

Then he cleared his chemical apparatus from the deal topped table and installed a high powered microscope on its surface. Using a forceps, he carefully teased a portion of the solid dregs onto a glass slide. Then he applied a thin cover slip. He slowly lowered the objective to the top of the cover slip, and then raised it until he had what he wanted to see in focus. He smiled and said, "I think that your diagnosis was correct. Take a look."

I carefully repeated his actions until the material was brought into sharp focus. It didn't take me long to recall the lessons that I had learned many years ago. There were tea leaves and what could only be stands of rye stipules.

"Holmes, what I find most revealing are fruiting bodies of the ergot fungus Claviceps purpurea. I never thought that I would ever need this knowledge." I said, "My physical diagnosis was correct. I'm pleased that I was able to predict the appropriate therapy."

Holmes replied, "Yes, Watson, you are to be congratulated for medical acumen. Tomorrow I will need to visit the purveyors of this tea for a conversation. I'm certain that they have closed their facility for the night, but I will visit them early in the morning. Meanwhile, you must tell your assistants not to alert the police. If they want to publish this account in a house medical proceedings and report it in Grand Rounds, where it will disappear from public sight but serve to further their careers, that would be fine."

I responded, "Why not bring in the police? They can help us gather evidence."

Holmes retorted, "If my supposition is correct, Bracket will benefit financially from my solution to the crime. If the perpetrators are jailed, which may be unlikely unless we can find more direct evidence tying them to the actual crime, no one will benefit from the misfortunes suffered by his wife and children."

Having accomplished all that we could, Holmes and I had our own high tea, being careful to inspect the label, sniff the contents, and to settle down for a rest. I was pleased by our conversation and in a relaxed frame of mind during the entire evening. As we sat, I asked Holmes why we didn't go to the tea merchant ourselves to get the information. He replied, "Everyone likes Commissionaire Bracket. They all use his services and trust him. Had we shown up, we might have encountered suspicion and resistance. Also, I think that I would like to light a pipe and cogitate upon the issues. Why would someone give John Alexander poisoned tea? Or if we are to believe his wife, why would someone give it to Sir James, or if we want to take it a step further, was the commissionaire's family the ultimate target? Then, is there a large supply of poisoned tea in the market? I'm certain that Bracket and his cohorts will round up all of the supplies. Then, we will need to scour the papers that I asked Billy to pick up for us as we enjoyed our tea and crumpets. And finally, why did the tea have a rye taste? I have a monograph on 226 blends of tea, including the appearance of cooked and raw leaves, and a description of each flavor. I have never encountered a tea that is flavored with rye, and I can't see why anyone would want it. Tomorrow, we will have accumulated enough data to guarantee a meaningful conversation."

Holmes's last act for the evening was to send our buttons out to acquire copies of all of the newspapers before he allowed the lad to leave for the evening.

I awoke at my usual late hour to find Holmes deeply studying the newspapers that were piled up next to his ham, eggs, and coffee mug. He had a glint in his deep gray eyes and a devilish smile in his face that predicted a bad ending to the perpetrators of this mischief. I quickly ingested my breakfast and left for my morning shift at St. Barts. Also, I needed to see to my four patients and handle any financial issues. Sherlock Holmes guaranteed that he would add this expense to whoever would end up paying for his investigative services.

As I left, Holmes said, "Are you up to a trip? I need to do a search of ancient British charters and you might enjoy the environs. We leave this afternoon from Baker Street Station."

I replied, "I will be packed quickly, a skill I learned in the army medical service." Then I rushed down to the street to get the cab that our buttons had reserved for me.

I arrived on time at St. Barts and met with my staff. I congratulated my students for a job well done and warned them about avoiding publicity. I brought a sample of the tea dregs for them to evaluate as background for their report, but told them that the source of the materials was still under investigation and could not be revealed. Then, with my interns in tow, I examined my patients, saw that they were now recovered from their travails, and released them from their involuntary hospital confinement. I informed Bracket and his wife that the poisoning incident must be kept secret so that Mr. Holmes is able to adjudicate the issue and obtain remuneration for them.

After two hours of patient rounds, I bid farewell to my staff, wished them a good day, and returned to my Baker Street lodgings for a well-deserved lunch and nap. However, the nap was not to be. As I arrived, my nose was overwhelmed by the strong odour of tea that masked the pungent smell of his vile pipe tobacco. Holmes's chemical table bore five opened cartons of Paladinium Tea, the same brand that was the source of the ergot poisoning the previous day. The entire surface of his work table was covered with microscope slides and cover slips.

Holmes said, "Ah Watson, you are just in time for our next pieces of evidence. All five cartons of tea that were recently delivered are free of rye particles and fungal spores. Only the box delivered to Sir James Green, who had later given it to Mr. Alexander, was so contaminated. It was not a random event. So, the source of the poisoned tea goes at least as far back as Sir James Green. Although it's possible that the servants despoiled the samples, I suggest that that is not the case. I sent the buttons to question Mrs. Bracket, and she said that the box did not look as if it had been opened, or if it had been, it was very well done.

Then he showed me the papers. In the interior pages of the Guardian, in the section devoted to agriculture, there was a brief account of cattle poisoning in a rye field near his famous university.

He cried out, "Quick, eat your lunch! A cab awaits our voyage of discovery."

And off we went on a journey that I found out would take us to the city where resides one of England's great universities, and former scholastic residence of Sherlock

Holmes before he left to complete his degree at London University and St. Barts.

As we dashed onto the train and entered the last available first class smoking carriage, I asked Holmes, "Where are we going? What is the purpose of this journey?"

He replied, "We are traveling to the area where I first encountered my university training. Therein is a library replete with official land charters, and a nearby field in which some poor cattle died from eating rye contaminated with the fungus of ergotism. These documents, and ownership of the land, may provide further information on the motive for the ergot poisoning that we discovered by accident, and the possible source of the deleterious material."

I immediately understood his objective, but I couldn't understand how this data would apply to a criminal event in far-off London. As usual, I was forced to stay on the sidelines, exploring the buildings and town of a university that was foreign to me, while my friend spent hours on the diligent search through dry records that may date back to the formation of the English nation itself. My perambulations and isolation, except for mealtimes, was only interrupted by the brief adventure concerning the copying of the Greek scholarship exam. After only two more days, Sherlock Holmes grabbed me off of the street. In his right hand he held a plethora of documents that were rolled in a bright blue ribbon.

"Come Watson, we must pack our belongings. I now have the solution to the mystery of the devious ergotism event!" he cried. "We must return to London before the trail turns cold!"

We ran for the train just as the whistle was blowing and the conductor yelled, "All aboard."

We hurried into a first class smoker and settled down for the long journey to Baker Street. Holmes busied himself with several newspapers that he had acquired from Professor Soames, and then began studying the documents that had been carried under his long, thin arms.

Knowing that my companion would not permit any conversation as he studied the papers in his hands, I sought out the dining car, had two glasses of dry white wine, and fell into a stupor. The gentle monotonous chug of the locomotive and the delightful view out of the window, after I had returned to my carriage, must have lulled me to sleep. I felt a gentle tap on my shoulder as the conductor cried out, "All off!"

I noticed that Holmes had now unfolded all of the documents and tied them into a neat pile. The newspapers were shoved under his seat. The edges revealed that several pages had been sampled with a pair of scissors. A smile on Holmes's face indicated that someone was not going to be happy in a day or two. The look of concentration thwarted my attempts to converse with him, and I quietly followed him to a hansom cab and our final ride to our quarters.

After we strode up the 17 steps to our suite, Holmes immediately went to his desk and began writing telegrams. I noted that he was also withdrawing his special expensive formal stationery and writing notes with his neat hand. He then called out, "Billy, drop these telegrams at the post office and pay for a reply to each. Then take a cab and hand deliver these to the addresses on the linen envelopes."

With that, Holmes looked at me and said, "Watson, as you see, I have been very busy. Please forgive me for ignoring you, but time was of the essence. Please get together your best set of city clothes. We will be entertaining tomorrow at high tea at five p.m. at the Paladinium Tea Room, in their special tasting room. I expect that we will make the acquaintance of two leaders of our society who, unbeknownst to our friends, have some dark dealings in their past."

"Should I call Gregson or Lestrade?" I asked.

"No, Watson, I think that justice will be served better without the intervention of the constabulary. Just be prepared to leave tomorrow at 4:40 p.m."

Then, opening his violin case, he continued; "Now, it is time for sweetness and light. Please fix each of us Scotch and soda while I supply some music before we order our supper from Mrs. Hudson."

The following day, I arose a trifle late, even for me, full of a desire to question Holmes about our coming adventure, but alas, he had already stepped out. I was required to fill the day as best I could, walking to Marble Arch and listening to the orators, and then returning for a solitary lunch of fish and chips, and a bitter ale.

Holmes arrived at four p.m. already attired in his conservative business dress. He glanced at my selection of dark frock coat, silk tie, and grey striped pants. He nodded in affirmation of my attire. We each picked up our most ornate walking sticks, walked down to the street, and retrieved a four-wheeler that our servant had secured for us.

Holmes winked at me and said, "We will make a stop along the way."

Then, we stopped at the residence of Bracket, who was now very elegantly attired in his military dress uniform. Our threesome pulled up at the chic entry to the most expensive tea room in the West End. A liveried footman emerged, opened our carriage door, and guided us past the little old ladies who populated the front room of the shop. We then were escorted up the stairs to the palatial rooms reserved for the special guests. The fashionable décor indicated that we appropriately dressed for the surroundings. The tables were set with glistening silver spoons and stylish imported tea cups and saucers, with matching pitchers and lemon service. The walls were adorned with masterworks of art, among which were several oil paintings by Holmes's great uncle, M. Vernet.

The heralded proprietor of the Paladinium Tea Room, Mr. Brooks, was garbed in afternoon formal attire. He greeted each of us individually as an honored guest. His thin moustache accented a very narrow nose on a slight well-shaven face that matched his slim build and tiny feet. He carried himself with the grace expected of a doyen of such a fine establishment.

When he approached Sherlock Holmes and shook his hand, he said, "Mr. Holmes, I have always wanted to meet you. I have been following your exploits closely."

Turning in my direction, he extended his hand and gave me a firm shake. "Doctor Watson, I'm extremely pleased to meet the famous author and biographer of Mr. Holmes."

He also greeted the Commissionaire with the respect usually afforded an aristocrat, shaking his hand and thanking him for his courage and service to our Queen. He then motioned to a tray of small glasses and invited us to join him in a sherry as we awaited our other visitors.

The two additional men arrived about five minutes later, separately, and each was accompanied by his man servant. After the valets removed the top hats and light overcoats of our visitors, they took away the walking sticks and went down the stairs to the servants' area. Sir James Green and Mr. John Alexander were men of a type who could be considered aristocrats and men of affairs. In many ways, they resembled Holmes's former school mate, Musgrave. Their attire was in the latest fashion from the best tailors. Their shoes were glistening in the light of the tea room. They were both very pale of skin, and had fair hair. They held their noses up as if to avoid any foul odours, and their faces bore the obvious signs of disdain. As they approached the earlier residents of the room, they bowed formally as a sign of recognition. However, they did not offer their hands. They especially looked askance at the uniformed military figure of Commissionaire Bracket, who gave each a military salute.

The man identified as Sir James Green said, "Mr. Brooks, I thought that this was to be a private showing. What are the other men doing here?"

Brooks responded as courteously as well as he could under the circumstances saying, "I thought that you would enjoy the company of other noted gentlemen at this event."

Mr. Alexander said, "Let's get this over with. As long as we are here, I can stand the company of Sir James Green for this short time. Next time, please make certain that you meet us separately. The other men are welcome to join us."

With that, Mr. Brooks clapped his hands and a waiter appeared, pushing in a large carboy sloshing hot water. The men were invited to take seats of their choice, and were each provided with a dollop of tea in a strainer. He then poured hot water through each.

Immediately, Sir James burst out, "Are you trying to kill us? This tea is poisoned!"

Shocked by this outburst, the other men pushed their chairs back. Sherlock Holmes asked, "How do you know this tea is poisoned? Is it the smell of rye?"

Sir James shouted, "Are you accusing me of something?"

"No," retorted Sherlock Holmes, "You are accusing yourself." And with that, Holmes finished preparing his cup of tea and began to drink. "Is it the smell of rye? I thought that this was a very pleasant taste."

At Holmes's signal, Bracket and I also drank our tea. Seeing that there was no danger, Mr. Alexander also consumed his tea. Chagrined by this, Sir James followed suit, but with some degree of trepidation.

"What is this about?" asked Sir James angrily. "You tricked me!"

"You tricked yourself," replied Holmes. "Now please seat yourself. I have a story to tell you."

Sir James stood up and attempted to leave. "I have no interest in your tales, you busybody. I'm leaving."

"We three will hold you in here until we have concluded the business of the evening. Mr. Brooks, I think that the Scotch and soda that I brought would be better suited to what follows. Thank you very much for your courtesy. Please sit and listen, since what follows many also be of interest to you."

Mr. Alexander said, "Yes, stay. I want to know what this is about." After each man had been supplied with their alcoholic beverage,

Sherlock Holmes began his recitation. "I received a desperate call from Dr. Watson that Sergeant Major Bracket's wife and children were stricken with ergot poisoning. Now, Dr. Watson is an expert in nervous system disorders. He was able to save the lives of the three individuals, all of whom had ingested tea smelling of rye. Neither Mr. Bracket nor his daughter was affected because they went to the hospital before they could drink any tea, due to an attack of pneumonia suffered by the youngest child. When Dr. Watson and I inspected Mr. Bracket's domicile, we noted a strong smell of rye. Subsequently, we examined the tea dregs in my laboratory and saw, in the microscope, fragments of rye wheat and Claviceps purpurea therein."

"What has that to do with me," yelled Sir James. "I don't even know this man or his family."

As he started again to leave, Holmes, Bracket, and even Alexander threw him back in his chair saying, "Somehow, I think that tea was meant for me. My cook told me that it was sent over and I refused it, telling her to destroy it."

"You have been after me all of the years as well. But you can't prove that I'm the source of the poisoned tea."

Sherlock Holmes resumed his professorial manner and continued. "According to Mrs. Bracket, she received the tea from Mrs. Alexander, who thought that she was doing a kindness. But the tea, which wreaked havoc with the Bracket family, was clearly intended for Mr. Alexander."

"Then where did the ergot in the tea come from?" asked Sir James belligerently.

"Thank you for the next entry to my story. It seems as if land belonging to you is infested with rye wheat contaminated with ergot."

With that, Sherlock Holmes passed around material clipped from the Guardian, and more detailed accounts of cattle poisoning from the local press in Holmes's university town. Holmes said, "I also visited the area with Dr. Watson, and looked at all of the land holdings in the area. You, Sir James, had access to the ergot-contaminated rye."

"If you think that is the case, why don't you turn this over to the police?"

"Because, I do not plan to besmirch your name or that of Mr. Alexander in the press. The society pages would have a field day. Also, it would harm the excellent and hard-earned reputation of the Paladinium Tea Room and its proprietor Mr. Brooks. I have another story that you may find interesting as well." went on Sherlock Holmes.

He continued, "I researched ancient English charters, almost to the beginning of our nation from the Norman conquest. There was a brave and ferocious knight who served William the Conqueror. As a reward for his service, the man was first made a baron of the realm, and later was awarded the position of Earl. This gentleman had a succession of heirs, each bearing the noble title and serving the kings of England. Unexpectedly, one of the men had twin sons. He died before the land could be officially awarded to the appropriate heir. After that time, descendants of both have quarreled over the ownership of the estates.

Gentlemen, those men were your ancestors. Your quarrel dates back to that time. You gentlemen are of the same blood, first cousins several generations removed from the great Earl, who is your ancestor. I now have the copies of all of the documents and land grants. I suggest that you join together in a court action and split the properties equitably, and to cease these useless attempts to murder each other."

"That is good news, Mr. Holmes. I had no idea that we were kin. I only knew that we each were told that the entire tract of land was ours to fight over," said Mr. Alexander. "It does not behoove us to fight each other when, in tandem, we can join our forces and reap the harvest that we deserve. James, I forgive your attempt to harm me if you can see it in your heart to do the same for my past actions."

Sir James stood up, held out his hand and said, "Cousin, it is time that we were partners. We are both very clever at affairs and could reap a great harvest. By now, the value of the land itself is far less valuable that our holdings in properties, money, and investments. "

To everyone's surprise, the two cousins shook hands in friendship and said, in unison, "To making our fortunes." Then, they embraced each other and started to leave arm in arm.

Sherlock Holmes ordered, "Just a minute, gentlemen. I'm satisfied that you have made a friendly alliance, but there is still the matter of Mr. Bracket and his family, who were the innocent victims of your rivalry. Mr. Bracket, thank you for your attendance. Now I wish to speak to the cousins in private, with only Doctor Watson as a witness. Mr. Brooks, would you please see the Commissionaire to a cab and pay his fare? I will reimburse you soon."

As they left, Mr. Brooks said, "It is the least I could do for saving my reputation."

After they left, Sherlock Holmes took some very formal looking documents from his pocket. He handed a copy to each gentleman, saying, "Here are contracts that I have had formatted by my attorney, binding you to an agreement to provide financial remuneration to Mr. Bracket's family. Please read them carefully. You may have a solicitor read over them, but I am firm on the requirements. You will collectively provide money to support a suitable home for Mr. Bracket and his family, and scholarships to excellent schools and a university education for his children."

Both gentlemen carefully read the short document, nodded their agreements, and quickly signed both copies.

Sherlock Holmes said, "Thank you gentlemen for your cooperation. I'm happy that everyone will benefit by this day's events. I will have my solicitor finalize these contracts for my signature, along with Dr. Watson, as witnesses."

Both men smiled broadly. "Thank you, Mr. Holmes. You are truly a miracle worker," said Sir James.

"Yes," added Mr. Alexander. "The words of Dr. Watson's narratives ring true. If ever I am troubled with a serious problem, I will contact you. Expect a check for one-thousand pounds for your expenses."

"I will add the same amount to that." Said Mr. Alexander, as he two aristocrats strolled off arm in arm.

Sherlock Holmes turned to me and said, "Now for some great food, wine, and repartee. We have both been invited by brother Mycroft to join him at his club for dinner."

I turned to Holmes and asked, "How does he know about this?"

Holmes replied, "Brother Mycroft seems to always know what is going on, sometimes before it takes place."

Then off we went seeking transportation to the guest dining room at the Diogenes Club.

The Man on Westminster Bridge

by Dick Gillman

I – Meeting Anthony Stewart

It was an occurrence during a cab ride, as we returned to Baker Street one pleasant evening in the latter half of May 1895, that was to begin the case that I have here recorded as that of "The Man on Westminster Bridge."

Holmes had become increasingly frustrated over the past weeks as nothing of great note had occurred to stimulate the great machine within his head that needed a constant challenge. For the last few days, he had prowled our rooms in Baker Street like a caged beast, avidly devouring The Times each day, hoping to find a case worthy of his talents. Each day, I had found the newspaper torn and tossed aside in disgust.

In an attempt to distract Holmes, I had suggested an outing to one of the Royal Parks. Holmes, after a great deal of persuasion, had grudgingly agreed. In truth, he himself could recognise that he was close to the edge of that abyss that would surely take him if his mind remained unchallenged and turned in upon itself.

We had spent a pleasant enough time strolling for perhaps an hour in the sunshine and, although the physical exercise had helped Holmes, the machine inside his head continued to race towards destruction. Having done all that I could, we hailed a cab and set off back towards Baker Street.

Throughout the journey, Holmes had remained silent and looked straight ahead, seeming oblivious to his surroundings. It was as we crossed Westminster Bridge that he suddenly cried out, "Stop!" and began hammering on the roof of the cab. The cabbie in response pulled back hard on the reins and the cab slewed to a stop. Holmes leaped from the cab and ran full tilt towards the stone balustrade of the bridge. For one dreadful moment, I thought that he had decided to end it all and leap headlong into the Thames.

As quickly as I could, I followed crying out, "Holmes! Holmes! For pity's sake, wait for me!" but it was to no avail. Holmes by now had mounted the balustrade and was seen to be reaching down towards something below him.

As I grew near, I heard him say, "You seem to be having some difficulty climbing back from there, friend. Allow me to help you." After a few moments, and as I watched, I saw a hand reach up and grasp the one offered by Holmes. Gradually, its owner came into view and Holmes assisted the figure back over the balustrade.

The figure before us was that of a middle-aged man and clearly in some distress. He was dressed as one would for The City, although some of his clothes had become unbuttoned and flapped like limp, black wings in the evening breeze. Looking at his face, I noted it was streaked with tears, and his eyes were wild with emotion. He nodded to Holmes, saying, "I do not know whether to thank you, sir, or curse you."

It was at that moment he collapsed before us. We were barely able to grasp his limp figure to prevent his head smashing onto the stone flagstones of the pavement. Propping the lifeless man against the balustrade, I reached for my hip flask and poured out a sizeable measure of medicinal brandy into the silver cup of the flask. Holmes took the cup from my grasp and poured a little into the mouth of the limp figure before us. Almost instantly the man coughed and became animated as the fiery spirit trickled down his throat.

Holmes grasped the fellow beneath one armpit and I followed suit. Together, we staggered with him towards the cab and somehow managed to seat him inside. I rode with him whilst Holmes joined the cabbie at the rear.

By the time we had reached Baker Street, our fellow traveller was much improved and was able to climb the stairs to our rooms almost under his own steam. Once inside, I immediately rang for Mrs. Hudson and asked her to provide a pot of tea.

Our guest sat on our settee, and for the first time he seemed able to make some sense of his hosts and the surroundings in which he found himself.

Blinking slightly, he said, "I am most grateful for the help you have given me this evening, gentlemen. It is far more than I deserve, for I am a wretched man. I do not deserve your kindness. Had you implored me not to jump, then I fear that that would have been the trigger for me to end it all. I don't even know your names, or indeed where I am. Allow me to introduce myself. My name is Anthony Stewart."

I looked towards Holmes and I could see that he was nodding in agreement. Holmes began thus, "I am Sherlock Holmes, and this is my friend, Doctor John Watson. You are a guest in our rooms in Baker Street."

A slight knock at the door announced the arrival of Mrs. Hudson with the tea, and after pouring out three cups, we settled back and sipped in silence. After perhaps five minutes had passed, Holmes leant forwards slightly, asking, "What has brought you to this position, Mr. Stewart?"

Our guest regarded Holmes with a face full of woe. "Mr. Holmes, I am a weak man. I have a good position in The City, but I have a weakness that clouds all my judgement and is the ruin of me. I am a gambler and, Lord help me, it has ruined me...or one accursed man has. I have lost everything:

my wife, my children, my home...everything. I know it is my fault, but he has taken everything in a way that is against all the odds. He is a cheat...I know it, but it is nothing I could prove...and it is not just my life that is forfeit. He has ruined others' too."

I could see a spark of interest in Holmes's eyes as he listened to our guest's story. "Who is this man that you accuse?" asked Holmes.

Stewart's face hardened. "His name is Cooke, Major Tobias Cooke. He is a retired army officer, and I rue the day I ever set eyes upon the man. He appears to have the luck of the Devil himself."

Holmes sat back in his armchair, his fingers steepled against his lips. "And where does this gambling take place?" asked Holmes.

Our guest looked up wearily, saying, "At a gentleman's club. Bairstow's, in Westminster."

Holmes's eyes now burned. He obviously knew the name and was eager to involve himself in this matter. "And where will you sleep tonight, Mr. Stewart?"

Stewart shook his head, saying, "I am unsure...I left the small amount of money that I have, together with a letter to my wife and children, in my rented rooms in Putney. I believed that this was to be my final day on Earth."

Standing, Stewart continued, "I have taken too much of your and the good Doctor's time. I must make my way back to Putney somehow."

Holmes reached into his pocket and from it he took half a crown. This he pressed into the hand of our guest, saying, "This will be sufficient for your cab fare, Mr. Stewart. Your story intrigues me. Have no fear, we will meet again, and I will enquire further into this Major Cooke."

Our guest was clearly moved by Holmes's gesture, and he took Holmes's hand, saying, "Have a care, Mr. Holmes, for the Major is a violent man towards those who do not pay their debts or have crossed him."

Holmes nodded and guided Mr. Stewart to the door. With a nod to Holmes, he was gone.

I sat a little bemused by the evening's happenings. "This Major Cooke seems to be something of a scoundrel, Holmes. What do you propose?" I asked.

Holmes had returned to his armchair and had taken up his pipe. Drawing steadily upon it, he replied, "I think I need to have some breakfast with my brother." Having said this, Holmes took a page from his notebook before dashing off a telegram and ringing for Mrs. Hudson.

This reply was of no help and did little to enlighten me... but I would have to wait until the morning and breakfast with Mycroft.

II – Major Tobias Cooke

I arose quite early and was looking forward to the visit of Mycroft to our rooms for a little breakfast. Often the intellectual interplay between the two brothers was sufficient to provide at least some small stimulation for Holmes. However, a brief look towards Holmes suggested that the previous evening's events had seemed to have only provided a temporary relief from his depression.

Mycroft arrived promptly at eight o'clock and I welcomed him on the landing outside our rooms. In a few brief words, I recounted my concern for his brother's health. I could see from Mycroft's face, as I took his hat and coat, that he had, with a single glance into our sitting room, immediately assessed the situation.

With a nod in my direction, Mycroft proceeded to seat himself on our settee and fill his pipe. Holmes was firmly ensconced in his leather armchair, his old dressing gown draped over his shoulders. He looked up briefly as Mycroft sat but uttered not a word of welcome. I rang the bell for Mrs. Hudson to bring up the breakfast tray and sat in my own chair and waited.

Mycroft moved forwards a little on the settee, saying, "I am most grateful for your invitation, Sherlock, for I, too, have something I wish to discuss with you."

Holmes did not look up. He simply blew out a cloud of blue smoke from his pipe and followed this with an unintelligible grunt. Mycroft looked across at me and I nodded to him in encouragement.

Mycroft continued. "This fellow at Bairstow's, I need to have your opinion of him."

Holmes again said nothing, but I was pleased to see some slight spark of interest appear upon his features.

"Bairstow's?" I questioned, as the name now seemed unfamiliar to me.

Holmes had shrugged off his dressing gown and looked towards me.

"Come along, Watson. It is the Gentleman's Club by the river in Westminster that Stewart spoke of. What is it, Mycroft? Has he also taken a liking to the club's silverware?" asked Holmes, somewhat testily. Mycroft gave a wry smile, saying, "Would that it were so simple. There are a handful of members at the club who like to place wagers against each other on the results of horse races. There is one member in particular, the one whom you mentioned in your telegram, who has had spectacular luck of late and has, in a matter of weeks, won some tens of thousands of guineas."

Holmes cried out, "Luck? Pah! As you well know, there is no such thing, Mycroft! The man is plainly a cheat and a scoundrel!"

Mycroft was now sitting back on our settee and nodding. "Yes, those are entirely my thoughts, Sherlock, but as of yet, I have been unable to determine how he does it."

Our conversation was halted by a knock at the door of our rooms, followed by Mrs. Hudson entering with a handsomely spread breakfast tray. Three places had already been laid at our dining table, and we were soon tucking into rashers of home-cured bacon, fresh farm eggs, and freshly baked bread. I have to say that I was greatly relieved to see that Holmes was enjoying the meal to the full. His appetite had recently dwindled to almost nothing. After the meal, we sat almost in silence and enjoyed a cup of Darjeeling. I could see that Holmes's interest had been piqued and he was now fully alert.

"Tell me more of this 'lucky' fellow, Mycroft, for I am intrigued," demanded Holmes.

With the briefest of raised eyebrows in my direction, Mycroft proceeded thus: "Well, Major Tobias Cooke is a retired cavalry officer. From what I have seen of his military record and my discreet enquiries at the War Office, he appears to have retired under somewhat of a cloud. Apparently, there seems to have been some unpleasantness regarding 'irregularities' in the officers' mess accounts."

Holmes nodded briefly before asking, "How and where does this gambling take place?"

Mycroft drew upon his pipe before answering, "There are, perhaps, five members of the club who gather in one of the side rooms off the main lounge, usually once or twice a week. Here they will select a race and, after consulting the runners and riders, they will wager against each other. It appears that they may place a bet at any time before the result of the race is known, even up until the very last second before the envelope is opened."

I was troubled. "Envelope? What envelope is this, Mycroft?" I asked.

Mycroft turned to me slightly, saying, "There is no telegraph at the club. A messenger boy is sent to a telegraph office nearby, and an arrangement has been made with the telegraph company whereby they will receive the result of the race and seal it in an envelope which is then brought to the club by the messenger boy."

Thinking for a moment, I asked, "I presume, then, that no-one will know the result of the race until the envelope is opened?"

Mycroft nodded, saying, "Quite so."

Holmes looked thoughtful. "This envelope, is it possible that it is opened and the contents conveyed to Major Cooke before the winner is announced?"

Mycroft slowly shook his head. "No, those were my first thoughts but I have seen it for myself. The chairman of the club was so concerned by the losses of some club members that he took me to one side and asked me to observe the proceedings. I was shown the envelope privately before it was opened publicly and all was intact."

Holmes had drawn his knees up to his chest and was now deep in thought. "What of the members? Are they free to leave the premises at all?"

Mycroft again shook his head. "They have agreed amongst themselves that none of them may leave the club once the race has started and until the result is known. This fellow, Major Cooke, has wagered thousands of guineas on horses with poor form only to have them win." Mycroft paused for a moment before continuing, "It is a bad business, Sherlock. Some of the members cannot afford these losses and may well be ruined if they continue."

Holmes blew out a thin stream of smoke, saying, "Yes, that poor wretch Stewart, for one! I have little pity for gamblers, Mycroft, but I detest cheats. I would like you to arrange to invite Watson and me to the club, as your guests, the next time these fellows meet."

Mycroft smiled. "It is already arranged. You are expected at 3:30 today. Their next wager is to be on the result of the four o'clock race at Lincoln."

Holmes could not help but rub his hands and smile, crying, "Splendid!"

Mycroft rose, gathered his hat and coat and, with a nod to me, he was gone. I have to say that I was indeed relieved to see that my friend was once more animated and looking forwards to the challenge ahead. It was apparent from his posture, his knees drawn up tightly to his chest and his eyes half closed, that even now he was considering a multitude of possibilities.

III – A Visit to Bairstow's

That afternoon, we dressed formally and made our way down the stairs to Baker Street. Holmes quickly hailed a hansom and gave the cabby an address in Westminster. Once on our way, I was curious about how these wagers were made, and asked Holmes to enlighten me.

Holmes sat forwards slightly in the cab, saying, "In my experience of these things, a group of fellows will wager on the winner of a race and perhaps also take bets on the minor placings. It is commonplace not to consider the bookmakers odds, but merely place or accept a bet on the horse's position at the finish."

I nodded...but in truth, I was still a little unsure.

Holmes saw my confusion, sighed, and then continued. "Suppose, then, that I think horse number three will win and I announce a wager of 500 guineas. You may accept the wager and if it wins, you must pay me 500 guineas. If it loses, then I must pay you 500 guineas. Of course, these fellows will know the previous form of the horse and so they will place or accept bets accordingly."

Again I nodded, confident that I now, at least, knew the rudiments of placing a wager.

In but a few minutes, our cab slowed to a stop at the kerb outside the rather grand façade of a fine Victorian building, having one side facing the river. A discreet brass plaque to one side of the arched and fluted stone doorway said simply "Bairstow's," and beneath that, "Members Only." On our approach, a liveried doorman touched the brim of his top hat with his gloved hand and opened the heavy, half-glazed, oak front door.

Once inside, I was immediately aware of the fine crystal chandelier that lit the elegant atrium. Sparkling brightly, it sent out shards of coloured light that highlighted the moulded plaster ceiling and the half panelled walls. We were clearly strangers and were straightaway approached by one of the staff who took the card proffered by Holmes. Almost immediately, we were whisked away to a smoking room where the familiar figure of Mycroft Holmes could be seen, seated in a deep-buttoned leather Chesterfield chair, drawing contentedly on a fine Havana cigar.

Upon our arrival, Mycroft rose from his Chesterfield and beckoned us to sit in the two empty chairs beside him. "Ah, Sherlock, may I offer you a little refreshment? I am told that they serve a very passable glass of sherry."

Holmes held up his hand, saying, "Thank you, no, but I would like one of your fine Havana's, Mycroft. A little sherry for you, Watson?" he questioned.

I nodded, replying, "Err...yes, a 'fino' would be most pleasant." I smiled and nodded at Mycroft.

With barely a raised finger, Mycroft summoned one of the ever alert waiters, ordering a glass of 'fino' sherry for me and a Havana for Holmes. Within moments, the waiter returned with a small silver tray which bore my sherry in a lead crystal glass, and beside it a fine Havana cigar. I carefully took the glass of straw-coloured sherry and sniffed at it before taking a sip. It was indeed very pleasant, like a mouthful of Spanish sunshine.

Holmes had taken the cigar from the tray and had used the cigar cutter proffered by the waiter to slice the very tip from the rounded end of his cigar. He now took a Vesta from his silver case, struck it, and then carefully toasted the end of the cigar before drawing contentedly upon it.

It was as we sat there that Mycroft reached over and touched the sleeve of Holmes's jacket. Inclining his cigar slightly, he used it to discreetly point towards a gentleman who was standing some ten feet away at the entrance to the room and now framed by the doorway, saying quietly, "That is Major Cooke, Sherlock."

I looked towards the doorway and there stood an impressive figure, every inch a military man, well-dressed and finely groomed. He stood some six feet in height, with hair that was iron grey. His slightly ruddy face was lined and bore fine almost mutton chop, whiskers. Looking around him, he gestured to three seated gentlemen who rose and left the room. With a sweep of his gaze, he left, seeming to have ensured that no-one else remained whose presence he required. As we watched, another member joined the group and the five now disappeared from our view into a side room.

Holmes turned slightly, saying, "An interesting fellow. The polo injury must be quite painful in the damper months."

Mycroft nodded. "Yes, those 30 guinea, hand-lasted shoes, undoubtedly from Harrison and Ball of Old Bond Street, must give his ankle some vestige of support, I would imagine."

Holmes nodded, saying, "Yes, but it is what he carries in his right-hand jacket pocket that intrigues me, Mycroft."

Mycroft nodded sagely in agreement. I sat amazed looking simply from one brother to the other. I, as had they, had only seen the man for, perhaps, barely 20 seconds. I had a brief impression of his face and clothes, whilst they had observed so very much more. As we sat, it became clear to me that Mycroft had chosen his position in the smoking room very wisely. From our chairs, we had a clear view of the atrium, and also the door to the side room where the five club members had gathered to place a wager and await the result of the race.

The rather grand, gilded wall clock in the atrium struck four o'clock. I had finished my sherry whilst Sherlock and Mycroft were still drawing contentedly upon their Havanas. It was a few minutes after four when I noticed that Major Cooke had hurried out of the side room, had turned left, and was now climbing the fine mahogany staircase. Holmes laid aside his cigar in the ashtray beside him and immediately gave chase...at a respectable distance. Perhaps two minutes later, the Major was to be seen hurrying down the stairs and heading towards the side room, followed by a now frowning Holmes.

Holmes approached us, clearly deep in thought. He sat for a moment in silence before turning towards the atrium, clearly impatient for something further to happen. I observed Holmes straighten and his jaw become firm, as a messenger boy crossed the atrium and walked towards the side room, clutching an envelope. Within moments, there could be heard a muted cry and, a minute or so later, the members from the side room emerged from their conclave.

As I watched, the faces of the five men were a testament to their fortunes. One was holding his head and, seemingly, almost in tears; another's face clearly showed anger and was almost scarlet, his fists clenched tightly by his sides. A third looked resigned to his loss, whilst the Major and another fellow were clapping each other on the back and had beaming faces.

Holmes turned slightly and stood with his back to the Major. Leaning forwards towards his brother, he said quietly, "I want to meet this fellow, Mycroft."

Mycroft nodded and waved a hand in the direction of the Major and shouted "Cooke! Come and meet my brother." The Major looked towards Mycroft, raised his hand in greeting, and he and his companion approached. Holmes still had his back to the Major and just as he drew level, Holmes turned abruptly and bumped awkwardly into him.

Holmes cried out, "Oh, I'm so sorry. I was tending to my cigar." Holmes smiled broadly and proffered his hand, saying, "Sherlock Holmes, and this is my friend, Doctor John Watson."

The Major looked us both up and down with a somewhat wary eye and shook our hands. Holmes continued, "My brother Mycroft, he is the sensible one, says that you like a flutter on the horses. My friend Watson also has a penchant for such things, don't you, Watson?"

In truth, I was flabbergasted by this sudden change in persona by Holmes. He had become this brash, casual fellow that I certainly did not recognise as my friend. I somehow managed to mutter, "Err...yes, I have been known to wager a few sovereigns."

"Nonsense, Watson! I have known you to drop a thousand or two at one go," cried Holmes.

I could only nod and smile, but, as Holmes said this, I could see that the Major had suddenly become interested in my wagering habits. Smiling broadly, the Major said, "Well, Doctor, as it happens, we are having a small wager on the outcome of the 3:30 race at York tomorrow. Would you like to join us?"

I looked towards Holmes and was about to open my mouth when he cried, "Of course he would. However, we are, of necessity, required to be elsewhere tomorrow, but Watson would be pleased to oblige the day after!"

The Major smiled, saying, "Splendid! We are having another wager that day on the result of the 3:30race at York."

"Excellent! Come along, Mycroft, I will treat you to some tea." Grasping his brother's arm, Holmes hurried from the room with me smiling and nodding a "good bye," and then hurrying in his wake.

As we left Bairstow's, Mycroft reached out and held Holmes's arm, asking, "What is it, Sherlock? Why this charade? Do you know how he does it?"

Holmes was once more his old self. Nodding, he replied, "I believe so...but I need a day to confirm my suspicion. I would be grateful if you were to meet Watson here in two days' time when he places his wager." Holmes paused for a moment before asking, "I take it, Mycroft, that you do not mean to ruin the man, but simply to recoup the other members' losses and warn him off?"

Mycroft nodded. "Quite so. The members do not want a scandal."

Holmes nodded and, after a good bye to his brother, Holmes quickly hailed a cab to take us back to Baker Street.

IV – Surveying the Course

Once more back in our rooms and settled in our respective chairs, I began to reflect on the events at Bairstow's. "Tell me, Holmes, what did you make of our new friend, Major Cooke? I am intrigued to know more of his polo injury."

Holmes blew out a cloud of blue smoke and laughed heartily. "After seeing him approach, it was clear that he was right-handed and lame in his left leg. From his slightly restricted movement in his right arm, he also suffers from arthritis. Now, a cavalry officer may carry a sword into battle, but as there have been none of late, it is much more likely that the damage to his shoulder is from the repeated use of a polo mallet."

I nodded, although in truth, I was still unconvinced. Holmes, of course, observed my troubled expression and added, "However, the Major's cufflinks which bore the distinctive crest of the Marylebone Polo Club did, to some extent, support my deduction."

On hearing this, I burst out laughing and then asked, "And the item in his jacket pocket?"

Holmes now grew more serious. "Now that is an interesting object, Watson. I managed to grasp it briefly when I engineered to collide with the Major. I have an idea as to what it is, but I need to return to Bairstow's early in the morning to confirm my suspicions."

Upon this, Holmes would say no more. We retired, and early the next morning, after a hearty breakfast of a pair of Scottish kippers, coffee, toast and some rather fine Seville marmalade, we made our way downstairs and out onto

Baker Street. Holmes hailed a cab, and I was perplexed when he directed the cabbie to take us to Westminster Bridge. During our ride, Holmes looked straight ahead and purposefully avoided my eye. It was clear that he wished not to be questioned as to what was afoot.

Arriving at the bridge, Holmes directed the cabbie to drive towards the centre span, almost at the point where we had saved Anthony Stewart. Here, he called out, requesting the driver to stop. Getting down from the cab, Holmes moved to the stone balustrade of the bridge and then withdrew from his jacket pocket a pair of field glasses. Raising them to his eyes, he used them to sweep, and then carefully examine, the buildings that abutted the bank of the Thames. As I watched, he paused in his observations. Looking towards one particular building, a thin smile appeared upon his lips. Replacing the field glasses, he leapt back into the cab, calling out to direct the driver to take us once more to Bairstow's.

Our cab ride was but brief, and before long we were once again within the atrium of Bairstow's. As we stood for a moment, we were approached by a tall, grey haired, slim gentleman, dressed very formally. His waistcoat was a delicate shade of dove grey, and it was adorned with a heavy gold Belcher chain and fob. His face was oval and sported a fine moustache. His eyes were bright, almost piercing – no, enquiring – and he spoke in a precise way.

Nodding briefly to us, he extended his hand and began thus, "Good morning, Mr. Holmes, Doctor Watson. I am Sir Terence Walters, the Chairman of the club. Your brother and I have already had conversations regarding your assistance in this matter, and I am at your complete disposal."

Holmes and I shook Sir Terence's hand and allowed him to guide us towards a more private area of the atrium. Holmes, I could see, was at complete ease with Sir Terence, and it took me but moments to recall that Sir Terence had, until but a few years past, been a senior figure at the bar.

Gesturing us to be seated, Sir Terence sat forward on his

chair, seemingly eager for Holmes to begin.

Holmes paused for a moment and then asked, "What do you know of this Major Cooke, Sir Terence?"

Sir Terence pursed his lips slightly. "Well, I know something of his military career, as all our members are scrutinised before being allowed to join the club. However, the business regarding his retirement from the regiment was obscured from us and only came to light, thanks to your brother. He is from an honourable family that has a country seat in Lancashire. His father bred racehorses, I believe, so I would imagine the Major's penchant for a wager stems from there."

Holmes nodded and from his expression, he seemed quite satisfied with this new information. "Yesterday afternoon when we were here, Sir Terence, Major Cooke took his leave from his companions and ascended the staircase to the first floor, disappearing into a room with an unmarked door. I was reluctant to follow, you understand, and I would be grateful if you might show me the room."

Sir Terence nodded and his face bore a slight smile as he led the way. Crossing the atrium, we passed through the lounge, where I could see the fine mahogany staircase with its scarlet Wilton carpet runner and brass stair rods ascending to the next floor. At the top of the stairs, Holmes pointed across the landing to a plain mahogany door. As I watched, Sir Terence's smile broadened, saying, "This way, gentlemen."

Passing through the doorway, we found ourselves in a panelled anti- room. Along one wall were arranged a row of dull, brass coat hooks. On the opposite wall was a large, mahogany-framed, bevel-edged mirror. Below the mirror were three wash basins which were furnished with a glass soap dish, together with a collection of colognes and lavender water. The third wall comprised a waist-high Travertine marble-topped counter. Behind the counter stood a liveried attendant with a small pile of freshly laundered towels. The final wall was simply panelled and contained a further door, behind which I was sure that I knew what I might find.

Sir Terence smiled broadly, saying, "You see, gentlemen, we all, at some time, must answer the call of nature. The outer door bears no name for our 'facilities,' as all the members know of its purpose and where it leads."

Holmes's face showed no humour. "I wonder, Sir Terence, if I might venture a little further and then, if you will allow, I would like to question your attendant?"

Sir Terence nodded and held out his hand with his palm to one side as a sign of his agreement. Holmes nodded politely and disappeared from our view through the second door. Within a minute he returned and walked over to where the attendant stood waiting. The attendant offered Holmes a towel but he declined, saying, "Thank you, but there is no need. I would, however, like to ask if you were on duty here yesterday afternoon."

The attendant looked towards Sir Terence for permission. Sir Terence nodded, saying, "These gentlemen are my guests, Wilson. You may speak freely and honestly to them as though you were answering to me."

The attendant looked relieved and answered Holmes. "Yes sir, I was here from one o'clock until late evening. I am employed here for six days per week."

Holmes smiled. "You, of course, know all the members here?"

Wilson nodded, saying proudly, "Oh yes, sir, I have been here these many years. I know them all."

Holmes smiled again, asking, "I was here at the club at a little after four o'clock yesterday, and I happened to pass a gentleman on the stairs whom I thought I recognised: Major Cooke?"

The attendant's smile became positively radiant. "Why, yes sir. You are correct. It was Major Cooke. I think of him as one of my regulars. You can almost set your watch by him, sir. He uses the facilities a few minutes past the hour or the half hour of an afternoon."

Holmes looked towards me with a knowing smile. Thanking the attendant, we left and returned downstairs with a rather bemused Sir Terence.

Once more in the atrium, I looked towards Sir Terence and noticed him rubbing his chin. He looked at Holmes, saying, "As a barrister, I am unsure as to what your questions might have revealed, Mr. Holmes."

Holmes replied, "Not a great deal in themselves, Sir Terence, but they are another piece of the puzzle which has dropped neatly into place. Tell me, if you would, which telegraph office provides the results for the races?"

Sir Terence thought for a moment before replying, "I believe it is the office on the corner of Bridge Street, a few paces from Westminster Bridge."

Holmes now had a grim smile on his face. "Thank you, Sir Terence. Doctor Watson and Mycroft will be joining the gentlemen who gamble tomorrow. I would be grateful if you might make yourself available at a little after 3:30...just in case there is any unpleasantness."

Sir Terence looked a little bemused but he readily agreed. Taking our leave, Holmes rushed out into the street, hailed a hansom, and tossed the cabbie a florin to race us back to Baker Street.

V – A Job for Wiggins

The journey was swift and uneventful, and barely had we reached our rooms when Holmes dashed to the window, opened it and shouted "Wiggins!" at the top of his voice. Barely two minutes passed before there was knock at our door and a lanky street urchin, accompanied by a clearly disapproving Mrs. Hudson, entered our rooms.

Mrs. Hudson looked Wiggins up and down before

saying, "This person said you had shouted for him, Mr. Holmes. Shall I send him away?" I watched as she began to roll up her sleeves.

Holmes smiled and then cried out, "No, no, Mrs. Hudson. Wiggins is quite correct, I did summon him. Thank you."

Wiggins curled his lip and Mrs. Hudson gave him a look which, had it been in Biblical times might, I believe, have turned him to stone.

Wiggins smiled at Holmes, saying, "Alright, Mister 'Olmes, what d'yer need?"

Holmes sat in his armchair and began to fill his pipe whilst saying, "A little detective work, Wiggins. I want you to go and keep a watch on the telegraph office on the corner of Bridge Street, just across the road from Big Ben. Be there by 3:30."

Wiggins nodded and with rising excitement asked, "What you expectin'? A robbery? A murder?"

Holmes's face had a wry smile upon it. "Not quite. Something a little more comical, perhaps. I want you to watch for anyone acting strangely, follow them to wherever they go next, and then send me word."

Wiggins nodded. "Usual rates, Mr. 'Olmes?"

Holmes again smiled and tossed Wiggins a shilling. With a touch of his cap, Wiggins was off, clattering down our stairs two at a time. I am certain that this display of bravado was only done to spite Mrs. Hudson!

After a delightful light luncheon of cold meats, pork pie, and pickles, we sat replete. I was eager for there to be developments in the case and, after half an hour, I began to pace irritably. Holmes, however, was the picture of serenity, sitting back in his armchair reading The Times and puffing contentedly upon his pipe.

Looking up from his paper and seeing my agitation, he gently rebuked me, saying, "Calm yourself, Watson. We will hear nothing until, I believe, four o'clock."

I consulted my pocket watch, and as this was some two

hours hence, I forced myself to sit and read. I must have dozed off somewhat, as the next thing I knew was our door bell ringing wildly and the clock in our sitting room now showed 4:05. The copy of The Lancet that I had been reading had fallen from my lap, and the thunder on the stairs announced the imminent arrival of young Wiggins.

Within seconds, Wiggins had burst through our door, his face wreathed in smiles. "You won't believe what I've seen, Mister 'Olmes!"

Holmes held up his hand to silence Wiggins and he turned to me, asking, "Be a good fellow, Watson, and go out and buy me a copy of the evening paper."

I looked at Holmes in shock. I was as keen as he to know what Wiggins had observed. Holmes inclined his head slightly and raised an eyebrow. Sighing, I took this to be a signal that he wanted to hear from Wiggins in private. "Very well, Holmes, I will be but a few minutes."

Having purchased the newspaper, I returned from my errand to find that Wiggins had completed his report and left. Holmes was now playing furiously upon his beloved Stradivarius. "What is that, Holmes?" I shouted above the tumult of sound that engulfed me.

Holmes smiled and paused briefly, saying, "What? You do not recognise it? Beethoven's "Battle Symphony", Opus 91. It celebrates Wellington's victory. I thought it quite apt for Major Cooke!" Holmes continued for perhaps two further minutes before sitting down, exhausted from his frantic bowing.

I must confess that I was relieved when he stopped. "Do I take it, then, that Wiggins provided some valuable intelligence?" I asked.

Holmes smiled and slapped the arm of his armchair, saying, "We have him, Watson! We have him! It is now down to you, old fellow, for tomorrow you must play your part as the innocent and inept gambler if we are to succeed."

I was now extremely concerned. It seemed that the whole

case rested upon my shoulders. I frowned, saying, "You will have to coach me in this, Holmes, for I have no experience in these matters."

Holmes leant forwards and patted me on my forearm. "There is nothing to learn, Watson, all you must do is be confident. Watch as the Major leaves the room, as he surely will, and on his return, listen to him. I expect him to make an outrageous wager. You must then engineer, in some way, to raise the wager against him to 20,000 guineas."

On hearing this, my mouth fell open. "Good Lord, Holmes! That is a fortune. He will never accept such a wager!"

Holmes wagged his finger in my direction, saying, "On the contrary, Watson. He will leap at the chance. Mycroft and Sir Terence will be present to see that all is proper, have no fear."

Although I was still unsure, I was comforted by the thought of their presence, given the Major's reputation for violence.

The following morning, Holmes and I breakfasted, and I watched as he sent off a telegram to Lestrade. He then excused himself, saying only that he would meet me at Bairstow's at four o'clock. I watched, bemused, as he placed a pair of white, opera gloves into his jacket pocket before leaving. I have to say that I was nervous for the entire morning. I could not settle and could barely manage a bite at luncheon before dressing for Bairstow's.

The cab ride was uneventful, and on entering the club, I was greeted warmly by Mycroft. Smiling, he held out his hand in greeting, saying, "Ah, Watson. A sherry, perhaps?"

I shook my head, replying, "Thank you, no, Mycroft. I would prefer a large brandy."

A wry smile crossed Mycroft's face as he said "Ah, I see you are getting into role."

I looked at him in a querying way. I imagined, from this comment, that he must already have had some communication with his brother, something to which I was not privy.

VI – Placing a Wager

At 3:20, Sir Terence joined us, shortly followed by Major Cooke. On spying me, the Major cried, "Ah, Doctor Watson! I am so pleased to see that you have been able to join us. Come this way." I was a little concerned when he took my arm and led me towards the small private room used by the group.

Once inside, the door was closed. The other four members that I had seen earlier were already assembled...plus another figure that at first I did not recognise. Looking more closely, I saw that towards the back of the group stood Anthony Stewart. I was about to greet him when a hand touched my sleeve. Looking towards its owner, I saw that Mycroft was very slightly shaking his head.

The room itself was expensively furnished with velvet covered chairs and rich, red velvet drapes. In the centre of the room there stood a large, oval mahogany table with eight dining chairs. To one side stood a drinks table, upon which there stood a silver tray and an array of bottles of spirits from which the group helped themselves. I felt the need for some Dutch courage and poured myself a large brandy. It was as I replaced the brandy decanter that I saw a sly grin form on the Major's face.

The members of the group all sat around the table and I joined them, unsure as to what was to happen next. I introduced myself to the gentlemen either side of me and nodded to the others.

Beside each person was a small pad of paper and a pencil. I took it that this was rather like a marker, showing the amount that you had wagered and to whom. Mycroft and Sir Terence stood some little distance apart, against the rear wall so that they could clearly observe the proceedings.

The clock in the room struck the half hour and the Major stood and addressed the group. "Gentlemen, today we are wagering on the 3:30 race at York. The race has begun. Who will place a wager?"

There then began some small wagers among the members: wagers of, perhaps, 50 or a 100 guineas. Slips of paper were passed between them as the wagers were made. I made a small wager of 20 guineas on horse number four with a gentleman sitting to my right.

It was then that the Major suddenly gripped his stomach, made an excuse and walked swiftly from the room. I looked about me and I was about to rise to see if I could be of some assistance when the gentleman to my right put his hand on my forearm, saying, "Do not concern yourself, Doctor. I have been told that the Major has some slight intestinal problem, apparently from his service overseas. The excitement of the moment aggravates it, but he will return shortly."

As predicted, the Major returned within four or five minutes. Apologising, he sat and then again addressed the group, saying, "I feel that good fortune is smiling upon me today, gentlemen, and although the horse has little form, I wager one thousand guineas on number seven. Are there any takers?"

I looked around at the incredulous faces of the group. A single voice spoke out...one that I immediately recognised as that of Anthony Stewart. "I fear it stands little chance today, Major. I am willing to wager five thousand guineas that it is not the winner."

The Major's smile was now like that of a wolf. "I thought you might have had enough, Stewart, betting against me. If you are so confident, will you not wager ten thousand?"

There was a gasp from the other members around the table as they waited for Stewart's reply. After a few seconds Stewart nodded, saying, "Very well, here is my marker." Stewart quickly wrote the amount of ten thousand guineas and signed it, passing it to the Major."

I felt it was now time to follow Holmes's instructions. I raised my brandy glass in salute to Stewart, took a hefty swallow from it and holding the glass aloft, cried, "This is an opportunity I cannot let slip. I will double that amount. I wager 20,000 guineas that number seven is not the winner. I feel the young gentleman has luck on his side today."

The gentleman to my right held my arm, saying, "Be silent sir, it is the brandy talking!"

The Major's eyes burned as he rubbed his hands together as if he were washing them. "Let him be! He has made the wager and we have all heard it. It will stand." Turning to Mycroft, the Major demanded, "Is he good for the money, should he lose?"

Mycroft nodded. "I will stand guarantor for the amount, Major...if need be."

It was at that moment that the slightest shadow of doubt passed over the Major's face. He shook his head as though to clear it and then looked once more supremely confident. I, however, was trembling like a leaf. If, somehow, Holmes's plan had failed, then Mycroft would stand to lose 20,000 guineas and I would be ruined.

For the next few minutes, the atmosphere in the room was stifling. I finished my brandy and found that I was still shaking. Several of the other members were easing their collars and mopping their brows waiting, as we all were, for the knock on the door that announced the arrival of the messenger boy with the envelope of results.

Suddenly, there was the knock and the Major moved to open the door, but his progress was blocked by Sir Terence, saying, "I think, Major, given the high stakes, an independent person should open the envelope."

Major Cooke's face was puce, but he kept control and managed to stammer, "Yes, yes...of course, Sir Terence."

The Major stood back and Sir Terence opened the door. Framed in the doorway was a uniformed messenger boy holding out an envelope. This Sir Terence took and, sliding his finger beneath the sealed flap, he opened it. There was a collective intake of breath as he withdrew the single sheet of paper from within it. Clearing his throat, he announced, "York, 3:30, first...number five, second...number eight, third...number 12."

Major Cooke lunged forwards, tearing the telegram from Sir Terence's grasp and reading it again to himself. "This is not possible! It is a trick!" Turning towards me, he screamed, "You are a ch — "

Sir Terence placed his hand firmly on Major Cooke's chest before he could say more. "Have a care what you say, Cooke! The libel laws in England are punitive, and I would happily represent any one of these gentlemen, for no fee, should you venture to tarnish his reputation. Be sure to leave a cheque for the full thirty thousand guineas in my office before you leave. Your membership of Bairstow's has been revoked."

Major Cooke glared malevolently at me and then at Sir Terence before storming from the room. The other members were still sitting open mouthed, unable to comprehend what had occurred. In truth, I would not have been able to enlighten them.

A few moments later, a familiar voice called out to me from the open doorway, "Ah, Watson! I understand that you are now a very wealthy man!"

Holmes laughed heartily and clapped me on the back. From across the room a figure approached with his hand outstretched. It was Anthony Stewart. Shaking Holmes's hand, a very grateful Stewart said, "Thank you, Mr. Holmes. I am forever in your debt and I swear never to gamble again."

Holmes's face was without emotion as he replied, "I will take you at your word, Mr. Stewart."

Holmes nodded towards Mycroft and Sir Terence, and I reached for my cheque book to pay the 20 guineas I had wagered. The gentleman who had been sitting to my right picked up the slip I had signed and, with a wink, he tore it up.

VII – A Pair of White Gloves

Taking Anthony Stewart by the arm, Holmes led the way out of Bairstow's, hailed a cab, and together we returned to Baker Street. I must admit I wanted to know everything, but Holmes would say nothing until we all were sitting with a steaming cup of tea.

Sitting back, I ran through my mind all that had happened. "Tell me, Holmes, how was this achieved?"

Holmes sipped his tea and began thus, "I became suspicious of the Major when I detected, in his jacket pocket, what appeared to be a small telescope. Now, why would one carry such a thing to a gentleman's club? Whilst Bairstow's is located on the banks of the Thames, it does not face it... except for one side...and why would a seemingly healthy man suddenly, and so predictably, have to make use of the club's facilities?"

I thought back to our first visit to the club, and how Holmes had questioned the washroom attendant. "Whilst in the washroom, you left Sir Terence and me whilst you investigated further. What did you discover, Holmes?"

Holmes smiled, "Tell me, Watson. Where in a gentleman's club might you be sure not to be disturbed and have perfect privacy...especially if you feigned to have an intestinal problem?"

It took me but a moment to realise. "Of course! In the lavatory!"

Holmes nodded, saying, "Quite so, Watson. I discovered that the rear wall of the toilet cubicles face the Thames, and have small, frosted, sash windows. I opened one briefly and had a most excellent view of the Thames and the bridges crossing it. Do you recall our cab ride to Westminster Bridge, Watson?"

I nodded and waited for Holmes to continue. "As I stood at the centre of the bridge with my field glasses, I was able to see clearly the frosted glass of the lavatory windows of

Bairstow's. Therefore, a person in Bairstow's would have a similarly clear view of the centre of Westminster Bridge."

I scratched my head, as I was still unsure how this discovery could benefit the Major. "Tell me, Holmes, how does this observation relate to the intelligence from young Wiggins?"

Holmes began to fill his pipe, asking, "Do you also recall the conversation with Sir Terence when we sought information on the background of the Major? Sir Terence thought the Major had developed his liking for a wager through his family connection to horse racing. Bookmakers who take wagers at a race course have to ensure that they can communicate with each other to ensure that they are all offering similar odds. They often have to do this over a distance of a 100 yards or more. How then is this achieved, Watson?"

I thought back to a race meeting I had attended at Epsom and suddenly remembered. "Hand signals! They communicate by some strange system where they wave their hands and pat the top of their heads...and...and they wear white gloves! Ha! The opera gloves! But why, Holmes?"

Holmes drew contentedly upon his pipe and blew out a thin stream of blue smoke. Pointing his pipe stem in my direction, he asked, "Why does a Robin have a red breast? To be seen, Watson! To be seen! The white gloves show up clearly against a dark background and the hand signals can be read over a long distance. Young Wiggins observed a man leave the telegraph office on Bridge Street, just as a messenger boy was leaving. The fellow ran to the centre of Westminster Bridge, where he was seen to wave his arms wildly in the air whilst wearing white gloves. Wiggins thought the poor man to be demented!"

I had almost forgotten about our guest until he suddenly shouted out, "So that was how it was done! Somebody received the results of the race from the telegraph office and then conveyed them, using hand signals, to the Major, who was using his telescope to observe from the lavatory window at Bairstow's!"

Holmes nodded, saying, "Precisely! That 'somebody' was a servant in the Major's employ. Wiggins followed him back to a house in Wimbledon which had the name 'Major T. Cooke' emblazoned above the bell-pull at the front door."

I was still puzzled. "But...but...that does not explain how you were able to deceive the Major today."

Holmes wagged his finger, saying, "Not so, Watson. Wiggins had described this fellow to me, and I determined that we were of similar height and stature. My telegram to Lestrade ensured that when this fellow appeared at the telegraph office and collected the results, a somewhat burly constable detained him. When I questioned him, he quickly told all. I had studied the bookmaker's code and from a distance of over a 100 yards, I would be indistinguishable from the Major's man. At any event, the Major would be concentrating hard upon my hand movements, not my identity. It was a simple matter to ensure that the number of the winning horse was changed in my message to him."

Anthony Stewart clapped his hands in delight. "Wonderful! Whilst Mr. Holmes was away from you this morning, Doctor, he tracked me down at my lodgings in Putney. He kindly offered me the chance of rebuilding my life by regaining all the losses I had made to the Major. He informed me of the part I was to play but, like you, I had not the slightest idea as to how the deception was to be accomplished."

Holmes leant forwards slightly towards me, saying, "I am indeed sorry that I was unable to tell you all, Watson. It was imperative that the Major's suspicions were not aroused by anything that you might inadvertently let slip. It was vital that you made the wager as though you believed it to be genuine and, it appears, you played the part perfectly!"

I shook my head. "Holmes, you will never comprehend how real that wager was to me. The prospect of being indebted to your brother for the rest of my life hung over me like the sword of Damocles."

On hearing this, Holmes slapped the arm of his chair and roared with laughter. After finishing our tea, we said goodbye to Anthony Stewart and earnestly hoped that he would honour his solemn promise to never gamble again.

Of the Major, we heard no more except for a mention in a note from Mycroft confirming that the cheque the Major had lodged on leaving Bairstow's had been honoured. Sir Terence had used the funds to make good the losses of the other members and, as a result of the Major's 'excesses', gambling was now prohibited at Bairstow's.

It was one morning, perhaps a week or so later, as I began to record this case in my notebook, that I remarked to Holmes that saving a man's life and bringing him back to his family was something of which to be proud. I noticed that Holmes almost blushed as I said this.

He shook his head, saying, "No, Watson. I take no pride in this. I saw it as my moral duty, for I, too, have been to the edge of the abyss on occasions...and, in any case, we have been amply rewarded for our endeavours. See what came in this morning's post!"

Holmes tossed an envelope to me and on opening its contents I read, "Dear Mr. Holmes, I am most grateful for your recent assistance. In recognition of this, it is my privilege, as Chairman of Bairstow's, to offer both you and Doctor Watson a lifetime's membership of the club for the great service you have rendered." The letter was signed, Terence Walters.

"I trust that you will accept, Holmes?" I asked.

Holmes's eyes twinkled. He appeared to consider my question for a brief moment before replying, "Yes, I believe so...if only to spite Mycroft!"

The Case of the Anarchist's Bomb

by Bill Crider

I have found but few joys in growing old. My great friend, Sherlock Holmes, no longer bids me to go adventuring, and spends his days keeping his apiary, while I, a superannuated physician, find that more and more often my afternoons are passed in looking over my notes on the many unrecorded cases that, for one reason or another, I failed to see into print in my younger and more enthusiastic years. There is, I confess, a bit of pleasure in recalling adventures long past, and for a moment I can almost hear Holmes's voice: "Come, Watson! The game's afoot!" Yet I know that in reality I am not likely to hear that voice again.

There is also a modicum of entertainment to be found in knowing that some portion of the public still takes the time on occasion to read one of my accounts of those long-gone days. Holmes often made light of those writings and sometimes resorted to what I considered ridicule; he would be quite amused, I am certain, to know that even now I receive an occasional letter about them, and that the letters often contain questions concerning what the writers consider serious discrepancies in the many stories, discrepancies in such things as the location of a certain wound caused by a Jezail bullet, or the precise order of various events in the lives of either me or Holmes or the both of us.

Having always thought that the answers to such

questions were obvious, I have seldom bothered to respond to the letters, but perhaps that was boorish of me. I shall now state the obvious this one time only, and that will have to suffice for all who would ask about these things. I happily confess that the stories I set down, while accurate in most of their details, were perhaps not accurate in all. This is true for a number of reasons, some of which need not be mentioned, though the most prominent of them is simply that there are times when I am not certain myself of just where or when a certain event might have taken place. My notes are often jotted down in haste and present only the merest outline of events. Trying to set them in order at a later date is not always possible, thanks to the fallibility of human memory.

To take just one example, I know that it is generally considered true that Holmes returned to England in April, 1894, having been absent for quite some time after the regrettable incident at the Reichenbach Falls. It is possible, however, that the date is in error. As I said, I am not always certain about those things. Just why is hard to explain, but in perusing my notes for a specific case, I can see why I am necessarily unsure about things in that particular year. Perhaps if I put the incidents on paper, I will clarify matters for myself, if not for others.

It was February of 1894 when I received one evening a note from a man whom I did not know well, but with whom I had previously had dealings through Sherlock Holmes. The man was no less than Holmes's brother, Mycroft, and his note was a request for me to join him at the Diogenes Club for a conversation about a matter of extreme urgency.

I was, of course, puzzled by this, and wondered what Mycroft could possibly want of me. He is, beyond doubt, one of the oddest men in London, and one of the most intelligent. He had even on occasion given advice to Holmes about one or another of his cases, though that was not his main interest in life. He was a gatherer and an absorber of information, so much information, in fact, and so well ordered in the massive files of his mind, that he had made himself virtually indispensable to the government, and a word from him could establish or alter national policy. Holmes had done him a favor from time to time, and I had been involved to some extent, but merely as an assistant who acted when called upon and directed. All the ratiocination had been Holmes's.

My curiosity being aroused, I made myself ready and took a cab to the Diogenes Club, which is located in Pall Mall, along with many others. The Traveller's Club, the Athenaeum, and the Reform Club are well known. The Diogenes Club is not. It is as odd as Mycroft himself, being a haven for people who as a rule would never enter a club. It is understood that everyone who enters must be absolutely silent. No one must take any notice of anyone else. Those who do not obey the rules are summarily ejected.

It was a dank February evening, with a gray fog that slid along the streets and shrouded the stone buildings in dampness. Lights flickered dimly in the windows. I paid the cabbie and entered the club. I found myself in a long hallway paneled with glass through which I could see the club itself, its members sitting apart from one another, reading silently or simply staring off into space.

There is a small visitor's room just off the hallway where talking is permitted, and it was into this room that I directed my step. Mycroft was already there waiting for me, and my first impression was that he had grown even larger than he had been at our last encounter. He is quite the trencherman if one is to judge by his appearance, and Holmes had once told me that his brother's only exercise was the short walk between his rooms and the Diogenes Club. As a physician, I suppose I should have taken it upon myself to give Mycroft some advice on how to better care for himself, but he was not the sort of man who solicited advice or took it unsolicited, so I never broached the topic with him.

"Ah, Dr. Watson," said he as I entered the room. "Do

have a seat. You'll pardon me if I don't rise."

"Of course," said I, removing my coat and hat and hanging them on a rack. It would have been difficult for him to rise, for he seemed to take up much of the small room with his bulk. The chair he sat in must have been especially made to accommodate him. I took a seat in the room's other chair, one of normal size.

Mycroft watched me settle myself with his peculiar light gray eyes. When I was comfortable, he said, "You have heard, I am sure, of this afternoon's sad affair of the Frenchman in Greenwich Park."

Indeed I had, but only because one of my patients had told me of it, for I, unlike Sherlock Holmes, was not a diligent reader of sensational newspaper articles. And this event had been quite sensational. A young Frenchman and known anarchist, Martial Bourdin, had fallen in Greenwich Park, and in doing so had exploded a bomb that he had in his possession. It had blown off his left hand and destroyed a goodly portion of his stomach.

"He was literally hoist by his own petard," said I, after asserting my knowledge of the affair. "An unfortunate fall."

"For Boudin, yes, but not for us," said Mycroft. "It is most fortunate that he did not reach his destination, for who knows what damage he might have done."

He paused and looked at me as if expecting me to speak. It was almost as if Holmes were in the room, for he often seemed to think I had the power to reason as he did. "You know my methods," he would say, and wait for me to bring forth some kind of response. Mycroft was fully his equal at waiting.

"What damage might that have been?" I asked after a while.

"Ah, that is the question," Mycroft said. "Or one of the questions, at any rate. Sherlock often said you had a way of getting to the heart of things, and I can see that he was correct."

I was flattered, though I should not have been, as I had no idea what he was talking about.

"You see," Mycroft continued, "we have no idea what Boudin's purpose was. Why did he have that bomb? Where was he going?"

"Surely he was going to the observatory," I answered. "He was a known anarchist and an associate of others of his stripe, possibly the leader of a gang of them. He had the intention of destroying the observatory."

"Highly unlikely," Mycroft said. "Think, Watson."

I thought, again trying to apply Holmes's methods. Eventually I thought I could see where Mycroft was aiming.

"A bomb large enough to destroy the observatory would not simply have blown away a man's hand and part of his stomach," I said. "It would have scattered him over a considerable area."

Mycroft smiled a thin smile. "You are correct. Therefore his intent was not to destroy the observatory. And there is more to the story. Bourdin was carrying a large sum of money. Where did the money come from? Boudin was a tailor, and he was not a rich man. Lately he had worked but little. He must have been given the money for some reason having to do with the bomb. Who gave him the money? Why? Bourdin lived long enough to tell us these things, but he refused to do so, and he soon died of his injuries. We need those answers."

It was a rare puzzle, indeed, but I still had no idea why Mycroft was discussing it with me. My association with Holmes may have sharpened my wits to some extent, but I was never his equal in the art of deduction. Mycroft was, of course, but he applied his powers to different ends, and besides, he could not be bothered to stir outside beyond his rooms or the Diogenes Club. With that thought, I began to see what need he might have of me, and he confirmed my suspicion with his next words.

"Within the hour," said he, "the police will raid the

Autonomie Club, where Bourdin was a member. Perhaps you have heard of it."

"A notorious nest of anarchists," I replied.

Mycroft gave a minute nod. "So it is said. At any rate, I need a man among the police. There is no one I would trust as much as you to report what they find. You might also learn much of interest that they might miss. They are, after all, only the police, and no match for Sherlock Holmes."

"Nor am I a match for him," said I.

"You may surprise yourself," Mycroft said, and began to struggle to his feet.

I rose myself, still somewhat at a loss, and offered to assist him, but he managed to rise on his own.

"You will find a cab outside," he told me. "I have arranged for the driver to be at your disposal this evening and for as long as you need him. He will be your assistant in this matter."

Ah, if only Holmes could have been there. He would have much appreciated this game I was about to enter upon, and to tell the truth, I would have been much more comfortable as his assistant than in having an assistant of my own, much less some cabbie I had never met. Still, if he had Mycroft's recommendation, he must be a good man. I donned my coat and hat and told Mycroft that I would do as well as I could.

"And you will do admirably," said he. "But you must hurry, for the raid is scheduled for nine o'clock. You need to be at the club when it begins." He handed me a folded paper. "This letter is all you will need to show the police, should they ask for your bona fides. Keep it safe."

I slipped the letter into an inner pocket of my coat and bid Mycroft farewell.

When I emerged from the Diogenes Club, I discovered that the fog had thickened and that the evening had turned much colder. I drew my coat around me and looked for the cab that Mycroft had said would be there. I spied a hansom at the curb a short distance from the door and made my way to it. When I reached it, a man stepped out of the shadows beside it and said in a raspy voice, "Good evening, guv'nor. Do I have the honour of addressing Dr. John Watson?"

"You do," I responded. "And what is your name?"

"You can call me Albert, sir. It's an honour to be lending you a hand this evening. I hear of you and Sherlock Holmes everywhere, and I have read of your adventures."

Albert wore a dark slouch hat pulled down low on his forehead so that the brim covered his eyes, and I could not make out his features. He was slumped in his heavy coat so that I had difficulty judging his height, but I had the impression that he was taller than he appeared. In a way he looked vaguely familiar, but I had ridden in many cabs in London, and I might very well have had this driver before.

"I am flattered that you have read my transcriptions of the cases of Sherlock Holmes," I told him.

"There's just one thing, sir," said he, "if you'll pardon the impertinence. Are not those tales of yours a bit exaggerated?"

"Nothing of the sort," said I. "And now we must be off to the Autonomie Club. Do you know the way?"

"Certainly, sir," said he, without further comment, and as I climbed into the cab between the wooden-spoked wheels, he mounted to his outside seat above and behind me.

"Ready, sir?" he asked when he was seated, his voice coming through the small trap door that was situated to aid our communication.

"Indeed I am."

He clucked to his horse, and we were off, the cloppity sound of the horse's hooves on the street being muffled by the fog. The leather curtains in front of me were drawn closed in deference to the cold, and as there was nothing to see out the side windows, all being shrouded in the fog, I used the time to speculate about what Mycroft had told me. As I saw it, if I could find out who had given Boudin the money, the other answers to the other questions posed by Mycroft would be easier to find. Unfortunately, I had no idea of how to go about doing so, and nothing came to mind during our drive to the Autonomie Club.

"I believe I should stop here," Albert said when we were about a block from the club.

I peered out the window of the cab, and although the fog was a barrier to sight, I could see that a number of vehicles were stopped ahead of us and that policemen stood outside the door of the club. It appeared that they were arresting late-arriving members, who seemed astonished but cooperative, at least for the moment.

Others were there, as well, many of them carrying signs. I had read of these people in the newspapers. The signs they carried all expressed approximately the same sentiment, which could be boiled down to "anarchists go home," as they believed that all foreigners were anarchists and they wanted nothing to do with them. I myself had no sympathy for anarchists, but I knew quite a few immigrants who had no interest in anarchy at all.

"Yes," I said to Albert. "Stop here. We do not want to interfere with the police. Perhaps I should introduce myself to their commander and see what I can learn."

Albert got down to assist my exit from the cab, and when I was firmly on the pavement, he said, "Sir, might it not be better if we did not announce ourselves? The police do not welcome outsiders."

I thought about some of the Scotland Yard inspectors, who had no love for me and Sherlock Holmes, but they did not appear to be among the policemen here. Even at that, Albert's advice was sound. We might learn more if we were discreet.

I noticed that he had said "we" should not announce ourselves. "Are you coming with me?" I asked.

"That was my commission from Mr. Mycroft Holmes," said he. "I am to accompany and assist you."

"Very well. Come along and we shall see what we can discover."

As we walked toward the club, I reached inside my coat to make sure that Mycroft's letter was still there, as indeed it was. I wanted to be sure to have it in case it became necessary to produce it. Already, there seemed to be a bit of confusion at the club, however, and I thought that Albert's suggestion would prove to be the best approach.

Just as we arrived at the entrance to the club, one of the tardy members took serious offense at his arrest. He began to fling his arms about, striking several officers, while yelling in French. All the officers closed around him in an attempt to pin him to the wall. One of the other men tried to strike the Frenchman with his sign, and his companions began shouting. They appeared much more dangerous than the supposed anarchists who were being arrested, and were clearly intent on doing the Frenchman serious harm. The police found themselves very much occupied in sorting out the confusion, though they appeared to be getting the situation under control.

"A happy diversion," said Albert. "Follow me, Doctor."

It seemed that Albert had promoted himself from assistant to leader, but I chose not to argue. Instead, I followed him as he slipped past the busy policemen and entered the club, which was not nearly so luxurious as the Diogenes Club, nor was it as quiet. Men stood in small groups, talking in loud voices and various languages. There was no doorman, and I suppose anarchists would not approve of such a thing.

"Did you recognize any of those men outside?" Albert asked me. "You mean the members of this club?" I responded.

"No. I mean among the others. The ones carrying the signs. It seemed to me that one of them was familiar."

I had often wished that I had the gift for faces that Sherlock Holmes possessed, but I did not. Still, I took a few moments to attempt to recall the men we had seen outside. The light had not been good, but I had glimpsed several of them. The one who had tried to strike the Frenchman with his sign did indeed look familiar, and after a several moments I remembered why.

"One of them was Henry Starnes," I said. "He is a leader of a group of nativists whose goal is to expel all foreigners, starting with those who have an anarchistic bent. I have seen his photograph in the newspapers. He is seeking a seat in parliament."

"I believe you are correct," Albert said, and then he sidled up to group of men in which the speakers were English, and I went along.

"The coppers will soon be coming in," Albert said when there was a lull in the talking and gesticulating. "Is there another way out?"

"Of course there is," said a big fellow with a red face and bristling hair. "But we shall not take it. We are not cowards. We have a right to assemble here and talk as we wish. And who are you, might I ask?"

"A friend of Martial Bourdin."

"Hah. The very rascal who's brought this raid upon us. Well, you might be seeking a cowardly way out, for the police will want to have more than mere words with you if you are his friend."

I had no idea what Albert could be up to, but he seemed to be quite comfortable in what he was doing.

"I do not fear the police," said he. "I do care about my friend."

"He was no friend of mine," the man said, and the others near him nodded as if to say he was not their friend, either. "Bourdin had few friends here."

"He must have had someone who cared enough about him to want to know the truth about what happened," said Albert.

"Perhaps Delebeck," said a short, stout man wearing spectacles. "He was Bourdin's landlord." He indicated a man in middle age with graying hair and a military carriage who stood alone near the wall opposite us.

"Thank you," said Albert. "Come, Doctor."

Once again, I followed. Albert had hidden depths.

Delebeck saw us coming, and while he did not appear eager to speak with us, neither did he flee. When we reached him, Albert nudged me in the ribs. Clearly he expected me to know what to do at this point, so I introduced myself.

"The very same Dr. John Watson who writes the amusing stories about his friend Sherlock Holmes?" Delebeck said. He looked at Albert. "And is this the great man himself?"

Albert and I chuckled. "No," said I, "this is Albert, who drives a cab, which we may be able to use, by the way."

"Use?" said Delebeck. "For what purpose? And for that matter, why are you here, Dr. Watson?"

"I am looking into the death of your boarder, Martial Bourdin."

"Indeed. In what capacity?"

"On behalf of Her Majesty's government," I thought to say as I reached for the letter from Mycroft, but then I remembered that Delebeck was an anarchist or at the very least an associate of anarchists. The letter would be more likely to anger him than to impress him.

"I am simply interested in the case," I said after a moment, trying to think what Holmes might say. "It has certain elements that intrigue me."

"I can understand why it might," Delebeck said. "I do not trust the police to find out anything about my friend's death. However, Dr. Watson, if your stories are not exaggerated, I believe I can trust you."

I tried not to take offense at his remark about the stories, though I thought I heard a low laugh from Albert.

"Your trust would not be misplaced," I told Delebeck.

"Then we should be leaving," Albert said. "For the police are now entering."

His hearing was sharper than mine, but I turned to see that he was correct and that the officers were now coming in through the front door.

"There is a back entrance, I believe," said I. "Let us take

advantage of it."

We edged around the men grouped in the room and found a dark corridor that led to a stair going down to a door. We passed through the hall and then the doorway without hindrance and found ourselves in an odorous alleyway, enfolded in fog.

"Wait here," said Albert, "while I fetch the cab."

I was not happy to be left there, and I could see that Delebeck felt the same. However, we had little choice, as Albert walked away and was almost instantly lost in the fog.

While we stood there, I tried to think of the kind of questions that Holmes would be asking, were he standing beside me, and in that moment I missed him more keenly than ever. However, even as I wondered how he would have managed the situation, something occurred to me.

"Were you at home today when your boarder left?" I asked.

"I was, but you must know that I had nothing to do with this sad affair. I was entirely ignorant of anything concerning a bomb. While Martial and I both distrust the government and would like to be rid of it, neither of us is violent in any way. We have made protests. We have agitated, but resort to violence? Never."

He sounded as if he were telling the truth, though one can never be certain about such things.

"Have the police searched Bourdin's rooms?" I asked.

"No, but I have been expecting them all day. Surely they must know by now where he lived."

Having experienced the methods of Inspector Lestrade, I was not so sure, and I was happy that we would have the first look at Bourdin's lodgings, even though my own search of them would never match one that Holmes would conduct.

"What about money?" I asked. "Was Bourdin quite rich?"

"Not at all. I have heard that he had a large sum with him when the bomb exploded, but I cannot say where the money came from."

"He did not have it with him when he left?"

"He may have," Delebeck said. "I broke my fast at the club this morning, and when I returned, he came out of his room and brushed past me without a word. That in itself was unusual. He had two parcels with him, but he was out the door before I could ask about them."

This was all interesting information, though I knew not what to make of it. I had no time to inquire further, as Albert came into the alley with the cab and stopped for us. He asked Delebeck where he lived, and Delebeck gave an address on Fitzroy Street. As soon as we were seated in the cab, Albert took us out of the alley and down the street at a sedate pace, turning away from the Autonomie Club and easily avoiding detection by the police, who by now were all occupied on the inside of the club. The men with the signs had all been sent on their way, and the foggy sidewalks were quiet.

I tapped on the small door between me and Albert, and he opened it at once. I smelled pipe smoke and heard him puffing away. On an impulse I did not quite understand, I conveyed to him what Delebeck had told me. He made no comment other than to say that we would do well to be careful of how we handled matters from this point forward, as it appeared that powerful forces were involved. I was about to ask his meaning, but he shut the door and cut off our communication.

"Have you and Bourdin talked often about the overthrow of the government?" I asked Delebeck. "In a theoretical way, of course."

"Of course. Naturally, we are opposed to the government. But we are also opposed to violence, Martial more than I. I cannot imagine him planning to use a bomb."

"Is it possible he would not have discussed such plans with you?"

"Yes, as he was a secretive sort, he might have kept it from me, especially knowing my nonviolent leanings. Yet I believe he would have told me of some plan to bomb the observatory."

Delebeck might have said more, but we had arrived at the address on Fitzroy Street. Albert stopped the cab, and Delebeck and I alighted. Delebeck let us into the house and showed us the rooms where Bourdin lived.

They were quite neat, and searching them would not take long, I presumed. There was something of an odd smell in the air, but it was so faint that I could not identify it. I could tell that Albert noticed it, too, though he said nothing. Delebeck seemed to be unaware of it.

I began my search by looking at the desk and its contents, I peered into the closets, into all the drawers, and even looked underneath the bed. "Excellent work," Albert said when I was done. "I can see why Sherlock Holmes relies on you in all his investigations."

"Er, yes," I said, "but what exactly do you mean?"

Albert walked over to the desk and pointed to a book. "To begin with, this book. When you moved it, you revealed the rail schedule underneath it."

I had not moved the book much, merely pushed it aside, and I had not noticed the paper beneath it. But before I could mention that, Albert had picked up the rail schedule and walked to the wardrobe.

"And here," said he, "you discovered that the arrangement of clothes suggested that some of them were missing. No doubt they are in the valise you spied under the bed."

In truth, I had not spied the valise, as the dim light of the room hardly reached underneath the bed, but Albert had bent over and seen it. His eyesight must have been incredibly keen. He pocketed the rail schedule and pulled the valise from beneath the bed. Setting it on the bed, he opened it.

"Ah. Neatly packed," he said. He closed the valise.

"Did Bourdin mention travel plans?" I asked Delebeck, who had been watching the proceedings.

"No, but he did miss his home in France. He had traveled

in America, and he liked it even less than he likes England."

"There is something more," Albert said. "Or something less. There is something missing."

"Missing?" Delebeck said.

"Yes," Albert said. "As Dr. Watson has so cleverly revealed to us by his search, there is nothing in this room, nothing at all, that could have been used to make a bomb. No plans and no chemicals."

I thought again about the smell I had noticed upon entering the room, but I could no longer detect it, so I made no mention of it.

"He could have made the bomb elsewhere," said I.

"Doubtful," said Albert, and he removed the rail schedule from his pocket. He opened it and laid it on the desk. "Look at this."

He placed his finger on the schedule. The times for departures to Dover were circled.

"Bourdin was going to France," I said.

"Excellent, Dr. Watson," Albert said, and I gave him a sharp glance. He had not removed his slouch hat, and it shadowed his face. I could not see his expression.

"He had money when he died," I said. "Along with the bomb."

"Yet we can infer that he had neither in his room until someone brought them here," said Albert. "He would not want to leave the money here, even though I am sure he trusted you, Mr. Delebeck."

"But who could have brought the money?" asked Delebeck.

"That is indeed the question," I said. "Perhaps we should convey our information to the authorities, Albert."

"Very well, sir," said Albert, and we prepared to leave.

As I passed through the doorway, I brushed the jamb with the sleeve of my coat.

"Ah!" cried Albert. "Dr. Watson, you have done it again!"

"I have?"

Albert pointed to a spot or stain of some kind on the door jamb about level with my elbow. Otherwise the wood was quite clean.

"See here," said he, looking at the spot. "As you have indicated, Dr Watson, it is likely to be of importance. Do you have an envelope?"

"Er, no, I do not."

"Never mind," Albert said, producing one from a coat pocket. "I happen to have one."

He carefully scraped a bit of the stain from the wood into the envelope. When he was done, he sealed the envelope and handed it to me.

"Keep it safe," he said, and I told him that I would.

"Good," he said with a satisfied air. "Now, is there anything more, Doctor?"

"I...do not believe so," said I.

I was not even certain about what we had, so after we had thanked Delebeck for his help and departed, I sat in the cab and tried to put things together as Holmes might have done. I had hardly begun my cogitations when Albert tapped on the communicating door.

"Have you reached any conclusions, Doctor?" he asked when I opened the door.

"Not yet," I replied. "It seems that we have a good bit of evidence, but where does it lead us?"

"What would your friend Sherlock Holmes say?"

Again I tried to apply myself to a solution. I wanted to begin at the beginning of things and move forward, but where to begin?

"The rail schedule tells us that Bourdin seemed to be planning a return to France," I said at length. "For that he needed money."

"How would he obtain it?" Albert asked. "By performing some sort of dangerous task, perhaps?"

"The bomb," said I. "Of course. He was not a violent person, according to Delebeck, but he might have resorted to placing a bomb for someone if the payment were sufficient."

"And who might have a motive to pay a known anarchist to place a bomb at the observatory?"

The horse plodded along. The cold damp air invaded the cab, and it seemed to clarify my thoughts.

"Someone who could gain something or advance his cause," I said. "Or both."

"Someone like Henry Starnes?" Albert asked.

"Yes. This incident will cause many more people in England to turn against all anarchists, but especially those from other countries. Starnes and his nativists will certainly gain a greater voice in politics. His seat in parliament would be assured."

"Very sound, Doctor," said Albert. "And if Starnes wanted to cause a commotion rather than do real damage, the observatory would be a sufficient target. Well known, but not essential to the nation's business."

"The death of Bourdin, though. He could not have predicted that."

"No. It must have been accidental. Perhaps Bourdin fell and activated the bomb prematurely, thus bringing about his own demise."

"It sounds very likely," said I, "but we have no proof."

"I think we do," said Albert. "Did you not notice a certain smell in Bourdin's rooms?"

"Yes, but I could not put a name to it. It was faint and had soon faded away completely."

"As if it might have been brought there on someone's clothing," Albert said. "Like whatever stained the doorframe."

Suddenly it came to me. "Paint," I said. "The smell was oil paint."

"Such as might be used to paint a sign," Albert said. "I believe that if the sample in the envelope were to be compared to the signs of Starnes's group, it would be the same."

I was momentarily elated, but something occurred to me. "Many people might have used that paint. We have no proof that it was Starnes."

"Mycroft Holmes will soon find out by examining his clothing," said Albert. "And he will question everyone along Fitzroy Street. Someone will have seen Starnes there."

He was correct, and I felt sure that now I had solved the problem Mycroft had set me.

"We have arrived at the Diogenes Club," Albert said.

The cab came to a stop, and I made my exit without assistance. I stood on the sidewalk, waiting for Albert to join me, but he clucked to the horse and the cab moved away.

"Wait," I called. "You must come in and speak to Mycroft with me."

"You have no further need of my assistance, Doctor. You have done a wonderful job on your own."

"It was not entirely on my own," said I, but he appeared not to hear me as the cab moved away and was swallowed up by the fog. I looked after him for a moment and then went inside the club to present my findings to Mycroft.

Perhaps now my readers are aware of why I have some misgivings about dating the return of Holmes to England as late as April of 1894. He was a clever man when it came to disguise, and during his career he fooled everyone, including me, more times than I care to enumerate. Could he have done it once again? If so, he never mentioned it after his recognized return. But now, after the passage of many years, most especially on cold winter nights when the fog settles over all, I still wonder about the case of the anarchist's bomb and just who was helping whom.

The Riddle of the Rideau Rifles

by Peter Calamai

As I write these lines, a dreadful darkness is descending over the civilized world. In Europe, only Britain, Ireland, and neutral Sweden and Switzerland remain free from the Nazis, and yet the United States of America remains on the sidelines as Herr Hitler extends his mailed grip around the Mediterranean and North Africa. Canada and the other self- governing Dominions are doing all they can to help our Mother Country. But without the industrial and military might of America on our side soon, I fear for the future of humanity.

This is not a propitious time to make public the tale which I recount here. Its publication now could arouse further those isolationist and anti-war sentiments already too evident among our neighbours to the south. But it is a story which the world should hear someday, and while I am still able I must record how brilliant detective work averted what would have been a calamitous international incident between Canada and the United States.

Yet I am getting ahead of myself. In writing this narrative I have drawn upon my personal diaries and other original documents in my possession. Once I completed my task I destroyed those documents, lest others reveal matters that I believe must remain forever secret. To my nephew Jonathan – or indeed to his progeny – I leave the decision about when to publish this account of the wisest man I have ever known.

Bartholomew Evans
Ottawa, November, 1940.

The little water remaining in the Rideau Canal was still frozen solid that March Tuesday in 1894 when the Private Secretary informed me that the Prime Minister, Sir John Thompson, wished to see me. I hurried along the corridor in the Centre Block where I, a very junior aide, was privileged to share a cramped office with several other young men. To my surprise, I was instantly ushered into the Prime Minister's office.

"Evans, I have an important task for you," Sir John said without preamble. "Read these."

From a pile on his desk, the Prime Minister handed me what I recognized, even at that early stage of my career, as a sheaf of state papers. Or more precisely, fair copies of those papers. They revealed an astonishing development.

That great Liberal, William Gladstone, then Prime Minister of Great Britain for the fourth (and final) time, had written my Prime Minister, soliciting his support publicly for a movement called the Anglo- American reunion, which sought the ultimate federation of the entire English-speaking world.

"We would thus repair the ruction with America caused by the folly of George III and the blundering of Lord North," Gladstone wrote.

Sir John had replied (no doubt also by diplomatic bag) that he was well disposed toward the idea, but domestic circumstances forbade any public show of support. His letter then marshalled facts of which I had been utterly unaware.

My Prime Minister said mysterious elements in Ottawa had begun fomenting anti-American sentiment within the past year, and their machinations had found favour in his own caucus and, indeed, even within his cabinet. Despite discreet yet concerted inquiries by Colonel Arthur Percy Sherwood of the Dominion Police, the source of this campaign remained unidentified.

"Until it is known and scotched, my hands are tied and I dare not act as you request," Thompson had written.

The third and last letter was the response from Gladstone. He well understood Thompson's predicament, he wrote, and had a possible solution to offer. With our approval, the British Prime Minister would dispatch a personal representative to investigate the anti-American phenomenon. Although the investigator was as yet unknown to the wider world, his detecting talents were highly recommended by Mr. Gladstone's closest advisor, a man who sometimes constituted the entire British government because of his unparalleled knowledge of every portfolio.

"I agreed, of course, Evans. What else could I do? I have just had a cable saying that this man is arriving by train in an hour. Apparently his name is Sigerson. Your task is to offer him every assistance, acting with my full authority. But keep me informed as well."

So overwhelmed was I by this sudden revelation of domestic unrest and secret prime ministerial investigations that it was all I could manage to stammer my assent and retreat from Sir John's presence, clutching the sheaf of papers. A quick consultation with the Private Secretary revealed that a suite of rooms had been booked at the Russell Hotel for Mr. Sigerson.

I met Gladstone's representative at the station what seemed like mere minutes later. My first impressions were favourable. Mr. Sigerson carried himself with a quiet authority beyond his years, which I judged to be about 40. Spaced widely above an aquiline nose, his grey eyes darted constantly, taking in details. When we shook hands his grip was firm, and his figure, while slight, was wiry. He stood perhaps an inch or more taller than my five-foot-ten. I judged that Mr. Sigerson would be a good fellow to have beside you in an altercation, should our mission come to that. Just as I completed this surveillance, he spoke, "I am going to address you as Evans and you should call me Sigerson, now that you've taken my measure," he said with a wry smile. "Our first order of business must be to gather data. I cannot make bricks without straw."

I was to discover in our short time together that Sigerson (as I indeed came to call him) was given to uttering such homilies leaning heavily toward Biblical and classical allusions. From this habit and his precise manner of speaking, I judged that he was a university man like myself, although a product of the English system and a decade my senior. Yet I failed utterly during the next few days to draw from him whether he had attended Oxford or Cambridge.

My own university connections from Queen's, however, could serve us well for this sensitive mission. Many of my fellows were now placed within the federal government as I was, not yet exercising great authority, but in positions where their fingers rested on many quivering strands of information.

We agreed that we would conceal Sigerson's real mission in Ottawa, telling people instead that he was an academic from Norway making a study of Canada-U.S. relations as a possible parallel to Scandinavia. We left his bags at the Russell and took the chance of calling on two of my Queen's connections without making appointments. In the first of what turned out to be continual surprises, not only did Sigerson immediately begin to speak English with what sounded to my ears like a Norwegian lilt, but he also somehow contrived to *appear* Scandinavian, if not actually

Norwegian.

Unfortunately, the first interview with a university contemporary elicited little more than some embarrassing sobriquets by which I had been known in certain undergraduate circles. The second classmate, however, suggested it might be worthwhile for us to talk with a friend of his, Jack Wells, who was with the detective service of the Ottawa city police.

"I will send a note saying that you will call this afternoon. If there have been any day-to-day incidents arising from tensions between Canada and the U.S., Jack is the fellow to know," said my classmate.

After a modest lunch, we walked to the police station and were quickly shown into the office of Detective Inspector Jack Wells. Events intervened even as we took our seats.

"I apologize if I seem somewhat distracted, gentlemen, but I received information of the most distressing nature only hours ago," said Wells. A few questions from Sigerson drew out the whole story.

A promising young detective constable named O'Reilly had been killed in a fall early that morning, apparently after a bar room brawl. His battered body, reeking of liquor, had been found on the stone bottom of a drained lock of the Rideau Canal, adjacent to an old government building known as the Commissariat.

"It's a black eye for the force, sure enough, but worse than that, his family won't be eligible for any pension because he wasn't on duty when he died. And the wife has two small children to rear by herself."

"What ought O'Reilly to have been investigating, Inspector?" I asked.

"Smuggling, Mr. Evans. We have reason to believe that someone is attempting to smuggle explosives into Canada. It could be some latter-day remnants of the Fenians."

I quickly informed Sigerson about the rag-tag Irish-American nationalists who had sought 30 years earlier to "capture" Canada and hold it hostage until Britain granted independence to Ireland. With the exception of one raid, their military forays into Canada had been failures and, by the early 1870s, the Fenian Brotherhood had vanished.

"I should like to examine the constable's body," Sigerson said without preamble. "My knowledge of advanced forensic techniques has proven useful to authorities in the past."

Wells replied, "I don't see that any harm can arise from that. We will do anything to get to the bottom of this tragedy."

In the station's basement mortuary, Sigerson drew from an inner coat pocket a magnificent brass-bound magnifying glass. Not that one was needed to see the terrible bruises, mottled yellow and purple, which covered almost every part of the constable's body. Instead, Sigerson studiously applied his glass to the man's hands, wrists, forearms and ankles. From one wrist he plucked something with a pair of tweezers, placing it in a small envelope. He did the same with a scraping from the sole of one of the constable's shoes.

"Your constable didn't die as a result of a bar room brawl or even a tumble onto the lock bottom, Inspector," Sigerson announced as we mounted the station stairs. "He was beaten to death by several men who used clubs and also their feet, and they delivered the fatal blows when he was bound and unable to defend himself. It was homicide, likely deliberate murder."

"You astonish me, Mr. Sigerson. How can you possibly know this?" asked Wells.

"Because the constable himself told me, or rather the evidence of his body did. The backs of his hands and forearms are cut and battered, the classic wounds suffered by someone trying to defend himself against a superior force which overwhelmed him in an initial assault.

"Rope burns around his ankles and wrists indicate he was struggling against restraints. I would hypothesize that he was beaten while bound in an attempt to extract some information. When your police surgeon performs an autopsy, he will likely discover many broken ribs, and possibly tibia and fibula as well. Those would not result from your standard drunken brawl."

The Inspector was beside himself with excitement.

"If this is true, it will be a capital piece of good news in this sorry affair, Mr. Sigerson. Not only would it remove the stain from the constable's character, and from the force's, but it would go a long way toward convincing the commissioners to award a service pension to O'Reilly's widow. Is there no way to obtain some evidentiary proof?"

Sigerson replied: "I took the liberty of removing a small sample of the rope fibre that was adhering to the constable's skin. With access to a dark-field microscope, I expect to identify its origin. I have written a small monograph about distinguishing fibres of the 73 most common ropes."

As luck would have it, another of my Queen's contemporaries had recently been seconded as an assistant to George M. Dawson, the second-in-command of the Geological Survey of Canada, which was Canada's oldest scientific agency. The survey was housed in a former hotel on Sussex Street and would have the latest in microscopes. I undertook to get in touch with my colleague and arrange access to the specialized equipment for a "distinguished scientific visitor from Norway." Sigerson and I agreed to reconvene Wednesday at the hotel.

That morning we called first upon Jephro Clarke, also a friend from college. He turned out to possess an ample supply of the sort of "straw" sought by the British/Norwegian investigator to form the "bricks" of his case.

"Yes, I myself have noticed anti-American sentiments about town, and not just the letters to the editor in the *Free Press*, *Journal*, and *Citizen*. They are particularly strong in a society to which I belong," Clarke confided.

"Pray tell us more, Mr. Clarke. Omit no detail, no matter how trivial it may seem to you," Sigerson urged.

"There is not much to relate, Mr. Sigerson. I am a member of the Hibernian Debating Society, an assemblage of good fellows who convene every Thursday evening for invigorating discourse about matters of topical concern. We normally gather in a meeting room of an inn on Duke Street and then adjourn downstairs afterwards to the public bar where the discussion continues, usually becoming somewhat more animated.

"Yet animus has never been a feature of our discussions, at least not until these past months. A few members began voicing opinions antagonistic towards our American neighbours, and the sentiment seems to have gained a hold, certainly among some of the more vocal members."

"Is there anything which distinguishes these particular men?" I asked. Sigerson shot me what I imagined was a look of approval.

"Not really, Bart. They're relatively new here in town but mostly from up the Valley, so there's the usual touch of Irish somewhere in their background. You hear traces of it when they talk. But they're solid fellows. I had occasion to recommend two of them, a father and son, to my superior for employment when we were faced with a sudden double vacancy at the Commissariat."

At the second mention in two days of this building, Sigerson raised a quizzical eyebrow, and Clarke elaborated. Like me, he was a personal aide, in his case to the Deputy Minister of Militia and Defence. The department was responsible for the Commissariat Building, a substantial stone edifice beside the lowermost locks of the Rideau Canal. Dating from 1827, the building had originally stored tools and equipment during the canal construction. For the past four decades, it had served as a storehouse for military goods, with an armourer and carpenter actually living on the premises. The current holders of those posts had been recruited from the Hibernia membership after the previous incumbents were discharged by the Clerk of Military Stores, the official with day-to- day responsibility for the building.

"I am heading over that way myself on a small errand, gentlemen. If you would like to accompany me I can show you around and introduce you to the Pattersons, father and son."

It was but a short walk to the west side of the locks and a gentle descent from Parliament Hill (formerly Barrack Hill) to the Commissariat. Somewhat to my surprise, Sigerson cross-questioned Clarke about the changing uses of the building and the various structural additions and subtractions. This inquisition continued as we toured the three floors, with Clarke throwing open doors to reveal stores of tunics, boots, infantry greatcoats, serge trousers, forage caps, braces, brushes for hair, shoes and cloth, button sticks, eating utensils, and all else necessary to keep a battalion of soldiers well shod, well clothed and well fed.

On the second floor, Sigerson opened one door himself. "This is far neater than I would have expected," he murmured.

"I believe that room is used for training purposes," responded Clarke, who did not look in. My quick glance revealed a dozen or so unmatched wooden chairs arrayed around three walls, while windows in the fourth gave a view out to the Ottawa River. Several coils of heavy rope were piled in a corner, leaving most of the floor unobstructed, probably for training demonstrations as Clarke had said. This interpretation was reinforced by the spotless nature of the floorboards, which were obviously scoured regularly.

On the main floor, a storeroom held rows of wooden crates of Snider and Martini-Henry breech-loading rifles, plus metal ammunition cases. Here Sigerson again withdrew his magnifying glass and proceeded to examine the rifle crates minutely, even dropping down onto the floor to look more closely at some detail.

He paid the same close attention to the work spaces used by the armourer and carpenter. As he was finishing that inspection, the Pattersons walked in and were introduced by Clarke. He and I moved off a few paces as Sigerson engaged the father and son in animated conversation.

"Well that was two hours very profitably spent," Sigerson said, rejoining us.

As we climbed back to street level, I informed Sigerson that he could call at the Geological Survey at his convenience to use the microscope, and he decided to go at once.

Meanwhile, I pursued my own line of inquiry. At Sigerson's request, I was to uncover everything I could about the Clerk of Military Stores, the official who had summarily dismissed the previous armourer and carpenter at the Commissariat.

This proved a more difficult task than I had imagined. Ottawa was then (and is even now) really a very small town, despite being the national capital. All persons of note are known to one another and information circulates quickly about their character and any particular foibles. But although several of my coterie could name this shadowy figure as Benjamin Saunders, none could provide any other details. Finally, through the friend of a friend of a friend, I was able to glimpse the personnel file of the man who effectively commanded the Commissariat and maintained an office there. Brimming with fresh information, I rushed back to the Russell Hotel.

Sigerson was curled comfortably into a basket chair in front of the blazing hearth in his sitting room, a darkened cherrywood pipe in one hand. From the opacity of the room's air, I hazarded that he had smoked more than one pipe.

"Yes, this is fully a three-pipe problem, my good Evans. Please tell what your inquiries have uncovered."

Restraining my excitement I marshalled and summarized the facts as logically as I knew how, for Sigerson seemed to prize ratiocination above all other virtues.

"The Clerk of Military Stores is Benjamin Saunders,

although perhaps I should say Colonel Saunders, for it was his military service in the British Army which secured him the post only last year. One of his letters of recommendation came from his superior, the commanding officer of the Irish Guards.

"But the most interesting fact lies in Colonel Saunders' outside activities. My friend Clarke confirms that the clerk is an active member of the Hibernian Debating Society. Clarke also now recollects that it was Saunders who first drew the Pattersons to his attention as possible replacement artisans at the Commissariat, whose hiring Clarke in turn recommended to his Deputy Minister."

"Did you discover anything further about the two men who left so precipitately?" Sigerson asked casually, blowing out a smoke ring.

"They have disappeared from town so I could not talk with them. But from all accounts, they had given satisfaction right up to the time when they were summarily dismissed by Saunders."

Sigerson appeared to be digesting this information and for a minute, his eyes strayed toward a violin case on the window sill. With a shrug, he turned again to me.

"My own inquiries were also productive, Evans. The Survey indeed possessed the requisite microscope and I was able to identify the fibres which I took from Constable O'Reilly's wrist. They come from a particular type of tarred rope manufactured exclusively for the Royal Navy, although it is sometimes also supplied to Britain's colonies if they are raising their own fleets, as I understand Canada is.

"Making use of this information requires us to have been especially observant. Would you please provide me with a description of the empty room we saw at the Commissariat, my dear Evans?"

It was a test, and I strove to come up to the mark, repeating the details mentioned earlier.

"Have I missed anything of importance, Sigerson," I

inquired.

"Only everything," he replied with a sigh. "You see, Evans, but you do not observe. In contrast, I immediately noticed a ladderback chair along the west wall which showed rope wear on the lower portion of the front legs. And in that pile of ropes, the top coil was a tarred hemp which I wager will match the fibres from the constable's wrists.

"As well, the spotless nature of the floor is suspicious in a room devoted to training. I fear the floor had been only recently scrubbed to remove blood stains, and that it was in that room that Constable O'Reilly received his fatal final beating. Despite poisoning myself with three pipes, however, I am no closer to understanding how he got there and why someone thought his death was necessary."

I was beginning to lose patience with this self-indulgent performance. "Is there anything else I should have noticed at the Commissariat, Mr. Sigerson?" I asked with some asperity.

"I draw your attention to the curious use of nails in the end pieces of the gun crates. Also worth a second look are the stocks of wooden dowels beside the carpenter's bench."

He could not be drawn further on that point. Over dinner in the hotel dining room, he instead expounded knowledgeably about an astonishing range of subjects, from the bimetallic question of Montreal to the great herd of bisons of the fertile plains and the breeding cycle of the stormy petrels of British Columbia.

"I have some private inquiries to make during the day tomorrow, so perhaps we can meet here in the late afternoon and partake of some more of the hotel's excellent cooking. As well, it would be best if you could acquire a set of clothes suitable for a labourer."

"What sort of labourer?"

"Oh, nothing too exotic, someone along the lines of a beamster, wheel tapper, drayman, pot burner, or knacker. Even a guard lacer would do, although it might be too early in the year for their activity."

I am positive that Sigerson was hiding a smile behind his hand as he ran through this list of occupations, still common then toward the end of the Victorian era but likely unknown to many as I write.

Late the following afternoon, dressed as a drayman, I called at Sigerson's rooms. Instead of the investigator, I was greeted by a fellow of coarse appearance, the lower part of his face obscured by a black beard and his stout body contorted from some sort of arthritic condition. His blackened fingers and stained vest front suggested daily toil with greasy machinery.

"Do you think I will pass as a plate-maker, Evans?" the apparition asked. His accent sounded like a kinsman to the Pattersons, father and son.

I was so completely deceived by Sigerson's disguise that it was some few seconds before I replied in the affirmative.

"We are bound for the Couillard Hotel, an establishment in one of the less salubrious parts of your nation's capital, an area called LeBreton Flats, I believe. The Hibernian Debating Society will be holding its weekly discussions upstairs and then adjourn to the public bar. We will watch them from a quiet corner. If there is any talking to be done, pray let me do it. As you may have noticed, I have some small facility with accents and dialects."

The new Ottawa Electric Railway did not yet service that area, so we took a hack and had the driver let us off a short distance from the Duke Street location. As local residents, a drayman and a plate-maker obviously would arrive on foot. There was time only to settle ourselves at a secluded table with our pints before a dozen or so men descended the stairs. Among that number were the Pattersons and Colonel Saunders, but not my friend Clarke. Equally fortunate, I had been in the background when Sigerson spoke with the Pattersons at the Commissariat.

Just as I was congratulating myself on the success of

our covert observations, Sigerson poured the remains of his bitter into my glass and approached the bar for a refill. While there, he made a point of talking with the Pattersons, who seemed to have no inkling of his true identity.

"Well, Evans, at last I am beginning to see the light," he said as he returned.

"I fear the case is still all dark to me," I replied.

"It is not my custom to divulge the outcome of my investigations until they are complete, a practice which sometimes causes distress to a regular companion in London." Sigerson paused and gazed briefly into the distance. A smile flickered across his bushy face.

"But matters stand differently with you, who have not had the opportunity to become inured to my difficult moods. So I will tell you the key to the whole puzzle. Those men are not, as you think from their speech, natives of the Ottawa Valley. They are in fact Irish Americans."

Not another word of explanation could I wrest from him that evening, as we sat and watched for another two hours until all the Society members had departed. As we stepped outside, Sigerson gave a triumphal cry and bent down to scoop up a finger's worth of the muddy clay protruding beside the boardwalk.

"The last piece of the puzzle," he ejaculated in triumph.

All I learned, however, was that I was to call at his rooms the next morning and also arrange through my friend Clarke for a ten o'clock rendezvous at the Commissariat to include the Pattersons, Colonel Saunders, and Clarke himself.

I remember that I did not get much sleep that night and called so early that Sigerson had only just completed his toilet. He insisted on ringing for breakfast, and shortly we were joined by Detective Inspector Wells. Yet Sigerson's only reference to the case was to ensure that three constables from the Ottawa force would be present at the Commissariat.

On our walk to the Canal, he spoke of Archibald Lampman, a poet who was a public servant in Ottawa and whose work appeared in *Atlantic Monthly, Harper's,* and *Scribner's*. Both the Inspector and I confessed that we had never heard of Lampman or his book, *Among the Millet*. But Sigerson was an admirer and had called upon the young poet at the Post Office Department, offering praise and encouragement.

"Art in the blood is liable to take the strangest forms," he remarked enigmatically.

At the Commissariat, a choleric Colonel Saunders and a brace of truculent Pattersons awaited us.

"What is the meaning of this? Why am I being mustered like this on the say-so of some pettifogging youngster," the Colonel demanded, glaring at Clarke and then at the three uniformed constables hovering in the background.

Sigerson took charge masterfully, abandoning his Norwegian persona. He led the group to the room containing the workbenches and crates of rifles. There he explained that he was acting on behalf of Sir John Thompson, and indicated me as the Prime Minister's private secretary (a post I would, in fact, occupy later but with a different man.) His remit was to investigate the origin of recent anti-American feeling and discover how deep it went.

"And I can now answer those questions," he announced in a restrained tone. "The anti-Americanism is an elaborate hoax, a ploy to camouflage a much more sinister purpose. That goal was to stage an inconsequential armed attack against the United States, one in which no one was harmed, which would appear to have been carried out by forces from Canada, acting with official sanction. And the Commissariat served as the planning and training centre for all this."

Bedlam erupted. Who was behind such a plot? What was the intention? When would it be carried out? How? And did he have any evidence for this fantastical suggestion?

"You are looking at it," said Sigerson, pointing to a crate labelled as containing a dozen Martini-Henry rifles. "Rifles have been removed and cached for the putative assault, after which they will be abandoned as evidence of Canadian involvement."

"This is preposterous," Colonel Saunders exclaimed, stepping forward. "Try to lift that crate with the rope handles on the ends, and the weight will prove the rifles are there."

Sigerson continued in the same quiet voice. "Yes, I concede that the crate feels heavy enough to suggest nothing is amiss. The men behind this plot, although in my opinion seriously deluded, are at least cunning. Yet they were undone, as in that old adage, by something as common as a nail."

He tapped the end of the crate with his walking stick.

"I tried to draw Mr. Evans' attention to the peculiar nails in these endpieces. They are of a larger size than the nails used elsewhere in the crates. That is because the original nails have been extracted to remove the endpieces, which were modified and replaced. If you look carefully, you will also notice a few holes from the original nails in which someone failed to properly place the larger nails."

Sigerson offered his magnifying glass and the Inspector took a look. "I dare say you are correct, Mr. Sigerson, but I don't see how this proves the rifles are missing, much less the serious plot you have alleged," he said.

"You have to ask yourself, Inspector, why nails were substituted in the endpieces. The most rational explanation is that longer nails were necessary to contain something extra added to the ends of the crates. My surmise is that this something extra is lead which Patterson senior, the armourer, crafted in sheets to fit. This additional weight was necessary to compensate for rifles which had been removed."

At this repeated allegation, Colonel Saunders erupted.

"This is a farrago of absurd suppositions and theories and I intend to expose it. Patterson, open this crate at once," he ordered the carpenter.

"Yes, please do," added Sigerson.

The cover was quickly off, revealing a top layer of three

neatly arranged bundles. Despite the thick cloth swaddling, we could discern the tell-tale shape of a rifle.

"Go ahead, take one out and unwrap it for this gentleman," the Colonel told Patterson.

In a moment, the young man held out for inspection a Martini- Henry rifle still shiny with protective grease from the factory.

Sigerson stepped forward. "Mr. Clarke, would you be so kind as to remove a bundle from the second layer and unwrap it for us."

The Colonel moved so quickly that he eluded the outstretched arms of the Inspector and two constables. The third brought him down with a classic rugby tackle. When we looked round, Clarke was holding out a wooden replica of a Martini-Henry. Further investigation revealed that the crate had contained three actual rifles, nine replicas and sheets of lead in the endpieces.

"Copying the rifle stock in pine was a simple matter for a carpenter," Sigerson said. "But he needed something ready-made in the shape of a barrel. I attempted without success to interest Mr. Evans in the absurdly large supply of wooden dowelling here."

Inspector Wells was motioning his constables to take away the Pattersons and Colonel Saunders. "We will get the details of this plot from them back at the station, Mr. Sigerson."

"I have no doubt that you will, Inspector. But there is something much more serious about which you will also want to question these men than theft and this half-baked plot, as it would be called in Devon."

Without another word, Sigerson then led the entire company to that mostly empty drill practice room on the next floor.

"Here is where Constable O'Reilly was beaten to death, and these are some of the men who did it," he announced with more emotion than he had shown previously. This was the story he then unfolded.

The constable was indeed on the job Monday night and he had followed one of his smuggling suspects to the Couillard Hotel. Sigerson matched soil from O'Reilly's boot to the mud sample from outside the inn. ("I have written a small monograph about soil identification," he said.) Somehow the "Society" members drinking there concluded, erroneously, that the constable had tumbled to their plot. They overpowered him and took him to the Commissariat, where they roused the Pattersons in their living quarters.

Sigerson walked over to the wall and lifted out a ladderback chair.

Then he gathered the top coil of rope from the corner.

"The constable was tied to this chair with that rope and systemically beaten to discover how much he knew. But it was all a terrible mistake. By the time the conspirators realized O'Reilly was following another trail altogether, it was too late. He now knew they were up to something even more diabolical. They felt they must kill him, which they did with blows to the head. They then doused his body with liquor to make it look as if he had been in a bar room brawl. After that, they dropped him head-first onto the stones on the bottom of the empty lock in an attempt to conceal the true cause of the fatal head injuries. The inference would be that O'Reilly had stumbled into the lock in a drunken stupor – which is in fact the conclusion leapt to by his superiors."

From the looks the constables gave the Colonel and the Pattersons, I feared it would go much harder for them now back at the station.

Before going our separate ways, we had agreed to meet later for a final summing-up. It was a sombre group which gathered that afternoon in a conference room attached to the Prime Minister's office.

Sir John himself was present and listened with great attention as Sigerson recounted the events at the Commissariat and explained his deductive trail. Inspector

Wells then reported that three other crates of rifles had been similarly tampered with, and that the missing rifles, along with numerous articles of official Canadian army gear and uniforms, had been recovered from a cache. Under vigorous questioning, the three men had confessed their participation in the plot and implicated others, including many members of the Hibernian Debating Society.

All but a few were American citizens, of Irish ancestry, who had been posing as Canadians from the Ottawa Valley. Colonel Saunders, however, insisted he was British, although of Irish sympathies, and denied any part in the fatal beating of Constable O'Reilly.

"I still can't quite fathom what they hoped to accomplish by all this," said the Prime Minister.

"Their plan contained far more passion than reason," Sigerson replied. "As latter-day Fenians, they were looking to thwart Britain at every turn. A strong federation of English-speaking people could only delay Irish independence, in their perverted view. So they came to Canada a year ago and began what amounted to a whispering campaign to make it seem that Canadians were becoming increasingly anti-American. The raid across the border would be the culmination, with your army's rifles and uniforms abandoned to implicate the Canadian government. No matter how strenuous the denials, there would be no way that the American public would accept stronger ties between our two countries under the guise of the proposed federation."

"What first alerted you to this plot, Mr. Sigerson?" asked the Prime Minister.

"The Pattersons' accents. It was obvious at once to my trained ear that the overlay on their Irish background was American, likely Eastern Seaboard, not from the Ottawa Valley. That started me along the line of investigating why Irish Americans might be trying to pass themselves off as Irish Canadians."

"I assume you will be heading back to London to report."

"Not for a few weeks, Prime Minister. My report to Sir William will be sent by diplomatic pouch. I have a good acquaintance who suggested that I visit his farm out West. But first I must stop in Toronto."

"Why is that, Mr. Sigerson," asked the Prime Minister as he rose. "My acquaintance urged me to get shod there. His bootmaker is Meyers. Perhaps you've heard of his establishment?"

Postscript

It was to be seven more years before Meyers the Bootmaker achieved immortality through publication in 1901 of The Hound of the Baskervilles, an adventure that actually took place in 1889, five years before our Ottawa story, according to Dr. John Watson's account. A reader of this tale today may well marvel how I could not have recognized an investigator who spoke of a "three-pipe problem", yearned to play the violin, employed a magnifying glass to such effect, and appeared to have written monographs on every aspect of criminal deduction.

In my own defence, all I can say is that the whole world believed that the Master Detective had died that terrible day in May 1891 when he plunged over Reichenbach Falls in a fatal embrace with his archenemy Professor Moriarty. In reality, he was to reappear to Watson's astonished eyes the month after the visit to Ottawa, but his return did not become general knowledge until October 1903, when The Strand magazine published a story entitled "The Empty House."

You can imagine my astonishment while reading that tale to learn that while Sherlock Holmes roamed the globe between May 1891 and April 1894, he often assumed the persona of a Norwegian explorer named Sigerson.

Ottawa References

The Dominion Police – Organized around 1870 to monitor and infiltrate the Fenian movement and protect cabinet ministers. Later responsible for security on Parliament Hill and for most federal policing services east of Lake Superior. Colonel Arthur Percy Sherwood became head in 1885 and held that post for a generation. In 1919, the force was merged with the Royal North West Mounted Police to form the RCMP.

Russell Hotel – Built in 1865 on the east side of Elgin at Sparks, the Russell was the fashionable hotel in Ottawa until the Chateau Laurier opened in 1912. It was first building in the city to boast bathrooms and steam heat. Prime Ministers John A. Macdonald, Charles Tupper and Wilfrid Laurier all lived at the Russell during their terms in office. The hotel suffered a fire in 1901, was rebuilt, but closed in 1925. It stood derelict until April 14, 1928, when another fire gutted the building and the land was cleared for the War Memorial.

George M. Dawson – Director of the Geological Survey from 1895 until his sudden death in 1901.

An inn on Duke Street – The Duke Hotel, later the venerable Couillard, was at 101 Duke Street.

Commissariat Building – Now houses the Bytown Museum.

Beamster, wheel tapper, drayman, pot burner, knacker, guard lacer, plate-maker – Tannery worker, railway worker who checked the wheels of locomotives, goods carrier by horse cart, pottery worker, dealer in old/dead horses, someone who laces up ladies' bicycles to prevent dresses getting caught in the mechanism, engraver of printing block plates.

Sherlockian References

- *Sometimes constituted the entire British government* – The phrase "sometimes the British government" was applied to Mycroft Holmes, older brother to Sherlock and a senior public servant.

- *Attended Oxford or Cambridge* – A contentious and unresolved issue in Sherlockian scholarship.
- *Have written a small monograph* – Holmes wrote monographs about the identification of tobacco ashes, tattoo marks, the tracing of footsteps, ear shapes, the effect of trades upon hands, and ciphers. He planned ones about the use of dogs in detection, malingering and the typewriter in crime.
- *You see, Evans, but you do not observe* – A recrimination Holmes directs at Dr. Watson more than once.
- *A three-pipe problem* – A classic Sherlockian description.
- *The bimetallic question, the great herd of bisons of the fertile plains,* and *the stormy petrels* – The names of three Sherlockian scion societies in Canada.
- *Meyers* – The title given to the leader of Canada's premier Sherlockian society, the Bootmakers of Toronto.
- *ACKNOWLEDGEMENTS: This story could not have been written without the plot advice and editing skills of J.A. ("Sandy") McFarlane. Valuable assistance was also provided by librarians in the Ottawa Room of the Ottawa Public Library, Gideon Hill, BSI, and Rideau Canal enthusiast Ken Watson.*

About the Contributors

The following contributors appear in this volume **The Lady on the Bridge and Other Stories**

Bert Coules wandered through a succession of jobs from fringe opera company manager to BBC radio drama producer-director before becoming a full-time writer at the beginning of 1989. Bert works in a wide range of genres, including science fiction, horror, comedy, romance and action-adventure but he is especially associated with crime and detective stories: he was the head writer on the BBC's unique project to dramatise the entire Sherlock Holmes canon, and went on to script four further series of original Holmes and Watson mysteries. As well as radio, he also writes for TV and the stage.

Wendy C. Fries is the author of Sherlock Holmes and John Watson: The Day They Met and also writes under the name Atlin Merrick. Wendy is fascinated with London theatre, scriptwriting, and lattes. Website: wendycfries.com.

Dick Gillman is a Yorkshire-man in his mid-sixties. He retired from teaching Science in 2005 and moved to Brittany, France in 2008 with his wife Alex, Truffle the Black Labrador, and two cats. He still has strong family links with the UK, where he visits his two grown up children and his grandchildren. Dick is a prolific writer, and during his retirement he has written 14 Sherlock Holmes short stories and a Sci-Fi novella. His latest short story, "Sherlock Holmes and The Man on Westminster Bridge" was completed in July 2015, and is published for the first time in this anthology.

Jack Grochot is a retired investigative newspaper journalist and a former federal law enforcement agent specializing in mail fraud cases. He lives on a small farm in southwestern Pennsylvania, USA, where he writes and cares for five boarded horses. His fiction work includes stories in Sherlock Holmes Mystery Magazine, The Sherlock Holmes Megapack (an e-book), as well as the book Come, Watson! Quickly!, a collection of five Sherlock Holmes pastiches. The author, an active member of Mystery Writers of

America, can be contacted by e-mail at grochot@comcast.net.

Carl L. Heifetz Over thirty years of inquiry as a research microbiologist have prepared Carl Heifetz to explore new horizons in science. As an author, he has published numerous articles and short stories for fan magazines and other publications. In 2013 he published a book entitled Voyage of the Blue Carbuncle that is based on the works of Sir Arthur Conan Doyle and Gene Roddenberry. Voyage of the Blue Carbuncle is a fun and exciting spoof, sure to please science fiction fans as well as those who love the stories of Sherlock Holmes and Star Trek. Carl and his wife have two grown children and live in Trinity, Florida.

Mike Hogan writes mostly historical novels and short stories, many set in Victorian London and featuring Sherlock Holmes and Doctor Watson. He read the Conan Doyle stories at school with great enjoyment, but hadn't thought much about Sherlock Holmes until, having missed the Granada/ Jeremy Brett TV series when it was originally shown in the eighties, he came across a box set of videos in a street market and was hooked on Holmes again. He started writing Sherlock Holmes pastiches about four years ago, having great fun re-imagining situations for the Conan Doyle characters to act in. The relationship between Holmes and Watson fascinates him as one of the great literary friendships. (He's also a huge admirer of Patrick O'Brian's Aubrey-Maturin novels). Like Captain Aubrey and Doctor Maturin, Holmes and Watson are an odd couple, differing in almost every facet of their characters, but sharing a common sense of decency and a common humanity. Living with Sherlock Holmes can't have been easy, and Mike enjoys adding a stronger vein of "pawky humour" into the Conan Doyle mix, even letting Watson have the second-to-last word on occasions. Mike is British, and he lives in Italy. His books include Sherlock Holmes and the Scottish Question; The Gory Season – Sherlock Holmes, Jack the Ripper and the Thames Torso Murders and the Sherlock Holmes & Young Winston 1887 Trilogy (The Deadwood Stage; The Jubilee Plot; and The Giant Moles), He has also written the following short story collections: Sherlock Holmes: Murder at the Savoy and Other Stories, Sherlock Holmes: The Skull of Kohada Koheiji and Other Stories, and Sherlock Holmes: Murder on the Brighton Line and Other Stories. www.mikehoganbooks.com

Peter Calamai, BSI, a resident of Ottawa, was a reporter, editor and foreign correspondent with major Canadian newspapers since 1966. For half those years he has worked five minutes' walk from the Rideau Canal and the Commissariat Building. When editor of the Ottawa Citizen's editorial pages, Calamai had the good fortune to spend an afternoon interviewing canal historian Robert Legget. He has been an active Sherlockian since the mid-1990's, concentrating on Holmes and the Victorian press. Honours include designation as a Master Bootmaker by Canada's leading Sherlockian society and investiture in the Baker Street Irregulars as "The Leeds Mercury", a name taken from The Hound of the Baskervilles.

Bill Crider is a former college English teacher, and is the author of more than fifty published novels and an equal number of short stories. He's won two Anthony awards and a Derringer Award, and he's been nominated for the Shamus and the Edgar awards. His latest novel in the Sheriff Dan Rhodes series is Between the Living and the Dead. Check out his homepage at www.billcrider.com, or take a look at his peculiar blog at http://billcrider.blogspot.com.